SHADOW STORM

JENNIFER AITKEN

To my family who've been reading my stories since I could write.
And my husband for his unwavering support.

Table of Contents

CHAPTER 1

A fire raged in my lungs, bringing me out of a deep, dense fog my mind had been hibernating in. Seconds passed while my consciousness crawled forward, taking over the driver's seat. When the fog cleared enough for thoughts to pass through without resistance, I looked around and recognized nothing. *Where am I?* I could hear someone talking but saw no one around. *Am I hearing voices*? "They're going to kill me. I have to run faster!" A voice said. A voice so familiar I knew it could only be mine, but my mouth was shut. I felt like a blank slate, not recognizing the thoughts passing through my mind as my own. I switched gears from my inner confusion to my outer situation.

My lungs continued to burn, my heart raced, and my body moved faster than I ever thought possible. I was running for my life; from who I had no idea. But I recognized without question the vibration of absolute fear coursing through this body and decided not to argue with it. I pumped my arms and thrust my legs forward as I raced through the countryside,
propelling myself as far from my pursuers as I was capable. Engines thundered behind me, gaining ground, but I dared not take even a millisecond to turn and look.

The sun beat down on this foreign landscape without sympathy. A light clear blue sky mirrored the tropical color of the ocean flanking the mountains to my right. *I am a long way from New York City*. Long blades of lush grass brushed past my legs. I was blazing a trail through this rarely-taken path. My brain was cramping in on itself trying to solve this puzzle, but there were too many missing pieces. It was creating a tidal wave of anxiety within me. And worst of all, my quads were seizing, and my lungs were white hot to the point breath was near impossible. As the sensation left my legs completely, I knew it was time to face the music. Music that I was sure had to be for someone else. *This has to be a mistake, right?*

Sweat poured from my forehead as I gasped for air, bending over in pure exhaustion. Fear still raced through my veins, but my body no longer had the energy to fight it. It was time to discover what was happening. While I worked to catch my breath, I looked at my hands, fingers, and feet and

recognized them to be mine, and yet, there was something off. Slight variances my brain couldn't pinpoint. But this was not the time to inspect this exhausted body. They were here. They surrounded me in every direction, waiting in their black-windowed SUVs. I didn't need to look up from the green grass to be certain of this. The ground beneath me quaked from their ramped-up horsepower.

"Don't move, Lucius. I am done chasing you. Do you hear me, brother?" A strange voice bellowed over the still roaring engines. One by one, they turned off, and my ears popped. *Lucius… yes, that's my name.* One memory found its way home, but a thousand more remained MIA. I decided the fear of not knowing myself was more significant than the fear of the men chasing me. I straightened and turned to face them.

Encircled by several large black SUVs, I saw that each was guarded by a single man. Not a man like me, a military man, or a bouncer. These men had massive builds and stern expressions and were armed at the hip. One man broke from the group, presumably the man who spoke seconds before. He knew me. His anger was more than a duty. It was personal, and this made my stomach clench. If this wasn't a mistake, what had I gotten myself into, and why couldn't I remember a single thing? Now standing face to face, I noticed some similarities between our features.

Something told me I, too, had these dark features. Dark, inset eyes, black hair, and tan skin, but the anger that burned beneath the surface of this man was his alone.

"Have you nothing to say?" His eyes burned into mine and I came up blank. A parallel version of myself came to life and answered the taunt without hesitation.

"Dax, I have nothing to give you! What you think I possess, I don't. It's time to give up this quest and go our separate ways. They have lied to you. Plain and simple." These words poured out of "*my*" mouth, but I was not responsible for them. This was not the self I dragged back from the deep fog only moments ago. Like a stranger in my own body, I watched and I listened. *What else can I do?*

"Lucius, we both know you're lying. Father was helping you before you left New York. You are not smart enough to make it here on your own. Let's just be frank. I am tired, people are dead, and I want what I came for. If you won't hand it over willingly, I have no problem taking it by force. We are done playing games with you. He is not coming to help you. You are all alone out here," Dax said with arrogance and no sign of doubt. He was certain he was getting whatever it was he wanted from me, and I was certain I was not the only "Lucius" inside this body.

"You killed those people, Dax. Don't put that on me. All I did was try to get away from you, from the Kai-Tangata. But you're relentless. What have I done to make you believe I have immortality? I am a college dropout who works in a library! There is nothing remarkable about me. Just because some sad old man told you I was something I'm not, you're willing to go to jail for murder?" I said, my voice rising in threat. But it wasn't me, really…the other version of Lucius knew more about what was going on here, but I couldn't sense him or reach his memories to get myself up to speed.

"Oh, how you are mistaken. You seem to think the police are arriving from Chile to capture us, when in fact, the giant international manhunt is for you, brother." Dax grinned and searched my face for the reaction he was hoping for. Of course, I obliged, providing the exact expression of shock, fear, and terror. How is this possible? I've killed no one. He must have been lying to manipulate me into giving myself up and following him to what I imagined would be days of torture and my imminent death.

"You're lying. I've killed no one. You can't manipulate me that easily, Dax. I won't be going with you today or any other day. You might as well just kill me now because I will die before I let the Kai-Tangata experiment on me," I whispered, afraid to voice my conviction. My heart believed it was the truth, but my mind was not interested in dying any time soon. Dax raised his hands as if to take me by the throat, but then rethought his approach and lowered them back by his side.

If only I could communicate with this other Lucius. But instead, I remained a prisoner in this body that looked like mine but didn't belong to me.

"Unfortunately, the fear in your eyes calls your bluff so I don't have to, brother."

"Stop calling me your brother! We have no such allegiance."

"How disturbingly uninformed you are, little brother. Father should have filled you in by now. Especially considering the danger he's put you in. Don't you think you deserve at least that?" Arms crossed over his chest, Dax awaited my response while analyzing my every reaction.

I felt even more compartmentalized inside this version of Lucius, and my fear and sense of claustrophobia was like a hand gripping my heart with all its might, constricting my life force. Not knowing if this was an act of the other Lucius or not, I stilled my mind and tried to reach out to him. If I was to have any chance of surviving this strange, mind-bending experience, I needed his memories

—his sense of self. I reached outside the tiny box within the mind of Lucius. I used all the strength my consciousness offered and felt the slight tingle of defeat. This single emotion was as close as I could get to Lucius, but it was more than I had only moments before. Bursting with frustration, Dax would not wait much longer for my response. His patience was spent. All he saw was a blank face on this shell of Lucius as two consciousnesses fought inside for dominance.

"Marsielles is dead. I expect you know this. What does this mean to you? Well, it means that the oldest, most decrepit member of the society is gone. It means I am now in complete control and I'm bringing you in, Lucius. I am done running all over the world chasing you. I have spent my entire life in your shadow, following your trail, and it ends here!" He exclaimed with a fierceness that made me wonder what kind of past we shared.

Dax took a small photograph out of his pocket and held it in the air. Inching closer, I wondered why he had anything I would be interested in seeing, but I accepted the bait, knowing my body was not quite ready for another escape attempt. Time tattered the tiny wallet-sized photograph around the edges, and the color was altered from wear and tear. I could make out two young boys in the photo, immediately wondering if this was nothing more than a ploy to get me within strangling range. I started backing away when something familiar struck me about the boys in the picture. The smaller boy smiled brightly, while the taller one seemed grim. But what drew my eye was a bejeweled knife hanging from the older boy's hip. It was mesmerizing and somehow familiar to my ruined mind. I looked back and forth from the face of the older grim-faced boy in the picture to the man right in front of me.

"When we gave you the dagger that night, I thought it would summon the powers hidden deep inside you. I know they're there. But it appears you've buried them for so long it will take more than an ancient dagger to reignite them. Regardless, whether you want to believe it or not, we are brothers, Lucius, but only one of us is the heir of the prophecy," he said, his anger retreating from the surface. Still, it was apparent how much he hated me, and clearly, he had years of practice—years of memories unavailable to me. A remote part of me understood that the same dagger was hanging from my hip right now—so close to sparking a memory, but not close enough.

I sensed anxiety from the version of Lucius who was so close to me, but not quite me. With no memories of family, friends, work, or anything from my life, these revelations of brothers, fathers, and prophecies evoked no reaction, no matter how desperately I wanted one. But I experienced the other
Lucius' emotions like a volcano erupting—out of control and wild.

"Let me put it to you this way, Lucius, brother." Never missing an opportunity to call me brother to agitate me further, Dax continued. "This person or voice, or whatever you have been following since New York City—and don't deny it, someone with brains has been helping you along—this person, likely claiming to be your father, never mentioned me? Why? Why would he hide me from you?" At the end of his rope, he motioned for one of his henchmen to join his side, and the two of them closed in around me with stark expressions and dark intentions in their eyes. They were looking to interrogate me and try to penetrate or break me into submission. Just as I was about to defend my not-so-secret companion, a ring of truth from Dax's words struck the other Lucius. Dax was right, it was a fair question. *How could he not have told me? Did he not trust me? How could I continue to trust him?* Dax was breaking the other Lucius, cracking the confidence he so clearly had in his father. Those fissures were spreading, enveloping both of me.

"That's right. Now you are seeing the whole picture. The police are coming, Lucius, and you are their only suspect. Members from several continents are now searching for you. Do you understand? There is no going back to your old life. Only we can help you now." His face filled with pity and I sensed the other Lucius bending to his words, leaning towards his logic and accepting his offer of defeat; the fight draining out of him.

A vibration shook me from my seat as a spectator. The other Lucius was reaching for his father, begging for him to communicate as they'd done in the past—

telepathically. But there was no response. What he found instead was me—an alternate version of himself. Preparing for the inevitable chaos, I imagined myself clenching my eyes and tightening my

stomach to brace for his reaction. But instead of fear or confusion, a sense of relief rushed through this body. Not only was he defeated by this Dax person, but he was laying himself down for me as well. Whatever this version of myself had been through, he was done, worn out, and crushed by life. Now it was my turn. His presence was waning. None of this made sense to me, and even though I couldn't rationalize it, I knew I was moving from my tiny box inside Lucius' mind to the forefront. At the same time, my parallel Lucius faded into transparency. Yet he was the one with all the knowledge, the memories, and the information, and I had nothing but a name.

This body raged with emotion from the other Lucius and me. His relief didn't outweigh my fear about what was happening to me and why. Not to mention what was coming next. If I had to speak to this person, what would I say? Yes, waking up in a body not entirely my own but so similar it might as well be, with another consciousness in the forefront was twisting my brain into knots. But at least I was only a spectator—trying to learn what was happening. Without the other Lucius, I would have to figure things out much faster.

I submitted to the defeat Dax and his men were waiting for. What else could I do? They had me surrounded.

I didn't recognize where I was or even who I was. It completely limited my options to surrender. As my shoulders hunched and my arms dangled by my sides, it seemed like just a few hours ago, I was somewhere else, living a different life, and yet the memories were just out of reach now, floating away.

"Finally, now we can begin," Dax said. In that instant, our eyes met and I didn't see the man lunge at me from behind. He forcibly tied my hands behind my back while I ate a mouthful of dirt and grass, struggling to breathe with the two-hundred-pound neanderthal kneeling on my back. Wrestling with my fear, I tried not to struggle, although anyone's natural response to a situation like this would be to fight. *Flight or fight, right?* I watched, trying to take in every detail—every facial expression—every whispered comment and match a name to a face. I needed to get myself out of this insane situation and back to my normal life. I needed information, and the more I collected, I hoped I could regain my lost memories.

****

Minutes, hours, and days blurred into one, but it didn't matter. Not sure if they'd given me drugs or if my mind had cracked into a million pieces. My confusion, anger, frustration, and disorientation fused into one pulsating blog inside my guts, and I was no longer Lucius Xavier but some other entity altogether. Someone's science experiment.

Fleeting images of a beautiful, lush countryside, full of bright greens and clear blues, flashed across my mind's projection screen. I heard whispers of a man's voice, encouraging me to do the right thing, but my memories were scattered, and I wasn't sure which memories were mine and which were the other Lucius'.

Feeling nothing but cold hard steel beneath my body, sticky electrodes stuck to my temples, and the repeated stabbing of syringes in the crook of my arm, I begged my mind to retrieve my memories. I needed help, and fast.

"He's not giving us anything, sir. We've been injecting him bi-hourly with the serum you brought us, but he's done nothing but mumble to himself since he arrived." A voice from a nearby corridor echoed into my room. Not one I recognized, but one I had heard a great deal since being abducted—when the other Lucius left me to fend for myself. Funny, I knew I was being injected, but hearing the word *serum* sparked a fresh fear that hadn't registered previously. My mind was working overtime on how to get out of this situation. *What are they injecting me with?* I couldn't come up with an answer, though. My thoughts were sluggish, and my extremities refused to answer the call to action my brain repeatedly sent them. I was numb, completely numb.

"Keep trying. I'm giving you one more week, Terrence, and then I am taking over. I can assure you that neither you nor he will be happy if that happens. Are we clear?" This was Dax's voice. At least I remembered that much. Sensing someone was about to enter my chamber, I tried again to reach for the other Lucius. I needed him. I needed to understand how we shared the same body, where I came from, and where I was now, but I felt nothing. He was gone. So instead, I shifted gears and focused with all the intensity I could muster to recall what happened after Dax's men slammed me into the ground, face first, and hog-tied me.

Random words and sounds came back to me—fragments of my other self. I pieced together what I could. I recalled being in one of the many SUVs that had surrounded me and there were dozens of people talking over each other. I remembered hearing "Easter Island" and "Kai-Tangata" and "Dagger" but trying to string these words together in a sentence that made any sense was impossible. The only thing I was sure of was that we were far from prying eyes, the way these men talked. Maybe it wasn't the worst thing that I lost consciousness?

The hinges of a door squealed in annoyance as someone sealed the room. I listened intently because I was unable to open my eyes. They were sealed shut by a thick layer of crust—one of the many side effects of this serum everyone spoke of. My wrists and ankles ached from my leather cuffs, not allowing even an inch of movement between myself and the steel table.

"You are going to get me killed. Is that what you want? Can you hear me, Lucius?" The voice cut through the silence of my torture chamber, answering my earlier question of whether I was alone. "Dax is going to kill me if we don't get the answers soon. I've overheard Orpheus is losing his temper as well. I hope we can get out of here in time." In a hushed mumble, he continued, "I'm not cut out for this. If you are getting any of this, Lucius, Maru sent me to get you out. We have little time before they discover I'm not one of them and kill me for not getting results—or just kill me, period. Either way, I'm risking my life for you, so please wake up!" His voice was low and urgent, and his message clear. If only I remembered who Maru was.

I hadn't said a word since before they captured me and wasn't even sure I could reply to this mystery man should I want to. He continued to mutter to himself while he tinkered with metal instruments and opened and closed a fridge, highlighting his distraction. The lights were vibrant in this room. I could see the glow of them behind my closed lids. It was relentless. The lights had been on since my arrival, and I was glad my eyes were sealed shut just to get a bit of relief from the blazing illumination.

"Alright, let's up your dosage, shall we?" he said, his voice suddenly booming as if he wasn't speaking to me, but to someone who might be listening. He approached with quick determination, and I held my breath, waiting for the injection to pierce my battered and sensitive skin. But it never came. He was constructing a ruse. Maybe this man will get me out of here. Regardless of who he was, or who

Maru was, I was thankful for their help, since I was helpless.

Then it hit me. Like a tsunami of images and sounds. Faces and conversations bombarded my mind. Memories flooded in so fast that my weak and foggy mind struggled to process them—or even identify them as my own. My first suspicion was that the other Lucius was back. These were *his* thoughts, *his* memories. But I didn't detect his presence. I had no idea where he went or if he was even capable of returning. I just knew that for the moment, I was alone in this body.

I saw images of myself cataloging books in a library —taking the subway countless times—buying the same old newspaper from the same newsstand on the street outside my apartment building. I saw myself reading alone in the near-empty loft by a single glowing lamp. I saw solitude and loneliness—and then I saw Dax. As the images continued to flood in, I watched Dax follow me through the library, check out books and return day after day until he finally approached me. These visions painted a picture of a life that was off track well before Dax came onto the scene.

Overwhelmed by the sheer number of snapshots flooding my mind, I struggled to drag my consciousness free of this event and bring myself back into the room. I focused on his words, on his actions and on his mission to get me out of here. *Could it be true?* I shimmied and wiggled to relieve one of my many bedsores. Just imagining the filth covering my lower limbs nearly caused me to vomit. With no grasp of time or any indication of how long I'd been stuck on this table, a new sense of urgency draped over me like a wet blanket.

From what I remembered of my first encounter with Dax, his anger had frightened me, and the thought of it now terrified me even more. He wouldn't stop. Whoever these men were, my mysterious friend would not deter them. I needed to remember more, and fast. So, I closed my eyes and focused on the stream of images that had flooded me moments before. I dove headfirst into those memories and tried to corral them—to claim them as my own. The deeper I dove into the stream, the quicker I realized that many of them were mine. The lonely man in the library and the solitary man reading in his apartment were all snapshots of my life before finding myself on Easter Island in a body that looked like mine but contained two different consciousnesses—two different versions of Lucius Xavier.

There was still no explanation for how I ended up on Easter Island, but by the conversations around me, I was confident that's where I was. Now, images and events helped form an idea of who I was before I ended up in a lab experiment halfway across the world.

"Lucius? Lucius, are you in there?" A rushed and panicked voice broke through my fog, bringing me back to the steel table and leather straps. "Listen to me. If you can hear me, you need to just give them what they want. Orpheus is coming. He is coming, understand? If he gets here before they get what they want from you, you will wish you were dead. Please, for your own good, just let them have it." The rushed breathing and high-pitched but hushed voice left just as abruptly as it arrived, the brief interaction causing massive turmoil in my stomach.

Not knowing who this frantic man was or if he was a part of this group called the Kai-Tangata, I had little information other than the name Orpheus. A name everyone whispered under their breath so the universe couldn't hear them. That I would hand over my immortality to them, which, of course, I don't have, is insane. It's nothing tangible to hand over because it doesn't exist. This is crazy. It was time to return to reality, forget this nonsense about immortality, and figure a way out of this situation. Yes, I had someone calculating a way to get me out of here, but how could I rely on someone I didn't know? If I was sure about anything, it is that words mean nothing. Only action counts, and it was time for me to take it. So I listened. I quieted the chatter in my head and took in all the details of my surroundings without using my eyes. The thick layer of crust still held them captive, but there was a lot I could decipher with the senses I had left.

A clock ticking, footsteps echoing in the distance, filtered air flowing in and out of the room, and the humming of what sounded like several electronic devices. I focused on the surrounding noises and painted a picture of a sterile hospital room. I saw white-tiled floors and large air vents covering the ceilings to pull out whatever toxins they were expecting to release here. Metal carts full of surgical equipment lined the walls, and right next to my bedside, an IV pole loaded with several bags of fluid. The scrape of metal against metal shocked me out of my head and back to the present. Someone was here. I smelled the same aftershave I had smelled since I arrived.

My calmness and ability to trust my other senses filled me with urgency and an increased desire to survive this situation. His arrival could not have been more on point. If he was, in fact, here to rescue me from these insane men, now was the time to talk about strategy before our window of opportunity closed.

"Listen, my name is Terrence. I am here to help you. Dax is demanding results, and I am not sure I can stall him any longer. Pretty soon, they will not care if you are alive or dead. Orpheus believes Dax is being too soft on you. I have a hunch you will soon be dissected, especially if Orpheus has to come here and outrank Dax to get results. I don't know what will happen to either of us if we don't get out soon." Terrence sighed, a hint of desperation in his slow exhale.

"Don't you have a plan? How did you think you would get us out of here?" I asked, my voice hoarse from being dormant for so long.

"Honestly? I planned to fake your death. Soak you in a tub of cold water long enough to bring on hypothermia. This way, your vital signs, and breathing would be so shallow you would appear dead to the untrained eye. Then I would drag you out of here to where Maru is waiting, revive you, and off we go," he said. As if his plan was foolproof, and he couldn't believe he was experiencing any roadblocks.

"And was there a Plan B?"

"If there was a Plan B, do you think I'd be freaking out right now, Lucius?" Terrence asked, his voice pitching frantically.

Whoever these people were, they had very little experience. Just as more questions formed on the tip of my tongue, I recognized the now familiar sound of scratching metal on metal. We had a visitor.

"Awe, so you are in there, after all. The men were beginning to think we had fried you beyond repair, but it seems there is a bit of you left." The grit and malice in Dax's voice was not something I would ever forget, and the sound of it so close to my ear sent tremors through my body. "I can see your eyes flicking behind your veiny eyelids. I know you're listening. You seem to thrive under your sensory deprivation. Maybe it's time to try something else." His insinuation was clear, but the idea of having my eyelids slashed open by the man who put me here sent my heart into overdrive. I listened to him fumbling with metal objects, imagining they were sharp surgical tools. My recent urgency to survive transformed into a new wish for death. Two quick movements had me screaming in agony; writhing in my restraints. "Oh, you can speak! We are already making progress!" He bellowed, enjoying playing the role of the torturer. A searing pain spread across my face, and the warm flow of blood covered not only my face but continued to pour down my throat and onto my chest. With my eyelids now slit open, I was rid of any sensory deprivation. I struggled to see through the debris of skin and blood.

Through my gory veil, I was unable to see the delight on Dax's face but could detect it from the sheer glee in his voice.

"You just don't have a clue, brother. Do you know what is coming?" he asked, pressing his lips against my ear, hissing his words, revealing his own fear in the process. Of course, he must be referring to this infamous Orpheus Terrence had already warned me about.
The hint of fear in Dax's voice only cemented the idea that this person was someone I did not want to meet.

"Lucius! Just tell me, for christ's sake!" Dax yelled in a guttural voice while heaving what sounded like a metal tray across the room in his rage. Anxiety burst to life within me at the whim of his hostility, and unfortunately, that felt familiar, but all I could do was remain still and try to choose the perfect words to get me out of this mess. Dax and everyone else in the Kai-Tangata believed I had immortal gifts that could somehow be taken, and I was hoarding them. Hemming and hawing, I had little time to figure out how to respond to Dax—but no response at all would deliver more pain. I had to say something.

"Dax…" I got his name out, so that was a start. I didn't know where to go from there, and my throat was killing me. It was dry and cracked from dehydration. My only option was to go the route the other Lucius had started. Denial. "I'm no one… I have nothing to give you, Dax." Having spoken more words in these last few minutes than I had in weeks was excruciating. All I could picture were exploding blood vessels and hanging dead skin on my esophagus walls. There was nothing I wanted more in this moment than a tall drink of water. The blood that poured from my face into my mouth was nearly welcome.

"Don't you dare," Dax whispered. The sound of a chair dragging across the room and stopping near my bed painted a clearer picture of what was happening around me. Now able to feel his breath on my skin, I had nothing more to add, so I waited for his next move.

"Father always favored you, Lucius. You were the chosen one since the second you burst into this world, screaming your little head off. Mother and father were both fixated on you while I slowly but steadily faded into the background. And if these memories aren't enough, how about how you've evaded the Kai-Tangata for the past six months? No one evades us. So don't tell me there is nothing special about you. I, of all people, know you have exactly what I am looking for." With a sigh of exasperation, he seemed to be out of ammo.

Shifting as best I could on the steel slab, I thought Dax's words sounded authentic. At least he considered them to be true. *Could we really be brothers?* The idea seemed insane, and even the other Lucius wasn't certain, but the events of my life lately had certainly been illogical. But it didn't make them any less real. At this moment, I decided I had no more time to wait for memories to return— memories I may or may not have access to. I had to fill in the blanks myself.

"If we are brothers, how can I have something you don't?" The only relevant question I came up with and the only question worth answering to determine the truth in all this. Confident, Dax heard me as the timbre of my voice returned to normal with each attempt to speak. The blood flow was lessening, making it much easier to get my words out. Silence. Either he didn't know how to answer me, or he was working on concocting a story I would believe so that I would divulge my secrets willingly. I fought against the drying blood covering my eyes, but still couldn't see Dax. I couldn't see his face, which I so desperately needed to in order to determine his sincerity or lack thereof.

As this thought came and went, Dax remained silent, but his actions spoke volumes. He placed a warm damp cloth on my eyes, letting the dried blood loosen. He gently wiped my eyelids, careful not to pull on the ruthless slit he had made earlier. After a minute or two of light cleansing, I was not only stunned by his actions but could almost see his face. I struggled to focus on what lay around me. It was as if I had never used my eyes before. The fluorescent lights burned my retinas. With persistence, though, Dax's face finally came into focus. That effort cost me soreness I never thought eyeballs could experience.

Dax and I stared at each other for the first time. Really looking at each other, each with our questions lingering but unspoken. His dark brown eyes were bloodshot and glossy. Lines jetted out at their corners, and a weary look spread across his face. He held a washcloth covered in my blood. Coming out of his trance, he appeared embarrassed by his sympathetic actions and returned to his stern demeanor, quickly concealing any vulnerability I may have witnessed.

"Now that we can see each other, I will answer your ignorant question." Shaking his head in disappointment, he seemed unsure how to continue. "I was always smarter than you. But it didn't matter—it didn't make one bit of difference. You had something intelligence could not replace, Lucius. Not to mention the complete love of mother and father, but that's beside the point. I found what I needed elsewhere, in Marseilles." Pausing again, Dax paced the length of my bed, running his hands through his brown hair and over his face before he finally said what was bursting to get out. "I know you've seen him. Our father. You've even been with him… somehow." Dax stopped and stared at me as if waiting for me to confirm his suspicions. Maybe I had seen our father or an image and voice of a man who claimed to be him—a fact I had yet to believe wholeheartedly. The fact remained that these events happened to another Lucius, and he was left holding the cheque, so to speak.

"Don't waste your energy trying to deny it. You have all the telltale signs of someone who has traveled the dimensions. Terrence may not know what they are, but I spotted them on you immediately. As soon as Terrence hooked you up to the heart rate monitors, I saw the additional heartbeat. Every third heartbeat contains an anomaly. Consistent with someone who has left this realm and landed in an alternate dimension." Fidgeting with the zipper on his cargo jacket, Dax looked every bit the part of a jealous brother. But all I cared about was the frightening truth he had just delivered. A truth that made complete sense, and once it was out in the open, it was clear there was no other explanation for how I came to be in this situation.

In my timeline, an event transported my consciousness to another version of myself in a parallel dimension. All of this was so beyond comprehension, but I knew I was closing in on the truth. From what I remembered of my old life, I was doing nothing but waste it. In this life, I'd definitely made errant decisions that had gotten me into this tight spot. Still, there was a fire inside me that I had never felt before. A fire that urged me to see this through, even though I understood very little about what was happening. As this realization sunk in, I had nothing to lose by telling Dax the truth, or my understanding of it.

"My memories are foggy, Dax, but yes, I heard a voice who claimed to be my father. This voice helped me get to Easter Island but at the moment, I couldn't tell you why I trusted it. Especially when this stranger inside my head didn't clue me in on what the hell was going on." Contemplating what to include in this tale and what to leave out, I continued, excluding the fact that I was a Lucius from another timeline, struggling to piece together memories from two very different lives. Then I realized. The more I wrestled with what to tell Dax, the harder my mind worked to find the missing pieces. In the midst of this turmoil, a memory fell into place—as clear as day.

At first, the recollection was just the sounds of people screaming, guns firing, and the wind howling. Then slowly, an image formed in my mind, followed by feelings of fear and grief. I saw myself standing on top of a giant crater amid men and women fighting and killing each other. Two men protected me from the chaos as I stood there, doing nothing to help and nothing to prevent it. A woman, whose name I couldn't grasp, screamed an order, and my two bodyguards rushed to take me down into the crater. We escaped through an underground tunnel system, and they left me alone in the shadowed cave full of strange artifacts and treasures.

Although the details are sparse, I knew that the woman was killed and that I spent time with my father down in those caverns. Even without the details, I could sense this truth in my heart. *How can I be so sure when these aren't even my memories?* An inner voice replied, *maybe they are becoming your memories.*

"Lucius!" Dax screamed, no longer tolerating my brief trip down memory lane. I spewed out my newfound memory, seeing no reason to withhold it. He already had the advantage of knowing more than I did. Maybe he would keep talking if I did.

"Who are you going to believe, Lucius? A real person standing right before you with photographic proof of our connection? Or a haunting voice who chooses when to help you or when to leave you to die in the dungeons of the Kai-Tangata?" His anger was palpable, but there was truth in his words as well. Where was this guiding voice? I thought about Dax's conclusions. I knew the other Lucius trusted this voice, but I had yet to communicate with it. And the facts remained clear; if he was my father, where was he?

"Well? We have little time Lucius. What's it going to be?" Arms crossed in front of his chest, Dax silently pleaded with me to believe him, and a part of me did.

"I remember little of my childhood. I don't remember that picture or my parents, but I think you're telling me the truth." It stung to agree with Dax after this abduction, but I couldn't deny there was validity to what he was saying, even if it wasn't the whole truth. I needed a strategy, and agreeing with Dax was the first move in my invisible chess game against the Kai-Tangata.

CHAPTER 2

Dax's interrogation left me drained and confused. My head was spinning with so many conflicting memories—emerging and blending two different lives, overlapping, and both were screaming for attention. The chaos in my mind pounded between my ears with such fierceness anyone walking by could hear it. Closing my eyes, I relished this time alone to consider all Dax had told me and all that had returned to my memory since our conversation. Terrence would be back before long, and I would need a clear head if we were to have any chance of escaping this situation.

Sleep grabbed hold of me. Not in a gentle, lulling way, but in an urgent and aggressive pull from the wakeful world towards darkness. My sleep had been restless and fitful since waking up in this stainless-steel room, but there was something so threatening about the dark now. The blank canvas that startled me previously was gone, replaced by a frightening painting splashed with memories from two lives fighting to merge—to create one clear picture. The chaos was palpable; heavy with fear and confusion. The entity of the two lives threatened to rip the breath right from my lungs.

Focusing on drawing deep and long breaths, I watched the canvas before me warp and evolve as the darkness lightened and the bedlam lessened. Continuing to breathe deeply, I watched like a man sitting in the audience at the theater, only it was my life story on the screen. *Can this really be a dream?* Even in my dream state, I questioned what I was experiencing. Never having had such an intrinsic impression before—what was it, if it wasn't a dream?

Finally, the surrounding scene calmed, allowing me to take in the canvas of memories before me. That conversation with Dax sparked something in my subconscious, revving its engines into high gear, allowing entry to old and new memories alike. I saw mundane things like me walking to work in the early morning and taking the subway across the city to see friends. Not interested in the boring details of my previous life, I needed to learn about *this* Lucius' life quickly. The fear of this illusion fading before I had the chance to learn all I could, pressed on my chest, forcing my long, slow breaths to notch up the pace.

There it is. I saw the continuation of the memory that surfaced during my conversation with Dax. A dirty and beaten Lucius stumbling through an underground tunnel system, looking for something—a particular cave. As an outsider, I watched as names and details burst into my mind like fireworks. But one stood out, "Maru." Maru is the one who saved me. She sent me down to those tunnels before she died on that crater ridge when the fighting broke out. She needed me to survive, to make it down to those caves and find my father.

Skipping ahead, I could see a Lucius who was frustrated, confused, and exhausted, sitting on a dirt floor in a cave beneath Easter Island, talking to a stone tablet. He held the tablet with reverence, staring at it sometimes with amazement and other times with rage. He believed he spoke to his Father in another dimension through the tablet. Sometimes he felt that. Other times he thought he'd gone mad.

I sensed the darkness growing thicker. It dragged my attention away from my canvas of memories. Losing time in this strange ethereal experience, I rushed to take in as much as possible before the recall disappeared. My eyes beheld thousands of square slides containing single images that connected the memories. As the darkness tightened its grip around my body, I spotted one last flashback. In an instant, my eyes connected with the image and the creeping grip of darkness abated. My senses exploded with the new environment around me. *I was there.*

The dampness of the subterranean world clung to me, chilling me. Standing puddles across a rutted dirt floor surrounded me. All around me were ancient stone artifacts, thousands of years old—some broken and tattered. But in the far corner of the cave was a glittering pile of treasure— not from this world. As much as the shiny pile of coins, plates, busts, and goblets mesmerized me, the plain stone bowl caught my attention as it slowly levitated from the dirt toward my chest. Instinct drew me to look into the bowl. *How could I resist?*

I saw blue skies, aqua lakes, and crisscrossing waterways. Golden structures dotted the landscape of this unknown location—this imaginary location. I scanned the images, taking them all in as they passed by me like a projector rotating through slides. People were laughing, talking, and building. Animals frolicked through lush vegetation as waterfalls spilled behind them. But what caught my attention was an opulent golden flower—a giant gilded building shaped like a tulip shone under the brightness of a sky so pure it seemed impossible to have been from Earth. Entranced by this scene, nothing could break my gaze away, trying to file each detail, each face, and all the bizarre flora and fauna. The images continued to scroll along and then they stopped on one man's face. That face drew a hint of recognition. *Is this you?* I asked the nameless voice I had been communing with. I couldn't, nor would I ever be able to explain it, but I knew in that instant I was looking upon the face of my father.

A man with a face no older than my own possessed long, flowing black hair and a dark complexion. His strength was evident from his thick build, and his stature in life seemed obvious. Even from a still-shot image, he was a man of power, a man who commanded and earned the respect of those around him—a leader. I could have stared at this image for hours, taking in every single detail, finally able to match a face to the voice, but it was too quickly replaced.

Before I registered any change, I was completely immersed in what I assumed to be one of the very imageries I had just viewed from the curious levitating stone bowl. I was at a complete loss. In the very far distance, I saw the giant silhouette of my body in the clouds. It was as if I were now both in the bowl of images and on the outside. Before my mind ran away with explanations, I immersed myself in scenery that could only be described as enthralling.

An ancient and mysterious city bustled around me, no one noticing the dirty man standing in awe in the middle of their cobblestone streets. I enjoyed this cloak of invisibility and strolled through what may have been only a dream. Regardless, the surrounding city was like nothing I ever saw in any history book. Golden statues, lush vegetation everywhere, blooming and growing without inhibition. Everywhere I looked, the city was alive in ways the twenty-first century never would be.

Wanting to take it all in before the dream ended, I darted through crowded streets, dodging past shops, houses, and restaurants, trying to see as much as possible before it disappeared just as inexplicably as it began. Every building glowed and glistened in the sunlight, all polished to perfection, made from a material the naked eye would perceive as pure gold. Enormous white pillars, awe-inspiring steeples, monumental staircases, and articulate symbols detailed every structure, not just those built for the rich. *Or perhaps everyone is rich here?*

After taking in as much architecture as my mind could absorb, my attention switched to the people. They could not see me running around like a madman in confusion and out of breath. This allowed me to scrutinize them in a way not possible in the crowded streets of New

York City. More than their appearance caught my attention. There was an air about them I didn't know a human being could possess. Yes, the streets were crowded, but there was no yelling or bumping into one another in haste. It was just the opposite. The populous of this mysterious city walked as if they had nowhere to be, at a gentle and leisurely pace, side by side with others. Some smiled and chatted while others displayed a look of contentment I had never seen before.

Standing amid these people made me feel self-conscious as if the answer to my question was clear—yes, there was something wrong with me, but there was also another way to live if I was brave enough to choose it. Losing sight of my original question of whether this city was real, I observed its citizens as if they were an exotic species. Women passed by wearing long tunics made of silk that flowed behind them as they walked. Back home, I would consider this attire from a higher status, but here it seemed every woman possessed the same luxurious garments. *Perhaps a city of equals?*

The men resembled what I imagined Roman soldiers to look like, although their expressions provided me with no details to make me believe they were warriors. Blank, serene faces passed me while I studied their short brown tunics, made of nothing as luxurious as the women's gowns. The fabric was similar to cotton, accented only by a thin rope around the waist to keep the garment secure on all shapes and sizes of men.

I walked amongst the crowd and saw their lips moving, but I couldn't hear their words. Even with this element removed, there was a soothing quality to walking in a crowd such as this. The layers of anger and sadness were blowing away with each step I took. Now the finer details of the city registered in my mind. Simple things like streets lacking garbage, having horses instead of automobiles, and solar panels instead of electric power lines—in some respects, the city represented the past and, in others, the future.

Like a lost sheep, I followed the crowd from the city center to the golden tulip building I saw in the bowl's images moments before. Upon approach, the people around me disappeared without a trace, as if they had never been there. Alone, I started towards the huge golden flower, but an unseen force held me back. I might as well have walked into an invisible concrete wall. The harder I tried to break the barrier, the more the scenery around me changed; drastically.

The beautiful greenery shriveled and burned under the immense sun. The streets were filled with screams of anger and hatred and ran red with the flow of blood. The houses crumbled. They no longer glimmered in the sunlight but appeared dark and dingy compared to what my eyes surveyed only seconds before. The sun faded when something thicker than clouds blocked its rays from reaching the city. Standing alone, shaking and confused, I watched the city transform into a nightmare. Tranquility was replaced with anxiety, and beauty transitioned into what could only be described as the aftermath of war. Tears welled in my eyes as I took in this shocking change, still fighting the invisible barrier trying to reach the golden tulip before it, too, was destroyed by this inexplicable wave of devastation.

The retort of cannons and gunfire rang in my ears, approaching quickly from the south. Desperate now, I placed both hands on the invisible barrier and pushed with all my might. I slipped as the sweat of desperation accumulated on the palms of my hands. I pawed and clawed at the wall. I didn't know where the impulse came from, but I felt I *had* to reach the golden tulip, and the more seconds that passed, the more desperate I became. Thousands of footsteps sounded in the distance, closing in on my location. The sky continued to darken, and with one last display of strength, I threw my body into the invisible barrier, and an explosion of light and sound erupted, knocking me off my feet and stealing the air from my lungs.

The discomfort of cobblestones poking my back awoke me from my dip into unconsciousness. Within seconds, I remembered some of what had taken place, even though the distinction between dream and reality remained blurry. I summoned enough bravery to squint cautiously before opening my eyes to some fresh horror I could not explain. My claustrophobia sped up at the sight of dozens of angry and frightened faces hovering over my body. On the verge of a panic attack, I succumbed to darkness, relieved to be within its grasp once again.

Out of the clutches of the dream, I instinctively surged upwards, trying to escape the darkness, only to be quickly reminded of the chains locking me to the steel table. Barely noticing the pain of the shackles ripping into the skin on my wrists, I recognized the sterilized room around me, but my mind hadn't caught up to my body, still trudging through the trenches of the strange dream I had just escaped. Calling it a dream made me feel like I understood what was happening. Deep down, I knew for certain that it was something else.

Before I had time to process the strange trip I had just taken, the metal door to my room made that familiar scraping sound. Someone was here. Now that my eyes were healing, I could no longer close them to all that was happening around me, and for the first time, I saw Terrence, his kind smile gave him away. He looked disheveled, like he'd been sleeping in a ball on the floor, wearing the same clothes as the day before. His face was pale but streaked with dirt, and his green eyes looked frenzied.

"What's the matter?" I asked. I squirmed up on my elbows as high as my restraints would allow me.

"Don't talk now. Listen." Terrence crept towards the metal door and placed his ear against it. Watching intently, I didn't speak or make a sound while he seemed to assess who, if anyone, was in our vicinity. The intensity of this moment delivered an explosion of clarity, reminding me of the danger I was in. Satisfied with his evaluation of the hallway beyond our doors, Terrence rushed over to my bedside and slipped a tiny key into the palm of my right hand.

"Under no circumstances let anyone see that. I will be back, and I hope you'll come with me. Understand that our time is running out, Lucius… be ready when I return." Terrence's stare was intense. His resolve was firm. *We are leaving.*

It took an entire day for me to work that tiny key into my wrist restraints, but when I finally achieved freedom, there were no words to describe my utter relief. I hadn't felt my hands in what felt like weeks. The pain was unyielding, but the more I wriggled my wrist and fingers, the more the sensation returned, and the pain receded. I attempted to rest my body weight on my numbed hands to pull myself upright. Several attempts were necessary before I sat up, breathing freely. I'd spent so much time lying flat on my back. It was amazing what such a simple posture change did to uplift my spirits and boost my resolve.

I stopped, holding my breath, listening as deeply as possible for any sign of movement toward my room. I could not risk someone bursting in and seeing me unchained; it would mean death for not just myself but Terrence as well. Not only was I free of my restraints, but I was also about to climb off this table. Legs shaking, I swung them over the side of my cot and allowed the frigid coldness of the cement floor to jolt them from their sleep.

Savoring my newfound freedom and feeling immensely grateful for my new alliance with Terrence, my blood coursed with adrenaline.

Hearing only the humming of the air conditioning unit, I took one last risk before reattaching my restraints. I attempted a quick walk around. Unsure whether my legs could handle the weight of my body, even though I had a hunch my weight was significantly less than it had been upon my arrival, I still doubted my strength. Already used to the bitter cold sensation of the cement floor, I hinged forward at the hips and allowed my legs to take my weight. My wobbling knees had me fearing the worst, but my arms flailed until I was suddenly stabilized.

I stood on my own two feet. I experienced the strength within myself I had almost given up on—almost forgotten was there. A burst of hatred sent a flame from the pit of my stomach to my throat. I didn't need some voice, fictitious or real, to guide me. I was a grown man with an inner strength to wield. My confusion and disappointment regarding my father's voice had not and would not leave the forefront of my mind. It was a constant struggle to focus on the problem at hand, which was to escape this scenario alive before the dreaded Orpheus arrived. I didn't know anything about the man, but I understood the fear his name struck in those around me. A few tentative steps took me from my bed to an IV cart only two feet away, further than I had been since my arrival.

High on newfound courage and rediscovered strength, I almost missed the sound of footsteps steadily approaching my door. Not daring to breathe, I listened for a split second before confirming the growing entity of fear in the pit of my stomach. Key clutched in the palm Terrence had left it in, I hurried as quickly as my weak legs could carry me back to my bed. Wrestling clumsily with the metal cuffs dangling from the bed rails, I was desperate to get back into position before that metal door swung open. It was no longer just my life that depended on it.

That tiny key was almost my death, but I calmed down enough to reestablish some of my hand-eye coordination and locked my restraints—all the while listening to the pounding footsteps getting louder and louder. With only seconds left to regain my composure, I was confident the color had receded from my face, and my breathing would appear normal. Clutching the key so tight within my right fist, I was sure blood was going to drip onto the table, but there was no way I was loosening my grip on what was now my literal key to freedom. As the doorknob turned, I prayed for Terrence—prayed it was time for our escape.

"It's time to talk," Dax said in a low, guttural voice. "Just the two of us." Closing the door softly behind him, he took a second to survey the room, confirming it was just the two of us. All he saw was medical equipment and stainless steel in desperate need of a polish.

"I don't know what game you think you are playing, but you aren't playing it alone. Orpheus is coming. He's on a flight tonight. Do you know what he will do to everyone in this bunker in order to get what he wants? He will stop at nothing." Dax's soft-spoken words quickly escalated into a rant, his fear shining through brighter than any sunrise I'd ever seen.

"Who is this Orpheus everyone is so afraid of?" One of the many questions resting on the tip of my tongue. But I couldn't just blurt them all out. I needed to be strategic. Dax could kill me with his bare hands, and I didn't want to encourage that.

"Orpheus commands the Kai-Tangata order. Not just the New York branch—the *entire* order—thousands and thousands of men all around the world. He is ruthless, Lucius. If you think what you've been through with us has been bad, you are in for a shock, brother." Dax said, the timbre of his voice returning to normal with a hint of sympathy I wasn't expecting. He leaned in close to my face, resting his hands on the bed rails. My instinct was to shift away, but I stood my ground. The smell of his tobacco breath nauseated my empty stomach, but I stayed firm. Dax was not himself. He had let down his armour since last we spoke. If ever I was to get any information out of him, now was the time.

"Dax, you know that I have nothing tangible to give you. I don't believe I have the abilities you're talking about. I am not immortal. I'm no one. Please, if you really are my brother, won't you help me get out of here? Don't you have any compassion for your own flesh and blood?" I asked, throwing it all on the table. Why wait? Orpheus was coming, and once he arrived, no opportunities would be left to weaken Dax. His armour would not only be back on, but locked shut.

My words appeared to hit him like a slap in the face. He jolted back, leaving more space between our faces, but close enough, I saw the flecks of red sprinkled across his black eyes. But these eyes were impossible to read, and his expression was blank, but that flinch hinted that my words had cracked his hard exterior. The humming of the air conditioner filled the room, sounding louder and louder the longer I waited for him to respond.

"Lucius, I came here to talk some reason into you. I came here to make sure you understand the sacrifice you're making. Don't for a second think your presence here is anything other than a human sacrifice. Once Orpheus gets here, your life will end. Simple as that. So, yes, I have some compassion for my blood. I'm here, aren't I?"

"Yes, you're here, but you're not offering me help. You're just here telling me Orpheus will kill me for something that is not humanly possible to possess, let alone give away." I said, working hard to keep my voice down. The last thing I needed was more Kai-Tangata members.

"Listen close, Lucius." Dax growled into my ear. The fervor in his voice masked my disgust at his cigarette breath. He had my full attention. "Since the day you were born, my life has been one defeat after another. Don't expect me to save your ass just because our arrogant father refuses to! Ironic, isn't it? When you were born, I ceased to exist. You were the most important thing in the world. And now, here we are, about to murder you in cold blood, and he can't be bothered to save you. Yeah, confuses me too, kid." With this, Dax dropped onto Terrence's office chair with a screech and a look of exasperation. His exhaustion and frustration were obvious as he ran his large, calloused hands over his face.

Not sure how to respond, I said nothing but watched him closely. His mannerisms were familiar. His inclination to rub his face when he grew frustrated was also my inclination. So many subtle things told me we were brothers, but my mind still fought to concede to the truth of it. Perhaps it still reeled from being dragged from one timeline to another, but the facts remained the same. I had a brother who gave me an ancient dagger in one timeline, which carried me to another. He'd tried to kill me on more than one occasion, and now I believed he was trying to help me.

"Why are you a part of this? Why are you so obsessed with becoming immortal? The idea sounds more like a punishment than a reward," I remarked after sorting through myriad thoughts and feelings. My question seemed to startle him. When he removed his hands from his face, I saw surprise and confusion, as if I should already know the answer.

"I need to prove I can do this, Lucius. I need to prove to Marseilles and our father that I can be immortal without either of them. They both abandoned me, but I won't abandon this quest. I am worthy of immortality, same as you," he said, his voice gruff with the intensity of his mission statement. His beliefs would not be shaken. This much was obvious. He needed to prove that he was worth something and at this moment, I felt sad for him.

The sound of the desk chair rolling across the cement floors shook me from my inner thoughts, and I watched Dax leave. His shoulders were hunched, and his breathing was quiet. I may not have convinced him to free me, but I learned Dax had weaknesses like anyone else.

****

I filled my dreams with images of Atlantis—the Atlantis I corrupted with my defective human mind. They were images of my old life, an entire dimension away, and homespun visions of what my future held in store, thanks to my overactive imagination. My mind could not decide if Atlantis was real or if I'd experienced a head injury and this entire experience was nothing more than a hallucination. These doubts cast significant shadows over my ability to make accurate decisions. *How can I make correct decisions with a flawed mind?*

Caught between oblivion and semiconsciousness, I struggled against these visions. Tossing and turning violently in my restraints, the pain of my torn skin brought me back to awareness. Out of breath and damp with sweat, the images of my dreams were far worse than the memories I carried from a life I didn't live. Still catching my breath and watching the remnants of my nightmare flit across my mind, I jolted away from these frightening images at the thought that I may have dropped my handcuff key during my restless sleep. No longer feeling its impression in my palm, dread yanked me awake. Only able to rise up on my elbows, I scanned the floors around my bed in a panic. Not seeing it brought no relief. *How could I have lost my only leverage?*

With my heart pounding and sweat dotting my forehead, I rummaged around the edges of my steel-framed slab. After many terrifying seconds had passed, I nudged the tip of the key with my forefinger. Thankful I hadn't lost it, I still had to edge it towards me before my morning visit from Terrence. I couldn't take the risk that he may not be visiting me alone. There was too much at stake. After several attempts and nearly pulling my arm out of its socket, I finally had the key back in my grasp. I was certain I would never sleep again in this place, dreading what might happen.

Too anxious to go back to sleep, I lie staring at the air vents dotting the ceiling, stroking my handcuff key, relieved that I hadn't lost it thanks to my fitful sleep. On the cusp of new nightmares, my fingers brushed over something on the side of the key. I uncurled my fingers from my sweaty palm and felt the engraving on the side of the key. Of course, most keys engraved manufacturer names on their sides, but something was different, sloppy about this etching I had not noticed before.

MARU

Someone, presumably Terrence, had taken the time to carve this name into the key, leaving me a clue I had taken far too long to notice, let alone deduce its meaning. Maru was a name floundering in the soup of memories from the other Lucius. Her name held immense emotion and power in his recollections, but to me, it meant little.

Before I could take the time to separate foreign memories from my own, my stomach muscles clenched at the sound of rapid footsteps approaching. Whoever was coming my way was in a hurry, and the odds of that boding well for me were slim. Terrence burst into the room, huffing and puffing as if he had been running for miles to get to me. I struggled to hear over his rapid breathing for other footsteps, in case he was being chased, but was relieved to detect nothing.

In as calm a tone as I could muster, I asked, "What's going on, Terrence? Are you okay?" Still hunched over, clutching his knees, he tried to regain his breath. Raising his hand towards me in response, I waited. I fiddled with the key and searched my memory bank for Maru and the part she played in the other Lucius' life. Only one thing was clear: Terrence had infiltrated the Kai-Tangata to save me. How he managed this I couldn't imagine, but the longer I looked at Terrence, the more I wondered if he, too, was a prisoner here in some form or another.

"He's coming, Lucius. His flight just landed. We need to leave. Now." His voice was calm, but his eyes darted around the room frantically.

"How? Do you have a plan? Does anyone know you're here?" I asked quickly, needing a five-second synopsis of what we were facing. Sensing we were short on time, I unlocked my wrist restraints, awaiting Terrence's response.

"Those vents you've been staring at for weeks, of course," he smirked. Terrence rearranged the medical cart, IV pole, and the lone chair as a blockade in front of the door. Of course, it wasn't nearly enough to stop anyone from bursting in if they wanted to, but it might trip them up for a moment.

Out of my restraints, I finally noticed the stepladder Terrence had brought in. He set it directly beneath the vents. I flung my legs over the side of the bed rails and realized immediately that I was wearing nothing more than a hospital gown. *Where are my clothes?* Sensing my question, Terrence threw a small brown paper bag at me that I also had not noticed. I chalked it up to my lack of sleep and top-quality nightmares. There was no time to dwell on the enormous holes in my observation skills.

"Thanks." I opened the bag and found a pair of jeans and a flannel button-down shirt. Neither was clean, smelling strongly of whiskey and motor oil, but it was better than the hospital gown that displayed my rear end to anyone who wished to see it.

"Follow me and don't fall behind. It won't be long before Dax heads this way. I overheard him last night at dinner. He has something new in store for you this morning. He wants to save face with Orpheus, and Orpheus is only three hours away." His words were rushed and inaudible as he clumsily unscrewed the four screws around the ceiling vent. "And before you ask, yes, Maru sent me. Now hurry." Carelessly flinging the metal air vent to the floor, he hoisted himself up into the ceiling. As his lower body disappeared, I knew this was real. This was happening and I had this mysterious Maru to thank for it.

My weakened body resisted every command, making it ten times harder to follow Terrence's lead as I fumbled up the stepladder. The air vent on the floor caught my eye, and although it took me three minutes to climb that ladder, I knew I had to collect that vent and replace it behind me once inside. I couldn't make it easy on them. Motivated to hurry by Terrence's urgent whisper, I stumbled down the ladder, grabbed the vent, and weaseled my way into the hole in the ceiling. The fluorescent light from the room below leaked up through the ceiling tiles just enough for me to see the outline of Terrence's face. His strange smile was one I couldn't place, but trustworthy or not, I was out of my restraints and away from my cell. A burst of energy zipped through my body for the first time since waking up in this timeline.

CHAPTER 3

Knowing enough not to speak, I took a deep breath, got on my hands and knees, and followed as closely as possible behind Terrence. Crawling carefully across the flimsy cardboard tiles, I tried not to make a noise or hit my head on the plumbing only inches above. I left only a few inches between my hands and Terrence's heels, not wanting to lose him in what appeared to be a labyrinth of twists and turns. Ventilation ducts and electrical wires ran every which way, creating the image of what the inside of the human brain might look like if I were crawling through it.

We turned right first and then a sharp left around a ventilation shaft. Right again, careful not to kneel on what appeared to be the underside of a light fixture and straight through a narrow ingress, inconsistent with the rest of the structure. "Do you know where you're going, Terrence?" I whispered as loud as I could risk. We heard voices from below, a constant reminder that the Kai-Tangata were still within earshot of our escape in progress.

"Yes," Terrence muttered over his shoulder. Irritability noted, I struggled against the many other questions I had on the tip of my tongue. How were we going to exit this building without being seen? Are we underground, above ground? Where are we going? I decided it was good enough to rotate through the questions in my mind to fill the silence and steady my anxiety. I pondered what situation I had gotten myself into.

We had been crawling through this attic labyrinth for what seemed like forever. We had to be getting close to an exit point. The longer it took to escape, the more time I had to concoct notions of how Terrence might betray me once we were out of this attic.

My thoughts engrossed me so fully that I began to ignore my surroundings and concentrated on hypothetical plans of escape from a man who had so far shown no signs of betrayal. The pit of my stomach leaped when my right hand teetered on a rotting floor joist. Worrying about dangers from Terrence that hadn't even presented themselves, I tried to focus. We were *both* escaping from the Kai-Tangata. It was not the time to daydream and expect the worst from someone who offered aid—someone who could've left me behind to save himself.

Now treading in complete darkness, it was clear we were in an uninhabited section of the Kai-Tangata base, a sign that we were close to whatever exit Terrence had planned. He halted in front of me, raising his left hand as a signal for me to stop. Doing as instructed, I tried to quiet my breathing so we could detect any sign of movement. Even the slightest noise could mean risking death if a member of the Kai-Tangata caught us. It wouldn't be long before Dax entered my room, realizing I was gone. We were running out of time. The image of an hourglass appeared in my mind, creating urgent panic I had somehow avoided until this moment, focusing so much on the hypothetical instead of the real dangers that loomed.

Silence. It seemed we were in the clear, but Terrence wasn't convinced, holding his position without moving an inch. I remained still as well. I had no idea our trajectory, so

I had to swallow my impatience. I watched while Terrence glanced rapidly from his watch to a ceiling vent less than ten feet from our current position. Terrence must have been waiting for a specific time, permitting us to move forward only then. But the sand in my imaginary hourglass was depleting rapidly, and my heart rate raced as fast as the falling sand.

I saw nothing but wires dangling from the plywood above my head and the odd ray of light shining through the drop ceiling tiles behind us. Darkness wrapped its invisible arms around me, constricting my ability to breathe. The longer we sat still—not moving away from the Kai-Tangata —the more my mind and emotions teamed up against me.

"Lucius," Terrence whispered, snagging my attention away from my angst. "It's now or never. Are you with me?" Again, he offered that strange slanted smile.

Waiting for my response seemed a moot point. I had escaped my room and followed him this far. There was no going back. Nodding, I tried to hide my irritation and confusion. I was dying to get moving. Anything was better than sitting vulnerable above hundreds of members of the Kai-Tangata.

Without another word, Terrence headed toward the ceiling vent he'd been eyeing—our exit. Carefully, he lifted the grate and set it on a plush pile of pink insulation beside it. Repositioning myself so I could peer over Terrence's shoulder, I stared into the abyss, trying to sense the environment beneath. The dark hole appeared ominous yet stimulating like we were lowering ourselves into the mouth of the beast. As we waited, listening to nothing other than our raspy breathing, I grew anxious to jump into the unknown and get the hell out of this building.

"Let's go. Lower yourself down. Be careful not to knock over the ladder that's right below. Any noise, and you will wish you were dead. We have less than seven minutes to get from here to the side door I unlocked last night for us."

"Why are you smiling?" Unable to control my volume, I regretted my outburst. But the more times I witnessed that strange smile, the more suspicious I became of him.

"Just get in the hole if you want to live," he chuckled as if this situation was amusing.

I was not amused. But he was right. We had to move forward. I placed my hands on either side of the ventilation shaft and prepared to lower my body to the ladder Terrence claimed existed in the darkness below. Immediately I noticed that some of my strength had returned during our journey, adrenaline fueling me, no doubt. Feeling the burn in my biceps, I kicked my feet around, searching for the ladder. Locking onto it, I climbed down.

Not realizing how hot and stuffy the attic had been, I took a few long drinks of fresh air while awaiting Terrence's descent. Standing together in complete darkness, the compact size of the room told me Terrence must've chosen a storage closet. Smart. "What now?" I asked, hoping my shaky voice didn't expose my nerves.

"Quiet."

"We are running out of time." I urged Terrence, ignoring his pleas for my silence. I had to remind myself that he was my way out of this place. I mustered all my willpower and stood silent, awaiting instruction. It felt like ages since we heard voices or a sound of any kind, but Terrence wasn't taking any chances. He listened with his ear pressed to the metal door before opening it just a sliver to confirm the hallway beyond was empty. Without saying a word, he threw the door wide open and ran. Not having to be told anything, within a few giant strides I was right on his heels, eager to escape these strange dungeons and get as far away from the Kai-Tangata as possible.

Running at full speed, we fled down a long, stark corridor. Painful reverberations charged through my body with each foot strike against the cement floor. Expecting to see stone walls and dirt surrounding us, I was stunned to find the corridor clean to the point of sterile, lined floor-to-ceiling with bright white paneling. Door after door zoomed past my peripheral vision as we sprinted. Each entry displayed the metal sheen I recognized from the room in which I had been held captive. No name plates or signs revealed what these rooms might be used for.

The corridor seemed endless. I realized how lucky we had been not to run into a single person—or have anyone on our tail. As this realization set in, it was as if my mind had ordered the very thing I feared when the sound of footsteps echoed through the abandoned hallway. Unable to tell whether they were coming from ahead or behind, the slowing of Terrence's pace revealed he heard them, too.

"Where do we go? Are we almost there?" I rushed my words out, struggling for enough oxygen to even speak.

"Hurry," Terrence urged over his shoulder as he picked up his pace. I feared that at any moment, he would run smack into a Kai-Tangata member, or one would come up and grab me from behind. I moved faster than I thought this body capable.

The parade of doors ended, and the corridor rounded to the right. Desperate to see our exit, I managed to urge a little more speed out of my legs, nearly stepping on Terrence's heels. With nothing to break up the monotony of the sterile white walls, I felt like the walls were closing in on us—as if we were struggling to exit a labyrinth we would spend the rest of our lives caught in. As the fluorescent lights and the white walls played with my mind, the sound of footsteps approached and I was certain they were right behind me.

"Terrence, they are getting closer. Where the hell is the exit?" Barely able to fathom how Terrence thought running this far inside the Kai-Tangata facility without being seen or caught was feasible, a new sense of despair overtook me.

"Just shut up and keep running. We're nearly there." *We're almost there*. It was a frequent chant, but its stamina was fading by the second.

Gasping for air, Terrence was able to get out a few more words. "There it is."

Twenty feet ahead of us stood a pair of double doors with the oh-so-desirable exit sign flashing red above. With our exit in sight, it became apparent how my body was screaming at me to stop. My lungs were burning so intensely that I half expected flames to come shooting out of my nostrils, and the pins and needles in my legs were becoming more painful by the second. Sensing I had only a few feet of effort left, my muscles cramped and seized. It became a mind-over-body wrestling match to make it to the door.

My despair diminished when I saw Terrence place his hand on the doorknob of our exit. The early morning sunlight burst into the corridor, and without thinking, I dove through the air, traveling the last few feet to the doors with not a single toe on the ground. The warmth of the sunlight and the shock of contact with the cold, hard cement hit me simultaneously. The pain didn't matter. It was a joy to inhale free air.

"Get up, Lucius!" Screaming and still running, I could see Terrence half a dozen steps ahead. The sunlight glared off his blonde hair and green pastures surrounded him. Scrambling back onto shaky legs, I was able to make it another foot before my body was violently shoved down from behind. Smacking head-first onto the concrete, I struggled to breathe. Whoever had been pursuing us was now placing all their weight on my back. I struggled to get up and free myself from the crushing weight of their body.

"Stay down." It was a gruff order. The voice was unfamiliar, but it was a voice I would never forget. I watched as Terrence hesitated at the sight of my capture and then turned and kept running. It was over. He made his choice.

Breathing shallowly, with a beefy man on my back, I knew this failure sealed my fate. Before I escaped my torture chamber, I knew that if we failed, it would mean our death, and here I was, defeated and alone with a Kai-Tangata member, ready to take me back to Dax. My captor leaned in closer to my face. His cologne nauseated me. White dots clouded my vision as my body screamed for oxygen.

"How does it feel to betray the entire human race, Lucius?" the man whispered in my ear.

"I've betrayed no one," I huffed. "Whatever Dax has told you, it isn't true." Were my words even worth the effort? The members of the Kai-Tangata followed Dax without question. They believed in their mission, and I knew I was dead because of this belief.

The attacker hoisted me up by the back of my shirt. I mustered enough strength to stand toe and toe with him. I had nothing to lose. My escape plan had been thwarted, Terrence was gone, and Orpheus was coming. The least I could do was stand up for myself one last time. But whatever anger this man had towards me when he tackled me, it was gone, and he was back to following orders.

"Let's go," he said, shoving his shoulder into my back to urge me into motion. We were heading back toward my room.

"I caught him trying to escape. I've got him cornered at the West wing fire exit." I heard the man say from behind. "He's coming to get you personally, Lucius." He sneered at me, spitting out my name like venom. He'd called Dax.

Knowing that the exit door was so close behind me sent urgent tingles up my spine. *What do I have to lose?* I side-eyed my captor. The second he dipped his head to scan his cell phone, I lunged towards the exit, stretching my body to its furthest extent. I grabbed for the door handle, but it slipped through my sweaty fingers. Commotion was erupting behind me; Dax didn't come alone.

"What are you doing? Grab him!"

"Hurry…"

"I've got 'em Dax. I'm in control here."

I could hear several men bickering back and forth as I struggled for freedom. One of them had me by the foot while I kicked and writhed on the ground, trying to shake loose from his grip. The sense of nothing to lose ignited my strength and determination. I kicked one of my captors and jumped to my feet, suddenly strong enough to bear weight on them again. The three men lunged at me as if I were nothing more than a cornered wild animal to be caged. In these short seconds, I thought NO and something extraordinary happened.

They had what they wanted, and I had what I wanted, but only I could see the two versions of myself. One in the Dax's grasp being dragged back to the room I worked so hard to escape from, and the other was standing outside the building in the lush green fields, scanning for Terrence, hoping beyond hope he was waiting for me— somewhere. I stared at my translucent and rippling doppelgänger with no explanation of how I accomplished this remarkable and illogical feat. But the longer my mind mulled over the situation, the more I saw how this could work to my advantage.

CHAPTER 4

The large metal doors closed with a bang behind me, and not a single person followed.

I am alone.

Confused, excited, and relieved, all in one lump sum of emotion, I looked around, hoping to catch a glimpse of a fleeing Terrence. The thought of being alone filled my veins with icy fear; there was so much I didn't understand, so many questions I wanted, no, *needed* to ask him. From that small crack in the open doorway when Terrence escaped, I was sure I saw a vast green countryside, confirming I was far from New York City. But now, I was outside too, and it was hard to be sure where I was.

Steep, angled slopes surrounded me. Some were partially covered in bright green vegetation, and the rest were brown—nearly black. Then it hit me. It wasn't dirt I was looking at but charred earth. Daring to take a few steps away from the refuge of the Kai-Tangata door, I couldn't help but feel insignificant, standing at the base of a giant crater. A small lake filled the center, and a name popped into my mind as I struggled to regain any semblance of orientation. Rano Raraku. The other Lucius' memories overtook me, providing answers I had no way of knowing. His knowledge of Easter Island was extensive, but it wasn't just facts flashing through my prefrontal cortex. These facts all had strings attached—attached tightly to the other Lucius'. And the name *Maru* was tied to it all.

Facts turned into memories of being atop this crater fighting the Kai-Tangata alongside two men, Po and Ariki

—and also Maru. I felt a tickle of excitement recalling memories that were not my own. It was empowering.

My situation was precarious, but I wouldn't give up hope. I scanned the crater, lake, and all, for Terrence. I couldn't imagine how he climbed to the top in such a short time. He had to be here somewhere. Shielding my eyes from the sun's glare, I saw no disturbance in the water or movement on the crater walls. I refused to allow defeat to claim me. I took some time, breathing in the fresh sea air, savoring the wind on my face, and just simply enjoying my newfound freedom, a tribute to my fleeting friendship with Terrence.

I had momentarily forgotten about my second self. Still trapped in the grasp of Dax and the Kai-Tangata, fate quickly reminded me. Images that were not my current reality flooded my brain. They were not the other Lucius' memories but something else entirely. Translucent images overlaid my view of the famous Easter Island crater. I could see, hear and even distantly feel what my doppelgänger felt at the hands of Dax and his men.

"... is there some kind of incantation? A spell? Tell us how we access your immortality!"

"I've already told you, Dax, I have nothing to give you."

Utterly shocked by the idea that this second image of myself was speaking and I had nothing to do with its reaction or choice of words was disconcerting.

"Are you willing to die for a man who will not stick his neck out for you? He's not coming, Lucius, if that is what you are holding out for. You are alone." Dax's words struck me with a veracity I didn't expect. Though I stood free and safe outside the underground facility, his words still wounded me. He was right, I was alone.

"You are not alone." An airy and cheerful voice broke through the many roadblocks of my distracted and severed mind. Looking from side to side and struggling to see through the translucent images projecting from my doppelgänger, I saw no one who might've spoken these words. It was prudent to open and close my eyes a few times and reconnect to my true self outside the Kai-Tangata's grasp. I saw a thick black rope being lowered inches from my face. Having taken only a few steps away from the steel door, I was still concealed within the steep crater's edges. Someone was above, offering a rope to climb to safety.

Behind me was nothing but death and torture. Before me was a deep chasm offering no shelter for when the Dax and the others realized they were torturing what I could only describe as a figment of my imagination gone wild. If this mysterious stranger wanted to kill me, I would've been dead already, standing in the middle of a crater, completely exposed. I grabbed the rope, gave it a hefty tug to make sure it was in fact secured to something and used all the upper body strength I had to climb.

Bloodied and blistered hands brought me onto the flat ground over the edge of the volcanic rock. Safety—I hoped. My chest was heaving as I tried to fill my lungs with oxygen after climbing what appeared to be fifty feet of rope with nothing more than my bare hands. After a minute of lying face down in the lush grass, hands and arms trembling from the effort, I looked around and saw a familiar face. Terrence. He stood smiling, his relief tangible. He waited for me, after all. Without realizing it, I started laughing. I was so overcome with joy that we had found each other. When my irrational chuckling subsided, I finally noticed the woman standing behind Terrence. The owner of the voice I heard? But it was not a face I recognized, and I was getting nothing from the other Lucius.

"Hello. And you are?" Trying to regain a bit of civility after too many days of fighting and scrounging to survive, I revisited my manners for the pretty stranger.

"We've met." Her smile widened to the width of her narrow, sharp-featured face as she spoke, studying my reaction. Feeling uncomfortable, I diverted my gaze to Terrence, hoping he might give me some kind of clue who this woman was, but all I got from him was an amused grin.

"Look at me, Lucius," she said. "Is there nothing you find familiar about me?"

Terrence nonchalantly began moving away from the scene, finding it hard to contain his amusement with my uncomfortable situation. The middle-aged woman drew nearer, silently encouraging me to oblige and take a closer look. I stood up straight, ignoring the pain of my bloody hands, and tried to put on a calm and confident air while I examined this woman who clearly knew me. Of course, she likely remembered a different Lucius, but how could I explain that to her when I wasn't even sure how I got here myself?

She stood confidently in front of me, her head reaching only my shoulders. Short brown hair rippled in the wind. When my eyes dropped to her face, a spark of recognition burst inside of me. It was as if someone had lit off a firecracker in my mind. Those deep brown eyes were ones I had seen before in memories that were not my own. Those were the eyes of Maru. *But isn't she dead?*

"Not dead Lucius! Reborn," exclaimed the woman barely ten years older than myself.

"Are you reading my mind?"

"Naturally." Her smile was just as contagious as Terrence's and in the background of this strange encounter, he still smiled, waiting for me to catch up on what was happening. Speaking hesitantly, it embarrassed me even to voice my thoughts aloud. They seemed ludicrous.

"Maru?" My voice cracked, but not out of fear— out of hope.

"Yes, my boy. Our mission together is not over." With a patient smile, she placed her hand on my shoulder and squeezed with the love that a grandmother would give their grandchild.

"But I am not the Lucius you know," I said, fully aware of the danger of speaking these words out loud. Once she and Terrence realized I was not who they thought I was, they would abandon me.

"Oh, but you are. There is only one Lucius Xavier. Even though you are a Lucius from a different timeline, you are here for a reason and this is still your story to finish," Maru said, her words and tone that of a guru. I believed her without question or hesitation, feeling safe and comforted for the first time since I awoke racing through a strange country in a foreign body.

"How is any of this possible? Why am I here?" I asked. She knew more than I did, including how I jumped timelines—hopefully.

"Now may not be the best time for stories. We are too close to your captors, and this Orpheus may be more perceptive than the Kai-Tangata members we've dealt with so far. He may know that the Lucius in their custody is not the real Lucius. We need to leave." Still speaking as if discussing nothing more than the weather, a tolerant smile never left her face. I had no clue how she knew the details of my escape. All I knew was there was something magical about this woman and the feelings the old Lucius had for her quickly morphed into my own. Or maybe there was no distinction at all between his and mine?

Back to reality. There was no doubt she was right. I'd lingered near this exit door for too long. Surely the infamous Orpheus had already arrived, and I would see him shortly through the eyes of the doppelgänger I involuntarily left behind. There were just too many things to say, too many questions to ask. My only option was to follow obediently in their wake, assuming they had a plan, and do as instructed.

"Yes, we have a plan. You can rest easy for a while… I can answer all your questions when we are undercover." Maru's emphatic nod, contagious smile, and petite stature in her new body made me feel like I was the only person in the entire world—the only person who mattered to her.

Clambering over volcanic debris and the challenging landscape of Easter Island, we trudged forward. Terrence remained the leader, and Maru and I followed him in single file, barely speaking a word, each so concentrated on the dangerous terrain that there was no room for distraction.

"Everybody down. Now." Terrence spoke softly but with enough urgency to hint there was not a second to waste. Dropping simultaneously, Maru and I hit the ground behind Terrence, sinking into the concealing vegetation. Before I even had the chance to ponder what or who may be coming towards us, a small personal aircraft flew over us at such a low altitude that I could read the side of the plane. 'Easter Island Air Tours', the aircraft read in bright green letters. A relief.

"Maru, I'm going to need your help here." Terrence had reached the end of his ability to lead our party, and it was now something only Maru could accomplish going forward. Looking at each of them, back and forth between their faces, I saw an unspoken conversation taking place between them.

"Are you guys going to fill me in?" I tried to hide the bitterness and jealousy in my voice that they were in cahoots, leaving me out on the sidelines, only feeding my loneliness.

"There is nothing for you to fear, Lucius. Do you trust me? Us?"

I had absolutely no hesitations about this. Of course, I trusted Maru and Terrence. They had aided in my escape, doing nothing to hinder my faith in them. Still, I hesitated, portraying indecision out of nothing more than childish jealousy.

"Of course I do. You both have done nothing but save my butt time and time again." Not being able to curb my smile, the three of us stood alone in the verdant Easter Island countryside, chuckling. "We will use the cave system again, but we cannot return to your family cave, Lucius. Your father has provided new instructions now that the Kai-Tangata has gained reinforcements." Nodding to me as they spoke, Maru silently tried to quell my fears.

"Don't ask more questions now, Lucius, unless you want to head back to your doppelgänger. We need to move. We have only a few more hours before the sun sets and we need to be on the other side of the island by then. Please, no more delays." Terrence patted my back as though trying to persuade a child to clean his room, and I immediately felt embarrassed by my behavior. Somehow, being able to forget my abduction, the deaths I'd witnessed, and the dozens, if not hundreds, of lethal men hunting me to the ends of the Earth, I had become complacent with my situation.

With the famous Easter Island head statues at our backs, there was nothing to orient us in the landscape that stretched ahead except the odd house dotted here and there among the tall grass. You had to know your way on this island when you left the main roads or the National Parks. This type of landscape made me feel primitive. Not in a negative way, but in a freeing way, unable to articulate until you are there with the wind on your face, the rocks under your feet, and seeing a vast countryside not populated by skyscrapers and concrete; natural.

Besieged by a blinding pain, I doubled over into the long grass, landing atop a sharp rock jabbing between my ribs while I tried not to howl in agony. Unaware if my friends had noticed my absence or not, I could barely breathe, and calling out to them was not an option. It had been hours since my last experience with those translucent and fleeting images from my doppelgänger. I was wondering if the illusion had faded, but all evidence pointed to the contrary.

"… You're too soft, the lot of you."

"Orpheus, we've been doing everything we can. We captured him, didn't we? That is more than the last leaders did."

"Don't make excuses… look at this imp. How hard could it have possibly been to capture him? He's weak, pathetic Dax. You gain no credit as far as I'm concerned. After all, I've been told this man is your brother?"

"What of it? He doesn't matter to me. That has nothing to do with anything."

"I'll be the judge of that."

Another blow of pain seared my right side. Scrambling to lift my shirt to examine my wound, it didn't surprise me to find anything but dirty, intact skin. Adjusting and readjusting my eyes, I could see nothing but the blue, darkening sky above me. Still, the voices were still ringing in my ears—voices I was sure were not near me, but back at Kai-Tangata headquarters.

"Lucius, are you okay? What's wrong?" Terrence jogged back, noticing my absence. "Maru! Something's happening to Lucius. I don't know what's going on." After only a few blinks of my eyes, Maru's face appeared, hovering above my own.

"I will teach you how to control this new ability, Lucius, but not now. If you need Terrence to help you walk, we only have about an hour's walk left before we reach our destination. Until then, there isn't much I can do for you out here."

I appreciated her honesty even though the pain threatened to take my consciousness from me the longer it drew on, forcing me to ask. "If my doppelgänger dies, what will happen to me Maru?" Scared stiff to hear the answer, I needed to know at least this while we carried on. This Orpheus everyone was so afraid of seemed to live up to his reputation.

"Your doppelgänger, as you call it, is nothing more than an extension of your soul, Lucius. It is not you, but a shadow of you. You are safe no matter what is happening in that Kai-Tangata facility right now."

I used Terrence as a crutch. At least I was relieved to hear that my life wasn't in danger. Terrence shared his strength with me, and I tried to focus all my energies on our destination, each step, and each breath, desperately trying to ignore the pain. Whispering in my ear so Maru couldn't hear, Terrence asked, "What's going on back there?" Still unsure of how Terrence came to be in the service of the Kai-Tangata, it was not surprising he was interested in what was happening since our escape.

"Orpheus is there. He is yelling at Dax for not getting what they want from me. He has a wrought iron pole, heated somehow to the point it's glowing that he is jabbing into my doppelgänger's side. Apparently, just the beginning of these new tortures."

"Thank your stars. It's only your Erebus taking the brunt of what Orpheus has to offer."

"Erebus?"

"It's what Maru calls your doppelgänger. It means your dark shadow. That's all I really know, though." It seemed to me that he knew much more than this, but it was also clear that Maru was the one who wanted to explain everything to me, so Terrence changed the topic.

"Lucky we came across each other, isn't it? It took me days to convince Dax I knew all sorts of medical techniques and completely bogus science to get your immortality out of you. Of course, I know nothing of the kind, but I was convincing enough; apparently," he said with a wink, visibly proud of his espionage skills.

"The pain is just about gone. Thanks, Terrence, but I can walk on my own now." With a simple nod, Terrence gently removed his arm from around my torso, and after a second of imbalance, I reestablished my strength and carried on. How could that excruciating pain dissipate so quickly? How could the visions and the voices come and go? *Do I have control over any of this? Where is my father?* The latter was the most important question to me. The words of Dax echoed through my mind. He was right. No matter what type of man my father was, I was alone, just like him.

"In here, boys. Just in time to see the sunset." Maru's smile remained a constant beacon of positivity, creating the illusion that instead of running for our lives, we were on a great adventure. Stopping midway through the countryside, we were, in fact, just in time to see the bright, fiery red sun setting behind the tropical landscape of white sands, palm trees, and seven Moai statues standing proudly on their monument. Anakena. We were just mere miles away from the famous beach of Easter Island, where the Moai stood guard to protect the island from the ocean's wrath, amongst other things. The three of us remained silent, smelling the sea air, even occasionally feeling the mist of the sea. The wind blew ferociously through us as if we were nothing more than another blade of grass. Within minutes, the sun disappeared behind the horizon of the vast ocean, taking its fire with it and leaving us with a twilight sky just as beautiful.

"Alright, we can sightsee later. Time to get undercover for the night. Come on, then," Maru said with a soft smile and a motherly touch that few women can claim to have so naturally.

"How are we going to get undercover in the middle of an open field?" I asked. Seeing the patient expressions of my traveling companions I knew once again I was behind. Terrence walked three feet to our left, while I stood watching his every move. I noticed him pull a sizeable chunk of grass until what appeared to be a trapdoor emerged from the soil. Obediently and without another word that would make me look foolish and unobservant, I jumped into the familiar darkness of the underground.

Once inside, Terrence pulled an industrial-sized flashlight out of his pack to guide our way. The new younger body Maru inhabited sprung into the cave system without fuss or embellishment, reigniting all the questions I wanted to ask. Being around Maru brought me relief. I no longer had any distinction from the old Lucius' memories to my own and the connection to her was so strong. I had no urge to contradict these feelings.

"Well, that was significantly easier than it's been in nearly seventy years!" Giggling, she relished in the easy motion of her new body. "Follow me, then. Just a few more minutes and we can all rest and refuel. We are heading to one of my many hidden sanctuaries on the island. After living here for nearly a century, you accumulate secret properties." The nostalgia and lightness in her voice made us both smile. Amazing, this young woman possessed a century-old soul.

"Oh Lucius, my soul is far older than that, my boy." She read my mind. "You are just a baby!" Laughing, she shook her head at my ignorance and began leading us *boys* once again.

Hiking through the damp cave system was familiar to me. It seemed like only yesterday the older Maru was leading a different me for the first time to my family cavern —the very place I was so keen to flee. Water dripped down the basalt walls from the surface above our heads. All I heard was the hypnotic trickling and the sound of our feet compacting the soft dirt with each step. Left, right, then left again, and another sharp right. *How on earth does she remember all of this?* Relishing in the silence, I tried to accomplish the same silence in my mind. I desperately needed the quiet. With more than a little effort, my mind quieted significantly and just in time.

"Lucius, light those candles for me will you, dear?" Maru said quietly as we made our last right turn around a large rock wall protruding much further than the rest. I could not see past it. Once rounded, I saw our new hideaway. Candle sconces hung on either side of the walls, one per foot for the depth of the underground room. Maru and Terrence trudged past me into the great darkness ahead, trusting me to light the candles without a match or lighter.

Standing in the grand rock entrance with dozens of candles on either side of me, I simply imagined lighting them. I pictured the flames in my mind—flares bursting out from nothing more than my sheer will. Intending to go to each candle and work my magic as I had done with my father, every candle was already alight when I opened my eyes. A flickering glow cast light onto walls as dark as midnight, illuminating the cracks, crevices, and luminous flecks of minerals. Feeling elated with my accomplishment, I revelled in it for a few seconds before following the others into the great cavern ahead. Somehow, without thought, I set ablaze a dozen or more candles. I didn't know how it was possible, but the evidence was right in front of my eyes; impossible to deny what I had just accomplished—all without the help of this *Father* the old Lucius was so reliant on.

"Lucius, come on. We've got food here," Terrence called out, his voice echoing, bouncing off the volcanic walls. Not able to remember the last thing I ate, I went from standing still to sprinting at the mention of food. At the end of the narrow tunnel was a cavern with ceilings well above twenty feet in height, its vastness a little terrifying. But the sight of Maru and Terrence feasting around a small wooden table in the center was a relief. I reached for it all, forgoing manners in my haste to eat. All that mattered was my ravenous hunger.

"Slow down, boy, you're going to end up sick. When was the last time you ate something?" Maru's voice was concerned as well as curious. As if to say, *was your father not feeding you all this time?* "I don't really know, actually." Considering it for some time, my memories came up empty. Of course, I wouldn't be alive today had I not been eating. "I guess my memories are too full of more important things to remember than what I've eaten—but obviously it was something!" I said with a curt laugh. I was the only one laughing. The seriousness on the faces of Terrence and Maru made me question just how bad I looked. As bad as I felt, apparently. "I hate to point out to you two that I wasn't exactly being served gourmet, balanced meals with the Kai-Tangata." I huffed, before shoving an entire biscuit in my mouth.

"No matter, no matter, eat up—but slowly." She smiled at me but exchanged yet another secret glance with Terrence. Nothing mattered but my hunger and thirst, so I ignored them and their strange glances and continued to fill my body with fresh bread, exotic fruits, and nuts until I could no longer eat or drink another bite. With one human urge satisfied, my urge for answers swelled to the point of explosion. Feeling safe and full for the first time in weeks, there seemed to be no better time to pummel Maru with as many questions as my mind could summon; there were hundreds.

Before any words escaped, the details of Maru's secret hideaway grabbed my attention. With a full belly, my focus became clear, and I saw so much more. Petroglyphs covered the surrounding walls, ancient drawings done in a time I could scarcely imagine. "Did you make these, Maru?" Not waiting to hear her reply, I wandered closer to the rock walls, running my hands over the strange images. They were colorless—simple scratches on the dark rock, leaving behind a white design. Delicate, winding shapes, my American mind struggled to understand. The longer I stared at the images, the more they made sense to me. Maru, or whoever carved these symbols, was depicting the ancient life of the islanders through art.

"I carved them oh-so long ago, curious boy." Maru, now right beside me, stared at the images in the volcanic rock with a look of nostalgia on her face that someone my age could never fully appreciate.

"Us islanders, the old ones anyway, have been using these volcanic tubes beneath the islands for centuries. I may have carved these symbols, but if you were looking closely on our journey here, the walls down here are full of stories told in a language very few still understand." Never taking her eyes off the basalt walls, she no doubt imagined the person who took the time so long ago to carve these beneath this mysterious island. Still finding it hard to fuse Maru's ancient words with her middle-aged body, all I could do was soak it in.

Her short, wavy brown hair was tangled and tousled from the journey. Her khaki hiking pants somehow remained crisp and clean. But it was her eyes I could not stop staring into. They were the eyes of the Maru from my memories, minus the gentle lines. But the idea they were in a new body made my mind reel with possibility and impracticality clashing together on a mental battlefield. I had no clue which side would win.

Terrence remained ensconced in the depths of Maru's cave while we took in the petroglyphs together. "Please Maru, tell me everything. I'm not sure how much more my mind can handle before it literally breaks." Whispering, my vulnerability was still exposed. But there was no hiding my desperation for answers.

"Let's sit, shall we? This isn't the type of tale that can be told in passing. It will take time, understanding, and patience, Lucius. Do you understand?" Pausing to allow her words to sink in, she continued, "It is imperative you shut down your mind. Open yourself to new possibilities, or my story will be nothing in the end if you are not willing to expand yourself."

Quickly I spoke to defend myself, "But I am willing, Maru. I have no other choices. I mean… I just lit candles with my mind, didn't I? Tell anyone else that, and they would lock

me away in a second! I have no more walls up, Maru.”
Hearing the defeat in my voice, I found myself enveloped
in a strong and loving embrace by my new, reborn Maru.
With her thin arm around my waist, she guided me back to
the wooden table we had eaten at earlier. Rather, the table I
had *inhaled* food at earlier.

“Where’s Terrence got off to? I asked, wondering if
my emotional exchange with Maru caused him to wander
off in discomfort.

“He’s preparing for the next leg of our journey.
He’s on our side, Lucius. You’ve no need to spend energy
worrying about that.” Motioning for me to take a seat, I
obeyed without question. The wooden stools were ancient,
perhaps just as ancient as the petroglyphs in the entryway—
old stumps someone had carved into a seat. The thought of
how many people had taken a seat here before me was
humbling.

“Now that we are comfortable… where shall I
begin?” Clasping her hands together, she lay them on the
table and appeared as calm and collected as any working
professional in the world. Yet the story she was about to tell
was one very few in the business world, or any other sector
would believe. Dozens and dozens of questions hurtled
through my mind. Which one was the more relevant, the
most important? When the images flooded my vision and
the pain returned, I knew I had to ask. “How did I get
here?”

CHAPTER 5

"As you have no doubt gathered, the word 'you' is not as singular as you were led to believe. Yes, of course, you are *you*, but you are not the only *you*. Many versions of ourselves travel through this vast universe on their own journeys, but not so different from the journey we embark on in our own dimension." She paused to sense how much of this strange commentary I understood. She watched me closely and likely saw nothing indicating we were on the same page.

"Right, so down to the basics, Lucius. When Dax inserted that dagger into your life in the timeline you are familiar with, an ancient force awoke, one that has been dormant for a very long time." Her eyes focused on the dagger hanging from my worn leather belt. Suddenly, I felt incredibly careless for leaving it hanging there with very little knowledge of its origin. I moved to take it out of its tattered holster and asked the only question I could. "What is so special about this dagger?" Turning it around in my hands, there was no doubt it was stunning, handcrafted at a different time with the kind of care that doesn't exist today. The hilt fit in my hand perfectly. It was decorated in vibrant colors, unique shapes, and seemingly authentic gems.

"That dagger is not of this world, Lucius. It belonged to your father so long ago. There is no measurement of time in your language to explain just how long that dagger has been waiting for you."

"Waiting for me," I repeated blandly, but there was definitely a question in there that didn't need to be articulated.

"That very dagger used to spend its days attached to your father's hip. One day it was stolen from right under his nose. Since that day, it has woven in and out of myth and legend from coast to coast and world to world. Until, of course, it was doomed to find its way into the hands of one of the Kai-Tangata members.

"Although we couldn't understand how he found it, once we learned Dax had the dagger, we knew it would drag you from your normal life into this timeline. What you must understand is that the dagger was created with a mission. To find the one soul in the universe prepared to save us all from the darkness. That soul was not the Lucius of this timeline, so it guided Dax right to you. In a timeline where humans no longer believe in anything I'm about to tell you." Without breaking eye contact and without malice in her voice, Maru grabbed a cracker or an ancient cookie from the table and snacked while I attempted to digest what was sure to be just the tip of the iceberg.

I paced around the small wooden table. Pacing calmed my nerves, allowing me to take control of the situation at hand, even if that was impossible. Many options flashed through my mind at lightning speed, from insanity to the deep dreams of an unconscious patient. But deep down in my gut, I knew she was telling me the truth, that she was real, the Kai-Tangata was real, and this cave underneath Easter Island was real.

"Your brain is fighting you right now, Lucius. My advice, don't engage. Allow it to process on its own. I am introducing a world of possibilities to you that your mind believed to be science fiction only moments ago. Come sit here. We don't have a lot of time and there is still a lot more to discuss before Terrence gets back and we must leave here." She patted the wooden stool gently. The kindness in her face, her eyes, and the sweet timbre of her voice was impossible to ignore. Obediently, I returned to the table. A small part of me was excited to hear just how much more the universe had in store for me, but most of my mind remained in chaos.

"Now, let's talk about the 'Lucius' you left behind in the Kai-Tangata facility," she said, watching me closely. I assume checking to make sure I hadn't completely cracked from this mind-bending tale.

"Only the Alvanata can perform Sachin, and it has been nearly millennia now since anyone outside the realm of Leto possessed these skills. You, my boy, have done so quite successfully. What you see now, before your waking eyes, is a transparent view of what your Erebus is experiencing, your doppelgänger, as you say. You can separate that reality from your own; it will take practice to master this skill, of course.

"Now before you ask more needless questions, stop. You know what happened in that facility, Lucius. Don't allow your mind to convince you it didn't or couldn't have happened. Just listen, please. Right now, the Alvanata are not our problem. Our immediate problem is Orpheus and the Kai-Tangata. All you need to understand now is that your father, Ameretat, has been one of the three guardians of the universe, the Alvanata, for centuries, if not longer. Chrychi, or dimensional beings, measure time differently, and some not at all. What you have accomplished with the Kai-Tangata proves that you are destined to follow in his footsteps." She took my hand in her own. She squeezed it with a grandmother's pride, even though her hand was very youthful.

"This is exactly what we, your father and I, have been hoping for. To silence the naysayers on Atlantis." Her last words fell out in a whisper as if she were speaking more to herself than to me. The mere mention of Atlantis brought back the horrid dream of what my dark and disturbed consciousness had done to the utopia, and I immediately felt unworthy of Maru's time, not to mention wracked with guilt. Perhaps the naysayers were right about me.

"No Lucius," she read my mind again, "what you saw in that memory was merely a reflection of what your consciousness looked like at the time, or more to the point, the consciousness of the other Lucius. It was *his* memory, after all. But I'd wager your consciousnesses are quite similar. What you need to know is it is within your power to change it for the better." Maru sipped from her banged-up grey metal cup. She drank fluids I knew my body needed, but it wasn't a priority. Maru was my priority.

"You're saying I can change what I saw?" Knowing that Maru asked for a ceasefire on the questions, I blurted it out without thought.

"That is exactly what I am saying. Your consciousness is always evolving, always changing, and we, the owners of those consciousnesses, have the ability to shape them—if only we have the sight to look into the heart of the universe—into *our* hearts, and take the leap, Lucius." Her voice was full of excitement, and her obvious belief in her own words nearly had me convinced.

"Now, getting back to task. It is time to teach you what I know about mastering your Erebus. Your father has spoken to me regarding this subject many times during our friendship, so I will relay what I know.

"You have the ability, as I've said, to separate your two realities. Now close your eyes, and focus on the images on your mental screen. Can you see what is happening in the Kai-Tangata facility?" she asked in a soft voice.

"Yes, I see it."

"Great, your Erebus is still strong, which means we have time. As you have no doubt figured out for yourself, the power of the Erebus is purely derived from your inner strength and your interconnectedness with the universe. Since you are new to this world, your erebus will not be at full strength. In time, it will fade, and the Kai-Tangata will find themselves with an empty bed and many questions.

"Take this. Cradle it in the palm of your hand. Sense it, Lucius. This is important—perhaps the most important part of your journey." Maru handed me something small, and smooth to the touch. With my eyes closed, I could only guess what it was, but I pictured a small, manicured rock, a gemstone perhaps. Still seated at the medieval wooden table, I did as instructed, grasping the small object in the palm of my outstretched hand. My fingers rolled the thing in all directions. I discerned its shape and enjoyed the coolness it brought to my skin. I focused my energies on it and, in doing so, somehow freed up an inordinate amount of space in my mind. I could easily categorize the images from my Erebus from the images of my reality.

"Yes, exactly! You've done it, Lucius. Keep hold of the object in your hand. Its power is now your own. Can you sense it? Coursing through you is pure energy straight from the core of the universe. With this object, you can easily control your Erebus and create as many as you would like. The possibilities before you are infinite in such a way that you may not understand now, but you will soon." Sensing I could open my eyes now, I saw first Maru's beaming smile and vibrant eyes looking at me as if I had just saved a child from a burning building.

In the palm of my hand lay an attractive yet ordinary-looking stone. Polished—yes. Smooth—yes. Its blue and purple facets shifted with every rotation. The more I stared at it, the more the color and fluid shifts entranced me. Blue, purple, green, pink, and white—a kaleidoscope effect every time I flipped the stone. Something about its iridescent qualities made me think Maru's words were truthful; this stone was not from Earth.

Maru's outstretched hand motioned for the stone, but the more I possessed it, concentrated on it, the more peace it brought me, and I was reluctant to hand it back to its owner.

"Come now, Lucius. That stone contains my universal power and strength. Soon you will earn your own. When the time is right."

It was hard to be angry or frustrated with someone who smiled like that, so I obeyed and relinquished the stone, immediately feeling a sense of emptiness.

"How can I control this Erebus if I don't have a stone of my own?" Worried about what it would be like to experience or watch my death from afar, I was eager to place all those images and thoughts into a compartment and lock the door.

"That is not how it works, Lucius. Your current Erebus is soon to die. That is true. Not likely at the hands of your captors, however. It will fade away. Your amateur powers can only go so far. This moonstone has many powers and strengths. It can bond with you, but it is not to be used for ignoring reality. It is to be used for living peacefully with whatever reality is yours." As she placed the moonstone back on a small metal platform resting on her ring finger, I could not imagine how I had missed it before.

"Now, we need to decide together, Lucius, since the three of us may spend a great deal of time together. I have one more story to tell before our time together is interrupted. Will you permit me?" she asked although it had to be rhetorical. Who would say no?

"Of course, please continue." Choosing to stand for the length of this new tale, I stretched my arms over my head and arched my back, relishing the safety I felt inside this underground cavern. It was a sensation I definitely took for granted in what I now considered to be my previous life.

"Dax is your brother, Lucius. I realize this isn't what you want to hear. The Lucius of this timeline refused to accept this. For your sake, I hope you accept this truth. If you don't, you will find nothing but pain and misery in your future. The reason you are here on this plane of reality is because that ancient dagger was drawn to you, Lucius. It is not a mere piece of metal. It is so much more. But like I said, time is short, and there is only so much we can discuss now." Maru abruptly walked from the table, a clear sign our discussion was over. Left alone, without distraction, I could detect the many facets of myself at war and wasn't sure which side to choose.

"Terrence in the house!" I heard Terrence bellow as he entered the vast cave, grinning and carrying half a dozen canvas bags. "Well?" he asked, looking back and forth between me and Maru.

"We haven't decided yet, Terrence. I was waiting for you." Maru replied.

My two travel companions watched me closely, scrutinizing me in a way that made me uncomfortable.

"What are we deciding?" I asked, trying to hurry them along.

"Well… Terrence has been off arranging our travel arrangements and doing a bit of reconnaissance on the Kai-Tangata members you left behind. We can no longer stay here. If you wish to continue down this path and learn who you truly are and what you are capable of, you need to come with us. If you prefer not to follow this path and want to blend back into the rest of humanity, now is the time to decide." So now their looks of evaluation made sense. They were each trying to gauge which avenue I would choose.

"How can you expect me to decide when I've been dropped into a story in the middle? I experienced nothing the other Lucius did. I've arrived here and am trying to piece together memories from someone else's life, Maru. This isn't a fair choice. I can barely tell what is real from fiction right now." I said, my tone rising the longer I talked to where I was nearly yelling. Clearing my throat, I continued, "I have memories of doing impossible things. But they're not mine. How can any of this be real?"

Maru and Terrence watched me carefully, and the feeling of being an animal in a cage did not escape me. "Lucius, what do you feel when you see these images and memories float through your mind? The ones that are not yours and that you did not experience firsthand." Maru asked.

I had been so busy thinking about those memories and categorizing them as someone else's that I had paid no attention to how they made me feel. I hated to admit it, but they felt like mine. Like I had done all these things while my mind told me I hadn't. "Lucius, there may be different versions of you across the universe, but when you travel through time, you accept the other's experiences and memories as your own. Your mind may tell you those memories aren't yours, but you know different, don't you?" She asked. Nodding to myself and her, she was right, even though I could explain none of this.

"It's time to begin your training and when the time is right, you'll be reunited with your father. Right now, you need someone who can withstand presence on the Earth— someone to be with you for proper coaching. Your father no longer has the strength to endure this world. What's it going to be, Lucius?" Looking back and forth from Maru to Terrence, I knew I had stumbled into something incredible, and even if none of it worked or came to fruition, it was still worth the risk. Dimensional travel, lost civilizations not lost, immortality, moonstone power, and who knew what else lay before me I was still yet to discover.

"When do we leave? I'm ready." I beamed with pride.

"Oh… you think you are ready?" They both grinned. My two new travel companions seemed to hold back a laugh, sharing an inside joke I wasn't sure I wanted to understand.

CHAPTER 6

We put our travel plans into swift motion after I declared my commitment to training and learning about the universe as no human had ever done before—at least none that I knew of. Within hours, we were boarding a private Hawker 400 jet from Mataveri International Airport. Fully expecting trouble from the authorities, to my surprise, we simply walked across the tarmac and entered the jet without a passport check or clearance needed. Terrence had clearly put their connections, favours, and any other leverage they had to work on arranging these plans, and I was glad for it.

Once in the air, I couldn't help but doze off. I never was able to stay awake on planes. My dreams were riddled with gunfire, death, destruction, blood, and screams. It was a fitful sleep full of faces, feelings, and echoes of my talk with Maru, all balled up into a fresh hell I knew nothing about.

"Ah, there is he. Finally awake. We've been flying for nearly twenty hours, and you've slept for, let me see…" pretending to ponder his answer, Terrence smiled, "nineteen hours!" Laughing at his joke, Maru smiled affectionately for a moment. I saw us as a family. Then his words filtered through my half-asleep brain… *twenty hours?*

"Jesus, twenty hours? Where the hell are we going?" I asked, shocked that we had been flying so long and still hadn't arrived—and that I'd slept for almost an entire day. Then something disturbing occurred to me. "We're still on Earth, right? This isn't some kind of crazy time travelling jet, is it?" Yes, I heard the words come out of my mouth and how crazy they sounded, but not any crazier than some things Maru had already told me.

"No, no, we're still on Earth. We are on our way to Kathmandu, Nepal. This is where your journey is to begin. Now, I want to make it clear to you and your subconscious mind that this is not a journey to enlightenment like you've seen in Hollywood films. This journey will take every bit of energy, strength, and soul you have to complete. It will be grueling, both mentally and physically, but in the end, you will realize you would have paid any price to reach *this* finish line." They both knew what we were getting into and had accepted the risks. I had to do the same even if I was going in blind. Was I willing to do anything to find the truth? To enter this new realm of the universe where anything seemed possible?

The answer was an unequivocal *yes*.

Choosing my words carefully, I wanted them to impact Maru. I wanted her to believe I could do this and complete this journey with her and Terrence. I focused on how to respond, and suddenly perceived open spaces in my mind and soul. Not something dark or negative, but a discharge of information. A freeing of thoughts and feelings I had been hanging onto, somehow released back into the universe, leaving me with a sense of relief that surprised and comforted me. There was no doubt changes were taking place within me. Unsure whether I was responsible or something cosmic was in control, the changes were welcome.

"Maru, I may not know what you've sacrificed for me, but I know that I will not let you down. I am going to see this journey through and will do everything I can to make sure I reach the end. I'm stronger now Maru, I think things are changing for me." My words hung in the lavish cabin of our private jet. No one spoke, and no one took their eyes off me. They were trying to determine for themselves if my words were true. I held their gaze, keeping my mind clear of the hundreds of doubts ready to burst through the front door. I was confident in my words and stood by them. After what seemed like an hour, which was more like a second, Maru broke the silence with her smooth voice.

"Yes, I believe you're right." She and Terrence smiled brightly. I felt like my journey was beginning, and the unknown was less scary.

We spent the rest of the flight eating, talking, and laughing as if we were a group of wealthy friends off to board a yacht somewhere off the Mediterranean coast. Of course, our actual destination differed significantly from that fantasy, but passing the time as if we had no care in the world was satisfying. *Perhaps there is no need for care or worries?* Pondering this, I watched as the others fell asleep and the cabin quieted, leaving me alone with my thoughts, questions, and memories. I couldn't help but think about Dax. My brother. He had tried to kill me on many occasions and was still in pursuit of completing that mission, but there was a sadness to him that provoked sympathy within me, regardless of what he'd done. Just as I wondered what he was doing and if my Erebus was still performing on Easter Island, the images flooded me like a dam yielding.

The visions were horrifying. It was uncanny to see oneself in duplication, living and acting as if the real you weren't safe flying over the Indian Ocean. My Erebus was not much more than a skeleton. Starvation and dehydration were clearly part of their torture as their frustration peaked. They covered its body in burn marks and stab wounds that had then been stitched up to make sure "I" didn't die. The look of hopelessness, pain, and misery was so palpable on its face that I couldn't help but wonder if I should help it. I had the power to create the Erebus. Maybe I could spare it more pain and send it back to the universe. Of course, Maru had been clear that I did not have the skill yet to create an enduring Erebus, but it had already been a week and the Erebus seemed to show no signs of fading, as far as I could tell. In fact, the more I considered it, the more the succession of events became clear. The moment I thought about Dax and the Kai-Tangata, the Erebus' images flooded my mind. *Did I call these images without realizing it?*

I shifted the images of my Erebus to a corner in my mind and looked around the jet cabin to see Terrence and Maru still sound asleep. My dependence on Maru was growing, and I decided I would not allow that to hinder me. It was time to make my own decisions and let the events unfold with no one's advice or input. Closing my eyes, I rearranged my thoughts to bring the Erebus to the forefront again. Dax and Orpheus were in the room staring at the emancipated body they had created, and for a split second, I thought I detected a glimmer of guilt on Dax's face as he stared at his little brother.

"You've failed Dax. Marseilles would be disappointed in the outcome here. We have tortured your brother to the limits of his life, and we still have nothing. The doctors don't know what to do. One has disappeared and for all we know, is naming us to the authorities right now. How could you let this happen?" Orpheus yelled at Dax, but there was sadness in his voice as well, revealing his own disappointment and thwarted dreams.

"There is something left. One avenue remains, but if it fails, the subject will not survive. It is the last resort and a long shot at best." Pausing, Dax seemed unsure or unwilling to share his secret with Orpheus. Of course, he would be forced to if he held back now. "There is an ancient text given to me by Marseilles. It speaks of an age-old offering to the gods. The immortal being in question must be laid out for the gods on an offering table and then lit on fire to release their immortal powers to those brave enough to stand the heat."

The two of them continued to discuss their last alternative, and I felt suddenly torn. Seconds ago, I wanted to free this shadow of myself from torture, and now a vindictive strategy overtook my thoughts. If Dax and Orpheus wanted to test this last resort and it didn't work— would they give up? This question floated like a delicate bubble waiting to be popped while I continued to listen to their argument.

"He would die. Is this correct? And, we wouldn't know if it worked until we burned him to ash? This is what you're telling me?" Orpheus asked Dax.

"Yes, that's exactly what I'm telling you. I have the book in my office. Marseilles gave it to me before he died and said our last stand is within it. We've tried everything else. Do you have any other ideas because I'm out?" Dax spat as if he were ready to wash his hands of this entire endeavor, perhaps this entire life.

They both stood staring over my Erebus, deciding how far they were willing to take this mission. The Lucius in front of them writhed in pain, half asleep or half-conscious. It was hard to tell. It disturbed me to know that my Erebus felt this pain. He was in fact only a shadow of myself, as Maru had described, but he was suffering and at my doing. The longer I watched, the more I wondered how a person could create multiple Erebus to do their bidding—to allow them to endure pain and even be killed for you. The idea appalled me.

"I have my orders too, you know, Dax. We have to continue. If this is our last resort, then so be it. We have to try. I can't go back empty-handed. We are running out of time." Orpheus appeared as afraid as Dax. It seemed they were both outside of their comfort zones. Now it was my turn to decide. Allow the Erebus to die to hopefully dissuade Dax and Orpheus to call off their hunt, or see if I even could dissolve my Erebus and put it out of its misery.

"It's an arduous decision to make and one your father struggled with time and time again." Maru's sleepy voice startled me. Forgetting I had been nursing a cup of water in my hand, I spilled it all over myself. Laughing, I replied, "Does this look like someone who can save the world? The guy who jumps at the slightest noise?" Not expecting a reply to my rhetorical statement, I mopped myself up as best I could with a towel and waited for Maru to continue. Wiping the residue of sleep from her eyes, she stared at me as if asking herself the same question. Her clothes sported wrinkles and dirt from the journey, and even her younger face appeared tired and worn. She looked so small and fragile, nestled in the large leather reclining jet seats, her feet dangling inches from touching the ground.

"Your father once created dozens of Erebus of his own to scout out the Kai-Tangata, but before making this decision, he thought through every set of consequences. He considered their deaths, pain, and perhaps even torture at the hands of our adversary. Essentially, these Erebus—or shadows, as I earlier described them—are pieces of the creator's soul. Therefore, when an Erebus dies or endures torture, these actions harm only one person."

"I don't feel any different though…" I whispered, considering these words to be true. I would've felt something if my very own soul were being damaged.

"It is not a sensation like a physical burn or cut. It is an injury that will not show itself for centuries or even longer, depending on how many Erebus you have created during your years. It will show itself when a weakness develops, one such as your father's. His inability to endure a presence on this planet shows a loss of strength within his very soul, a sacrifice made to put an end to this prophecy and protect you." Nodding slightly, as if seeing her words had gotten through to me, she nuzzled back into her seat, curled her legs beneath her, and resumed her sleep.

Let's assume I believed Maru's words, which I was inclined to do. Then there was really no question about whether to let Erebus die at the hands of the Kai-Tangata and prove to them that immortality cannot be harnessed or stolen. Funny that now I believed it did exist. Regardless, the thought of the torture that the poor shadow of my soul was enduring was distressing. I'd never been responsible for the death of a living thing.

Unable to quiet my thoughts enough to sleep… I wandered about the cabin. Back and forth, I paced the length of the jet from the cockpit to the larger-than-normal airplane lavatory. It was only a fifty-foot walk, but enough to burn a bit of energy and give my long limbs a well-deserved stretch. Restless, I rummaged through the empty overhead baggage compartments. We boarded with nothing on ourselves. After opening six of the twelve compartments, I was surprised to find three small leather carry-ons in the last bin. Hesitant but curious, I reached for and unzipped the first bag and found women's clothes and provisions. Oh, thank God, Terrence and Maru were thinking ahead. Fresh clothes were waiting for me in one of the remaining two bags.

Eager to clean myself up, I hauled the bags out of the overhead bin and rushed into the lavatory. A quick glance in the mirror and I barely recognized myself. My brown hair was so greasy that it appeared to be black. Dirt, debris, and grime covered my scalp, face, and every visible inch of skin. With about ten square feet to work with, I had more room than I would on a regular airplane. I stared into the small square mirror hanging over the aluminum sink, and took the lone white washcloth and soaked it in soapy hot water.

After nearly half an hour, I scrubbed my entire body, repeatedly rinsing out the cloth. It was no longer white, but I was refreshed in a way only a person genuinely deprived of such amenities could understand. Maru was kind enough to pack toiletries as well, allowing me to shave, brush my teeth and apply deodorant like a civilized being. And it felt wonderful. Stubble removed, odour eliminated, I stepped into a fresh pair of jeans and pulled a clean t-shirt over my head. Maybe they were trivial luxuries back in New York City, but these items were appreciated now on route to Kathmandu.

"We are beginning our final descent. Our expected landing time is 11:02 am local time," the pilot announced over the loudspeaker, waking both Maru and Terrence.

"What a sleep. I feel like a million bucks. How 'bout you, Lucius? Did you get some shuteye?" Terrence asked while he stretched his arms above his head and yawned loudly.

"I think 20 hours was more than enough." Smiling, I handed Terrence his carry-on and Maru hers. "Now, which of you is responsible for this gift? So glad someone was thinking ahead for me."

"Maru, of course," Terrence said, smirking at Maru, acknowledging she was the brains behind the operation.

"Well… thank you, Maru. I haven't felt this good since…well, what should we call it? My body switch?"

"If that helps you, I'm glad you found it. Now, Terrence, you get cleaned up, and I will jump in when you're finished."

Terrence didn't hesitate and disappeared into the bathroom.

Maru and I sat in silence, listening to the water running while Terrence cleaned up. Maru possessed a state of peace that eluded me—had always eluded me. Back straight, feet dangling off the edge of the high chair, and a serene smile spread across her face, she looked completely at ease with her surroundings. This was my goal. She was the mentor I wished everyone could have.

"I allowed the Erebus to follow through with the Kai-Tangata's last resort mission," I said. "If it goes the way Dax described, the Erebus will die and they will get nothing. Perhaps finally convincing them that immortality is not available for theft or removal."

"A wise decision. A small part of your soul for the greater good. But I must tell you, Lucius, have little in the way of expectation when the results reveal themselves. I have acted similarly in the past on countless occasions and no matter what I've done, the Kai-Tangata cannot be deterred. I'm not sure anything can convince them of the truth anymore. They are in too deep." Not moving a muscle, or even her head when she spoke, she stared ahead, focused in front of her. *What is she looking at? I have no idea.*

I could see her point. It had been centuries, if not longer since the Kai-Tangata began their search—and if nothing could stop them all that time, perhaps nothing would.

"Oh, we can stop them, dear, but not by suggestion or coercion. They cannot be tricked or deceived. They must be completely annihilated for our mission to succeed." Outwardly calm, her words were fierce, which stunned me. Her declaration we must 'annihilate' the Kai-Tangata made my breath catch in my throat. Maru was always a symbol of peace and unity. I couldn't reconcile her words with the image of her on the pedestal in my mind. Finally, I blurted out, "We can't just kill the Kai-Tangata. There are hundreds of them, if not more. I will not have that blood on my hands." Breathing heavier than normal, I tried to regain my cadence while nervously awaiting her reply.

"Did I not say our journey would be grueling? Both mentally and physically, Lucius?"

"Yes… you did."

"No one can prepare you for what is ahead, but you can't afford to be this naïve. There will be casualties when our quest includes saving humanity, Lucius. People will die, and not all will be with the Kai-Tangata. Innocents get in the way." Terrence creeped out from the bathroom at this moment and stood in the center of the aisle way, sensing he had intruded on yet another serious conversation.

"Our journey includes two primary goals, Lucius. Goal number one is to train you to think and act like a dimensional being and, if we are lucky, procure your acceptance among them. Goal number two is to use these new powers and intelligence to defeat the Kai-Tangata and their allies… by any means necessary. Do you understand?" Standing, bag in hand, Maru was ready for her turn in the bathroom but waited to hear my response for her own analysis, no doubt.

"Yes, I understand, Maru." Nodding to further cement my allegiance with her, I watched her turn and close the bathroom door without a sound. "I'm always causing trouble, aren't I?" I said, trying to defuse the tension. With Maru ensconced in the bathroom, Terrence sat down and shook his head at me. "What? I shouldn't have said anything, I suppose…" Sure, this was what Terrence was thinking. I believed it to be true. Why argue with someone as insightful as Maru, a dimensional being?

"That's not what I was going to say. There is nothing wrong with having your own thoughts and questions, Lucius. That's what we are here for, but you need to keep up, man. How did you think we were going to defeat the Kai-Tangata? Hand them a muffin basket and ask them politely to move on with their lives? Come on, man, we are at war here, even if the rest of the world doesn't have a clue. That's exactly what it is." Fiddling with his bag and adjusting himself in his seat, he also seemed to be completely comfortable with what lay ahead. Perhaps that was because he was more informed; had time to absorb what we were embarking on.

"What else aren't you telling me, Terrence? I have a right to know what we are getting ourselves into. What's waiting for us in Nepal?" Running my hand through my freshly-rinsed hair felt good. It made me feel like myself again, but perhaps that wasn't a good thing. I seemed to be losing my insight and regaining my stupidity.

"In the depths of the Himalayan Mountains, Ourania is waiting for us… for *you*, really." He sipped from his plastic cup of water. His new clothes and fresh shave made him look even younger. His round face was one of the features that made him so endearing—so likable. You looked at Terrence and knew he would be a loyal friend who would always have your back.

"Final checks before landing, please," the pilot said gruffly into the speaker system. Right on cue, the two flight attendants who had assisted in our boarding emerged from their secret hideaway at the back of the jet and fastened us safely in our seats. A knock on the bathroom door resulted in Maru's emergence, and, with these few quick actions, we were all ready to land in Kathmandu. But I was *not* ready for whatever was waiting for us there.

CHAPTER 7

Chaos ensued once our hasty customs rituals were complete. The airport in Nepal offered nothing of note except the usual relief of de-boarding a plane and the excitement that your final destination was near. All standing with carry-on bags in hand, I only at this moment realized Maru had changed like the rest of us, but she thought ahead to tailor her attire to our new environment. Terrence and I still looked like Americans in jeans and t-shirts. Standing beside us, she looked every bit the local wearing a bright red, floor-length skirt covered in intricate golden designs. Her top was nearly hidden behind yet another piece of fabric draped over her shoulder and crossing her torso. Noticing I was staring, Maru showed off her outfit with a twirl. The hem of the skirt swirled around her. She was a true marvel.

Maru took the lead and led us from customs to the exit, where dozens of transport options awaited us, their proprietors eager for clients. The men waiting with rickshaws were the most interesting to me. They were not deterred by the cumbersome luggage on their backs. Stepping out into the madness, I stuck close to Terrence while Maru perused the crowd, searching for someone, all the while smiling, waving, and greeting the locals in fluent Nepali. No one would ever guess she was not one of them. Then it occurred to me. Perhaps she had been… once.

We walked, shuffled, and squeezed our way through a maze of people and vehicles, blatantly searching for a specific person, although I had no idea whom we were searching for. Clinging to the brown leather strap of

Terrence's carry-on bag, I followed closely, often being grabbed and sidetracked by a driver desperate to get a paying fare for the day. On the other side of the paved airport road, Maru appeared to have found who she was searching for. Waving to Terrence and me to meet her, we quickly sidestepped several small, but brightly-painted tourist buses to reach her.

"This is Mataio, everyone. He will guide us over the Tibetan border." Maru stood beside the man as if displaying a prize of great importance. Terrence and I shook hands with the lanky figure closely guarding his tour van. Mataio smiled and shook my hand vigorously. At about my height, maybe an inch taller, his height clashed with the diminutive crowd. Khaki pants and a stained white golf shirt hung off his gaunt body.

Greetings completed. It was a relief to be ushered into his van, escaping the noise and chaos of the arrival gate. Bright green and white letters covered the rusted exterior of the bus. *Chrychi Tour Company*. I'd subconsciously absorbed those words while shaking the man's hand and then climbing in to buckle my seatbelt into the wobbly bucket seat. The interior was simple. Brown stains scarred the ripped grey fabric of the seats, and the radio blared music filled with tambourines and kettle drums. It was both beautiful and overwhelming with its diverse sounds. Once Terrence buckled in beside me and Maru took the front seat, I had to voice my thoughts on the familiar word. *Chrychi*. Dimensional beings, as Maru had once explained.

"Chrychi Tours? That can't be a coincidence, right?" I asked, leaving the question hanging in the air for anyone to grab, anyone who could or would provide the answer I was looking for.

"No coincidence, Lucius. Mataio is your… *cousin*… I guess you could say." Maru's reply was even more hesitant than my original question.

"Why do you say it like that, Maru? Like you aren't sure? Is he my cousin, or isn't he?" I asked. Only able to see the backs of their heads from my seat, it was impossible to tell if Mataio and Maru were silently communicating in an attempt to exclude me. My paranoia grew in the silence while I awaited what I believed to be a simple answer. Mataio turned in the driver's seat to face me.

"Lucius, I am a dimensional being from Atlantis. Your father tasked me with transferring our people into the borders of Tibet in order to meet with Ourania. I have been a tour bus driver officially for five years now, but I've been waiting to meet you. It's a genuine pleasure," he said, flashing white teeth. Nodding his head excitedly, his shaggy blonde hair tossed over thin shoulders.

"I'm sorry, I don't really understand. Why are there dimensional beings wandering around Earth in need of transport? I thought they could travel anywhere and be anything they wanted?" I tried to recall my conversations with Maru on the subject; certain this was the one thing I clearly understood, out of the many things I didn't, which made me even more confused and frustrated.

"Well, look at Maru, for example. She has spent nearly half her dimensional life on Earth, living as a human. When we travel to different times, dimensions, and planets, it is always our goal to amalgamate ourselves fully with the local customs, and that means traveling as they travel, eating as they eat… you get the idea." No longer smiling, Mataio assessed me with narrowed eyes. "We can talk more on the way. We better get going before things get too crazy. We're already bumper to bumper, so there will be loads of time to chat." Turning his attention to the chaos beyond the windshield, Mataio belched and maneuvered the tourist van out of traffic.

"It's over 100 hundred kilometres from here to the border, taking the Araniko Highway, Lucius. Get ready for the adventure of a lifetime… if we make it, that is."

Slapping my arm, Terrence laughed loudly at Mataio's unnerving joke.

The Araniko Highway rang familiar to me, but I couldn't place what, if anything, I knew about it. There couldn't be that many highways in Kathmandu. We were certainly taking the primary route to Tibet. While I racked my brain for what I thought I might know about this highway, Maru intervened.

"It's been voted one of, if not the most, dangerous highways in the world. But not to worry, dear, Mataio has been driving this highway nearly every week for five years. We are in excellent hands."

"Well, it's never my driving that's the problem," Mataio added, laughing and shrugging. Success or failure, either outcome was the same to him. My mind jumped back and forth from worrying about whether my Erebus was still alive and wondering who this Ourania was and why I had to meet her. I looked through my dirt-fogged window at the scenery. Mataio was not exaggerating when he said we would be bumper to bumper. Sitting in traffic, I could stick my arm out the window and touch the vehicle next to us. Lucky for me, claustrophobia was not a problem because our tiny tourist van seemed to be getting smothered. Men with rickshaws zigged and zagged through the narrow spaces between vehicles, making more headway than we were.

After only twenty minutes in the van, it suddenly seemed devoid of oxygen, and I found myself, along with my fellow travelers, panting as if I were running beside the van instead of sitting in it. The sweat dripped from my forehead and off the tip of my nose. The sensation of clean, dry clothes was about to be something of the past. After moving only a few feet in ten minutes, I figured we might as well have a conversation to get everyone caught up— mostly me, of course.

"So, does anyone want to discuss this journey? I know we are going to Tibet, but where? How are we going to get there? Is Mataio taking us the whole way? Why do I have to meet this Ourania person?" It was either 99 Bottles of Beer or these relentless questions. Something had to fill the silence. Tapping my fingers on my knees, I thought, *They all know, but why won't they tell me?*

"The entire purpose of this journey, Lucius, is for you to learn the ways of the dimensional beings and to become who you are destined to be. If I were to tell you the trials that lie ahead, it would defeat the purpose," Maru said.

"What purpose exactly? You said I am to be trained to be a dimensional being. Okay, I understand. But what is the secret purpose? Because I don't think this is all about my training." I had been sensing a deeper meaning to everything Maru said, but could still not pin down what was happening. But at least I knew something was up.

"It's a journey you must take in order to gain the trust of the others, Lucius. Your brother has tainted your family legacy, and now the rest of the Atlanteans doubt your ability to be assimilated into our society. They all know what happened with your father and the simulation in the cave, Lucius." Turning in her chair to look at me, I could see sincerity and concern in her eyes. "This is not the end, Lucius. I have no doubts you can complete this journey with absolute success, and Ourania will help you once we get there. But *getting there* is definitely part of the training." She glanced at Terrence to reaffirm her statement. He simply nodded in my direction and continued watching the people and traffic outside his open window.

Sensing this was all I would get from Maru for the time being, I watched the pedestrians as well. Bikers weaved through traffic, and merchants walked up to the van windows, trying to sell nuts, fruits, and local delicacies. The culture in Nepal amazed me. So much more colorful, and uninhibited compared to Western society. Watching from the van, I got a sense of their casual attitudes, like Mataio. They allowed events to unfold naturally, capturing any opportunity for a sale, but in no hurry to cross a street. Their eyes were wide open, never missing a beat, and I wanted to achieve that same enlightenment.

"No landslides this week, guys, so we should be good to go," Mataio announced, shattering my daydream about the Nepali people.

"What do you mean?" I asked, seriously wondering what kind of danger we were heading towards.

"They cut the Arniko Highway out of the Himalayan mountainside. During the rainy season, landslides can happen almost daily. Luckily, we are traveling in the dry season, but even now, the risk of landslides exists. A washout can happen at any second, blocking the road with fallen rocks or car pile-ups from accidents, or people who have gone over the side." Mataio spoke calmly. These details were part of his day-to-day lifestyle but to me the sound of this treacherous highway bordered on insanity.

"It's the only way into Tibet, kid, so hold on tight. It can get rough."

I did not respond. Instead, I spent a few minutes deciding if I wanted to look out the window or not, and see just how close we were to the mountain's edge.

"Look out the window, Lucius. The view is amazing," Mataio said. His breath fogged up the window, decreasing his visibility. He rubbed the condensation with his hand, making a clear hole. Looking out my window, I saw the mountains and the narrow road we traveled, imagining it was nothing compared to what lay ahead. I needed to have more courage. Lots more.

I grabbed the bottom of my t-shirt to wipe clean a small section of the window, hoping to expand my view. However, all I accomplished was smearing the dirt and grime around. I abandoned this and mimicked Terrence. Face pressed tightly to the window, I noticed that our rear tires had less than an inch of contact with the road before rolling over nothing but air. It was small comfort to see a transport vehicle nearly twice our size traveling the very same narrow death path. The more I watched, the more the transport seemed to gain on us, becoming aggressive and bullying us to drive faster.

"Mataio, there is an enormous truck trying to drive through your van right now. Do you see this?" I asked, worried as the insistent driver inched close to our back window.

"Oh yes, it's part of the Arniko highway driving game. These transport drivers get paid on delivery, and per load, so they are always in a big hurry to get to China. This is a major trade route, but guess what? He can't get around us, so he's just going to have to calm down unless he wants to go over the edge." Mataio's unbothered attitude was slightly comforting but not enough to completely forget the giant truck trying to edge us out of its way.

Using the bottom of my fist, I expanded the circle on my window and could now see the Himalayan Mountains for the first time. The snowcapped range, not so far in the distance, was enough to amaze anyone. Majestic peaks as far as the eye could see. In the foreground stood an impressive dome-shaped building perched atop a grassy hill with the formidable Himalayas as its backdrop. As the road widened, so did the number of rocks covering the sides of the road.

"Are these rock piles to keep people from driving off the road, Mataio?" I asked, never taking my eyes off the scenery. Chuckling before responding, he finally said, "No, Lucius. Someone has moved those rocks off the road from the landslides and rock fall events. The piles keep getting bigger, so I guess it is helpful in that way—now that you mention it." After an hour of smooth sailing, we came to a sudden halt. Just as within the city of Kathmandu, we were bumper to bumper. As far as the eye could see were tour buses every color of the rainbow.

"There sure are a lot of tours heading to Tibet." I remarked, looking at the buses line up ahead and behind us.

"You are required to be a part of a tour company to gain admission to Tibet. There is no other way in." Terrence explained. There were people all over the road now. They exited their vehicles to stretch and take pictures of the famous mountain range in the distance.

"It will be at least another two hours before we make it to the border. This is the line. You guys might as well stretch your legs. I'll stay in the vehicle," Mataio suggested. Not even a second had passed before Terrence threw open the van door and stepped out into the hot air. It wasn't as hot as within the van, but he fanned his hand over his face.

"Why can't Mataio come out with us?" I asked as we all stood on the edge of the road, looking out at the vast green landscape, so lush it was mesmerizing.

"Someone will steal the van. Loads of people walk this highway from Kathmandu, hoping to sneak onto a tour bus and cross the border. We can't expect to cross with a stowaway, so someone always has to guard the van." Terrence talked as we paced alongside the highway, taking in everything from the rocks to the sky. It was beautiful beyond what I experienced on Easter Island—a whole other kind of natural beauty.

"Hey guys, get back here… we're moving," Mataio yelled from the tour bus. Terrence and I turned when we heard his voice. Maru had somehow made it back to the front seat while Terrence and I were busy marveling at the nature around us as if we were not inhabitants of this world, but visitors.

Back on the tour bus, the vehicle was able to pick up a brisk pace. "I thought we were stuck in line at the border. Why are we moving so fast again?" I asked Mataio.

"I guess I was wrong. Now that we are moving, I am inclined to say there was an accident ahead of us or a car got crushed by a fallen rock."

"Sure, sure… just another day, right, Mataio?" I joked halfhearted while gazing up towards the mountain on our right side, checking for loose rock. Noticing my glance, Maru said, "Don't bother. They always come from much higher than we can see from here. Besides, seeing it doesn't mean we can do anything about it now, does it?" Everyone else in the van laughed while my stomach twisted in knots. Their ability to constantly remain calm in the face of danger or when our lives were at risk intrigued me. It made me suspect that regardless of my fears and worries, I must be on the right path.

Moments later, on the left side of the road sat a completely demolished tour bus, just like the one we traveled on. Unable to see inside, I figured the passengers were fine and waiting alongside the road somewhere ahead for help. After driving a few kilometres, there was no sign of anyone waiting for help. Had those unsuspecting passengers fallen victim to a rockslide? Both afraid and saddened by the lives lost, lives that could have easily been our own, I turned from the window and closed my eyes for the rest of the journey.

"Only twenty clicks to go now. We can take a quick break in Kodari if you guys want something to eat or drink," Mataio said, delighted we made it this far without incident.

I was extremely curious about how they thought we would cross the border since I had no recollection about where my passport had gone. This question hovered on my tongue before deciding to keep it to myself. They had made it clear to me that they had everything under control and I was more of a dimwitted cousin they were forced to drag along with them. It was best to leave my less pertinent questions unsaid.

"Lucius, look, we made it to Kodari. Not far from the border now." Although Terrence's words seemed optimistic, his tone was anxious. For the first time, he appeared apprehensive about our journey, which made my tension sky rocket. I wondered if their fate rested in my hands once this journey through Tibet began. I could understand his worry if that were the case.

"Let's stop for some water, please, Mataio," Maru asked. Something in her cagey tone made me suspect this stop was for more than water, but I was learning to keep my mouth shut for a change. And to observe…. *closely*. It was a relief to pull off the highway. I didn't realize how tense my body had become over the course of our dangerous ride, but I immediately relaxed as the van pulled away from the mountain's edge for the first time in hours.

The village was very much like Kathmandu, but on a smaller scale. The architecture was the same, with buildings constructed of odd materials in various colors. Nothing like the blocks of steel and concrete in the city I spent most of my life. Mataio pointed us toward a local vendor who would sell us fresh water, fruits, and nuts. The streets were not nearly as packed as Kathmandu, but the traffic sounded just as loud. Thousands of travelers trying to reach Tibet through this tiny portal town seemed to keep it active. The vendors knew who to target and did so easily, walking out into the streets with baskets full of the most delicious-looking fruits I had ever seen.

We all acquired fruits and beverages, me a bit more fruit than I could possibly eat, but I couldn't refuse the little boy selling. Not having a clue about what I just purchased, I wondered if I would like it. We sat at a small aluminum patio table in front of the vendor's tent and ate and drank in silence. There was a tension between us that hadn't been there before. The atmosphere weighed on me. Again, I remained silent, giving them the opportunity to let me in on what was happening. I was sick of asking questions that they refused to answer anyway. I sliced into my strange pink fruit with green tentacles emerging from all sides. The inside was the completely opposite—juicy white pulp with tiny black flecks spread throughout. Using the tip of my knife to extract a tiny piece of the fruit to test, I felt like a child again. It was so refreshing to be in such alien territory, to be a complete stranger to my surroundings.

"Delicious," I mumbled with a mouthful. Juicy and refreshing. After spending hours in a hot and sweaty tour bus with nothing to hydrate with, I savored this pleasure. Thinking of nothing else but my next bite of this delicious, exotic fruit, I caught the wide-eyed stares of my traveling partners. They gawked at me as if I were a monkey in a zoo exhibit. I hesitated; the fruit suspended before my open mouth.

"What's the problem?" I tried to eliminate the irritation in my voice. Their tendency to hold back information from me was pissing me off. With the strange fruit still in hand, juice dripped down my wrist as I awaited their response. Oddly, they continued staring at me as if I had said nothing. Anger growing, I threw my fruit down on the rusting patio table and said, "What the hell, guys? What is it now?" Clearing my throat, I was embarrassed when I realized how loud my words came out and how many other tourists were now watching curiously.

"What do you know about Shambhala Lucius?" Afraid of those curious ears, Maru leaned across the table, whispering. Concern cast shadows in her eyes. I took a second to consider my answer. I knew the legends and myths of Shambhala, known to some as Shangri-La. Feeling a new sense of unease, I collected my thoughts before speaking. But suddenly, before I could even utter a syllable, a familiar pain overtook me. Lost to Maru and Terrence and the foreign world before me, I found myself in a familiar, sinister place.

<h1 style="text-align:center">CHAPTER 8</h1>

"We're doing this! Move the body now or I'll give you the honor of being included in the ritual yourself," Orpheus screamed at a young man—not even a young man—a boy, trembling in the doorway. A member of the Kai-Tangata I had never seen, but one who seemed to be more than a little uncomfortable with the sinister twist this entire situation had taken. The more he argued with Orpheus and Dax, the more likely they would kill him once he fulfilled his duty of transporting my Erebus to the ritual site.

"I just think it's an enormous risk, and if it fails, it leaves us with nothing but *you know who's* wrath," the young man said quietly, nearly under his breath. Making his opinions known was the limit to his bravery. One eye swelled shut, my Erebus struggled to obey my will and scan the room for more information. I already allowed Dax and Orpheus to continue with their absurd plan, and if I was going to let my Erebus burn to death, I needed to get as much information from the situation as possible. It eased my conscience this way. I needed to know this 'you know who' the men kept referring to in whispered tones and under their breath.

Dax and Orpheus stared at my Erebus while I made sure it didn't move a muscle but allowed its good eye to survey the room. It looked as I remembered, all cold metal and precise surgical instruments and that large ceiling vent from which I was able to escape. The difference was an abundance of chairs next to my bed, as if members of the Kai-Tangata had opted to view my slow demise and torture for their own pleasure. I was still sitting with Terrence and

Maru in Kodari, eating fruit at a small patio table awaiting passage into Tibet. Still, I wanted to get all the information I could from my Erebus before returning to my full self. I snapped back and forth between my full self and my Erebus. This took an immense amount of mental strength and energy and I was already feeling the drag of it—the drowsiness taking over.

Shooting daggers of pain rocketed through my lower back as my Erebus was carelessly lifted from the hospital bed. It had been occupying it now for over three weeks after my escape. The stranger held my Erebus in his arms and looked down at it with pity and sorrow. I had never seen such a reaction from a member of the Kai-Tangata. The tears in his eyes conveyed that he did not want to be doing this. He disagreed with his leaders, but his body went through the motions, regardless; his survival taking priority over my own.

"Bring him to the ritual room. Everything is ready." Orpheus' voice reverberated down the hall to the young man carrying my battered Erebus. Weighing not much more than a hundred pounds himself, my Erebus could not have been over seventy pounds of bones and flesh, barely alive but alive enough to burn to ash. I reminded myself this small sacrifice of my soul was worth it. This sacrifice would hopefully get the Kai-Tangata off our backs for good, even if Maru didn't believe it was possible.

"Here we are, Lucius. I'm sorry, man, I didn't know…" The man's words were barely audible, his whisper so low and soft I hesitated to interpret the sounds as words at all. Whether 'he didn't know' meant he didn't know what he was getting into with the Kai-Tangata or how far they would go, I realized this man didn't fit. He also had little time left to live if I knew Orpheus.

Half watching the scene through the eyes of my Erebus, the 'ritual room', as Orpheus called it, was something out of a gothic nightmare. The cold slab of stone rising nearly five feet from the ground sent shivers through the bones of my Erebus. The room offered no tiled floors, sterile-looking walls, or modern light fixtures. Instead, the sacrificial altar stood on an archaic dirt floor, and the walls were not painted and drywalled, but a collaboration of small rough stones stacked one on top of the other to create a barrier between rooms. Tall brass candlesticks stood on either side of the stone slab, holding slim white candles that cast this strange chamber in the flickering light.

"Get that damned book, Dax. I will not wait another minute. This is happening, and it's happening right now. We are out of time! Don't you get it, man? His vengeance will exclude no one." Orpheus bellowed at Dax, who stood only feet from him when they entered the ritual room together. Without a word, Dax turned back towards the main corridors in search of the book left to him by Marseilles.

"Get out of my sight, boy, or you'll be next. Ritual or not, the fire will burn hot enough." He smirked, proud of his retort. Orpheus watched as the young Kai-Tangata member ran from his position next to the stone altar and sprinted down the long hallway until he was out of sight completely. Chuckling to himself, Orpheus paced the dirt floor back and forth, creating a small, worn pathway in front of the altar. Never speaking a word to 'Lucius' and never taking his eyes off his feet. Arms crossed, his patience for Dax was running thin.

"Dax!" Orpheus bellowed in a tone so full of anger my Erebus shuddered at the sound and the unfortunate echo that made its way through the Kai-Tangata layer. "Where is he? Well, it's over, it is over… that's for sure. He's coming for us all now, and Dax is clueless about what's coming. Clueless!" Orpheus' whisper turned into another bellow just as Dax entered the room, pale and wide-eyed, book in hand.

"So this is it, is it? The book that's going to save our asses?" Orpheus questioned mockingly. I struggled to get a view of the book that Dax was so protective of. It had a thick, supple brown leather cover, worn throughout, suggesting it had been through hell and back with many travelers and somehow found its way into this secret torture chamber of the Kai-Tangata. Orpheus reached out to touch the book, but Dax yelled at him to stop, hauling it away from Orpheus's long fingers. "Don't. I will hold the book. You are here because you must be, but I am still in charge of this operation. If you don't like it, the book goes back to the safe, and you can explain to *Him* what went wrong here." The confidence in Dax's voice was palpable, and he never wavered once during his practiced but compelling speech. And there it was again, a reference to a "Him" that seemed to cause every man to hesitate. Orpheus took a step back, fuming but cornered into silence.

"Are you alive, Lucius?" Dax waited for a response he would not get. "I hope you are because this is going to hurt, and we need your suffering, your pain, and your anger to flow out of you right 'till the end. I never wanted it to come to this, but you've given us… *nothing*!" Dax's soft-spoken words grew louder and louder as his frustration mounted. These two men were out of their element and losing their grip. Emotions running high, Dax opened his sacred brown book and searched through the pages for the ritual Marseilles had once told him about. Carefully touching the fragile pages, he grew hasty, turning page after page with growing impatience. I could see through my Erebus that Dax was becoming annoyed, searching for the tale his beloved Marseilles had trusted to him and only him. When finally, a glimmer appeared in Dax's eye that seemed to soften his hardened edges for a moment.

"Found it. Here it is."

Fully ensconced in my Erebus, I slowly shifted its body to the right to get a better look at Dax and his book. He stood only feet from me, completely engrossed by the words in front of him. Watching closely, I witnessed the slightest tremble of his hands. Sweat accumulated on his brow. Signs of guilt or remorse? I would never know, but there was something behind those eyes—a private struggle he would likely never admit to.

He slammed the book, and I rolled back into position. There was no reason to provoke further violence against my Erebus. I could no longer see Dax, but I could hear the light tread of his footsteps inching their way to my side on the ceremonial altar.

"I don't want to do this, you know. You got yourself into this mess by believing, father. He's not who you think he is—not anymore." His lips were so close to my ear that I could feel the warmth of his breath. He would not risk anyone else hearing this confession. I couldn't help but wonder what he was implying about our father and whether or not to believe him. Before I could ponder the question any longer, Orpheus' bellow cracked the tension in the room like a brick through a window.

"Let's go, Dax," he growled.

Dax quickly reopened the book, placing it on a small stone table in the corner of the room. It was far away from the ritual table and my Erebus. "Bind him, Orpheus." Dax's words were simple, but his voice was soft. Orpheus was moving towards my Erebus before Dax finished speaking and snapped the metal cuffs around my wrists and ankles with no ceremony or remorse.

"Right now, pile that wood around the altar. Quickly. We need to perform the ritual before he dies," Dax said with a bit more anxiety in his voice than before. He piled armload after armload of sliced wood around the altar and in the hollow place beneath the middle to build a fire hot enough to condemn a human to ash. The men in the room seemed anxious my Erebus might die before they finished, and yet none of them dared to come and actually check if it was still breathing.

With the wood stacked for optimal bonfire status, the ritual could begin. "The second I'm finished reading, I will give you the signal to light the fire. Got it?" Dax asked Orpheus. A quick nod was his answer. There was nothing left to do but start. Clearing his throat, Dax read aloud,

"O great Devaraja, I beg of thee, I implore thee,
Purification is upon us. We need the power of your spirit,
I offer you Earthly infinitude, by fire and ash,
The world is putrid; the world is dark and lost,
I praise your purity and beg of thee,
Sanctify those among me and myself,
Eternal servants you will have. Devoted and Pure."

Nodding his head towards Orpheus, Dax took out his packet of matches and walked towards the firewood. With two strikes, he created a flame fierce enough to set the wood ablaze. With the fire stoked, there was no stopping it now.

The flames caught inordinately fast. The heat was so intense, I wondered if I would be burned by it through my Erebus. Dax and Orpheus must've soaked the wood in an accelerant for the fire to ignite so fiercely and so quickly. Within seconds, the flames were taller than the altar, encircling my Erebus completely. I knew Dax and Orpheus were close. I could barely hear their muffled voices. Perhaps they were completing whatever they had left of the ritual. As the fire raged on, it finally occurred to me that my Erebus would burn, and when that happened, I would no longer have eyes in that room, and no way to know what would happen to Dax and Orpheus. If they would, in fact, accept their defeat. The temptation to create another Erebus was strong and in this moment, it made sense why my father would've created so many—to have eyes where he could not be.

I endured the pain with my Erebus, but it was not as agonizing as experiencing its heart and soul fade deeper and deeper into unknown darkness. A place in the universe no mortal could know during life, but one that every mortal would face in their death. This body was failing, and it was only a matter of time until death took the Erebus and the ritual would end in failure. I could not fathom how Dax and Orpheus would react, but I hoped they would end their conquest in defeat. Light enveloped my vision and heat invaded my body, or rather, the body of my Erebus. A few missed breaths, an irregular heartbeat, strangled by lack of oxygen, and the Erebus surrendered. It was too weak from weeks of torture to possibly fight this inevitability. It was gone, ash just as Dax and Orpheus had wanted, and I found myself staring into two very perplexed faces; Maru and Terrence.

****

A few slow and deliberate blinks of my eyes brought me back into myself. Back to Kodari and my friends. The realization instantly hit me I had killed off a part of my soul and received nothing in return for this sacrifice but hope that the Kai-Tangata would abandon their search for immortality once and for all.

"Lucius, are you okay?" Terrence's concerned face was a welcomed sight. The atmosphere of the Kai-Tangata layer was one of tension, anxiety, and fear, and to be rid of those feelings was a relief only experienced once you were free of them. "What's happening back on Easter Island?" Correctly assuming I was experiencing something through my Erebus, Terrence was eager to find out what was happening, and from the expression on Maru's face, so was she. Shifting uncomfortably in my tiny metal chair, I realized just how many more people had entered the market since we had sat down, and I had checked out to cross to another part of the world.

"Come on now, Lucius, we have little time left before we need to cross," Maru urged. "The ritual is complete. But I didn't think it through, Maru. I thought if I sacrificed my Erebus to this ritual, I would learn the Kai-Tangata's next move, but that part of me is dead, and I no longer have eyes in that facility. Any leverage we had is gone." I dropped my head, as defeated as Dax and Orpheus were halfway across the world, hidden in their mountain layer surrounded by smoke and ash.

"Perhaps you envisioned the outcome to be different, but it doesn't mean your sacrifice was for nothing, Lucius. How often do our thoughts and imaginations line up with what happens out here in this world?" Maru asked gently, leaning over to clutch my shoulder. With a squeeze of love and friendship, the gesture conveyed her support. Knowing she was right, of course, I was so embarrassed. I never learn.

"The Kai-Tangata will never stop, Lucius. I've told you this. Centuries of killing and plotting, one act of death, and one sacred ritual gone wrong is not enough to stop them. There are larger forces at work that you are not yet aware of, and only the Alvanata can stop these forces." Seeing my confusion, Maru shook her head. "Now is not the time. We have more important and pressing matters, Lucius. These are issues that have outlasted time itself… they can wait a little longer for our attention." Her perfect white teeth flashed beneath thin lips as she smiled brightly. Her happiness was contagious. It brought a smile to my lips as well.

"Do you understand you are a wanted man, Lucius?" Her words hung in the air as if caught in a giant invisible net, allowing me the opportunity to stare at them, to ponder them and their foreign nature. "What do you mean? Wanted man?" As the words spilled out of my mouth before my mind had a chance to process them, it all made sense. There were dozens of people, if not more, killed in my wake by the Kai-Tangata. If they had in fact been operating for centuries, as Maru had suggested on multiple occasions, then they were not fool enough to leave these murders unclaimed. They would pin them on me to make my travel more challenging and make my journey and conscience more burdensome.

"Yes, that's right. Every major police and government agency is looking for you, my boy. They believe you killed a lot of people and are armed and dangerous to anyone you may encounter. We cannot cross at the conventional border into Tibet, Lucius. Your face is enough to have us all arrested; locked up with no key is my best guess. Dusk is approaching, and we can't linger here much longer without drawing attention. No one lingers in Kodari. To the locals, we are all travelers awaiting the border, and we can appear to be nothing else." Maru stopped short of completing her sentence and scanned the marketplace with an urgency in her eyes I had not seen before, not even during our incursion with the Kai-Tangata months ago. "Let's move this meeting back to Mataio's van, the crowd is thinning and the border line is moving." Maru and Terrence rose agilely from the table while I snapped up as if struck by a bolt of lightning. I banged the tiny patio table, knocking all its contents to the dirt ground, attracting even more attention, not to mention a bit of disdain from Maru for my carelessness.

Still looking around at the few locals whose attention I had captured with my clumsy display, Terrence urged me back to the road only feet away, where Mataio was guarding our ride. For some reason, my blunder on the patio seemed to enrage Maru when, to my eyes, the locals looked like no threat, just old men selling exotic fruit to tourists.

Mataio waved exuberantly at the sight of us as he paced the length of his tour bus from end to end and back again. The line for the border was not moving. "Hey guys, back so soon? We're still a good hour away by my estimation. Haven't moved an inch since you left." His cheery tone and nonchalant nature contradicted Maru's fierce mood. When the two clashed, Mataio simply took a step back and allowed her to enter the bus without another word, but not without a questioning glance towards Terrence. A shake of his head told Mataio to leave it alone, and we too entered the back of the tour bus without a word.

"Lucius, I am trying to be patient with you," Maru said. "I have been told since I was a young woman—a young woman in my very first body—that *you* would be the one to bring balance to this world and yet here I am centuries later, many bodies later, and I am having doubts for the first time in all those long years." Half-turned in the front passenger seat to face me in the back with Terrence, her face was full of disappointment. Some of her anger had dissipated, but the disappointment was far worse.

"I'm sorry I bumped the table, Maru. But I think it is the least of our problems. I am a wanted mass murderer, apparently, and I don't really think the people of Kodari are that interested in any of that." Anger constantly bubbled and simmered with some measure of control beneath my surface, but the more I was yelled at and disciplined like a child, the less controlled that simmer became. It boiled. I leaned forward on the edge of the torn fabric seat, ready to let it all out. To scream at Maru for not telling me the entire truth, for constantly throwing me breadcrumbs that made no sense without the complete picture, for continually making me look subpar, unworthy to even be on this adventure. With the words on the tip of my tongue, Terrence's firm grip on my arm held me back. When I turned to him, his eyes pleaded with me to stop and think, to stop and breathe, to just *stop*.

It was precisely these moments that fueled my rage, increasing my feelings of inferiority. But I always caved, always buried these feelings deeper, hoping eventually all would become clear, but the further into the journey we went, the harder it became to keep this anger hidden from the others. I nodded at Terrence, easing myself back into my seat, feigning agreement, and pushed my argumentative self into the basement.

"I'm sorry, Lucius. I am having a bit of trouble acclimating myself to this world and this dimension again. I was only gone a few short months, but keeping their pain at bay was a full-time job at first. It's been so long that I forgot how hard it can be." Maru spoke to me from the front seat but stared out her window at the hundreds of others waiting to cross into Tibet. Her eyes drifted from man to man, family to family as she spoke, as if their specific pain affected her, and it was her job to shield herself or become one of them; become the human she so desperately wanted to avoid.

Stuck now in my astonishment, I could not think of a single word to say. So busy being mad at Maru it never occurred to me for a second that she was struggling to be back on Earth. Come to think of it, I never really considered anyone but myself and hadn't since I found myself in this new world. This journey was meant to make me a better person, something superior even, and it seemed to only bring out the absolute worst qualities in me. Mouth hanging open, I struggled to think of something better to say than that pitiful and overused word, *sorry*, which I already used far too regularly.

"There's no need to say anything, Lucius. This journey is going to test us all, in different ways, but test us all you can be sure of that. We all have something at stake here Lucius, although you are the star of our journey, it is about more than just one person." Abruptly, she exited the tour bus, opened the sliding door to the back where Terrence and I sat, and hopped in. Kneeling in the wide vacant space in front of us, she continued, in a hushed voice. *Who could be listening?* I couldn't even imagine but her prerogative.

"Okay, back to priority one. We need into Tibet and we need no one to know about it. Any thoughts?" Maru asked, one knee on the gross carpet floor of the tour bus and the other crunched beneath her as she awaited our ideas. For the first time since jumping timelines, someone wanted to know my thoughts and what plans I had, and it embarrassed me to admit I had nothing, not even the slightest idea, to contribute. "Come on, Lucius. You're always saying we don't treat you like an equal partner in this group. Let's hear your ideas for a change," Maru said with a smile, but not a happy smile, more like the type of smile you receive when you know someone has just bested you, beat you at your own game, and they're loving it. I racked my brain and bullied it into coming up with something on the spot. Even a pitiful idea was better than nothing at all. Their gazes bore into me, filling me with the shame of my inability to help. Always wishing they would include me, but never taking my attention off myself for even a second to contribute. Finally, Terrence broke the silence. "There's a forest nearby, isn't there, Maru? Seems like suitable cover?" Terrence's eyes were on Maru, but his peripheral glance kept bouncing toward me. While his half-idea hung in the air, it finally clicked. He was providing me a base to jump off of.

"Right, good start, Terrence." I jumped in as soon as my brain processed what he was trying to do for me. "If there is a forest, all we need to do is get there without being noticed and disappear in the trees." Thankful for that confidence boost provided so generously by Terrence, I felt alive. This was my adventure. I was, in fact, more than a tag-along getting in everyone's way.

"Alright, alright…" Maru drifted off, pondering our elementary plan, but it was a place to start at least. That's the way I looked at it. "Well, you're right about the forest, but getting to it and using it as cover may be challenging. First, it's going in the wrong direction. Ourania is North-West, and that forest flows South-East." Rubbing her chin, furrowing her brow, and clicking her teeth, Maru lost herself in thought. I was sure she had her own plan. She always did. This was just a charade to make us feel involved. Like a faculty retreat or team-building event companies put their staff through to make us think we were a part of the system and not just minions for hire.

"We need to get out of this line now, and we will need cover. Crossing this border is no joke. The officials are serious about who they allow to enter and will show us no mercy if they catch us trying to sneak across on our own. Terrence, let Mataio know it's time," Terrence said brusquely and then, without a word, pulled hard on the sliding door of the tour bus and exited to speak with Mataio.

"Grab your bag and Terrence's, please, Lucius. There's about to be a diversion, and we cannot miss it. It's our only opportunity to slip away unseen. Hurry now, Mataio is ready." Jumping up without hesitation, I rummaged haphazardly through the backseat to find Terrence's bag and then my own and fled the van as quickly as possible. Maru stood on the side of the road, a picture of serenity and refinement. I joined her, but could not have looked more out of place—a rough-looking backpacker with a pristinely dressed local woman of class. The line into Tibet still wasn't moving. It was filled with travelers getting in and out of their vehicles for fresh air and to stretch their legs. I just barely glimpsed Terrence and Mataio shaking hands in a hilariously shady fashion and knew instantly. A good portion of our plan had already been in place.

"All set, we have ten seconds, and then we are on our own. Mataio says he will see you soon, Lucius." Patting me gently on the back, the three of us stood side by side on the gravel road amongst hundreds of other travelers. "Mataio isn't coming with us?" I asked, glancing back and forth from Maru to Terrence. "No, Mataio is a charter man, Lucius. His part in this journey is over, well… nearly over, that is." Maru smiled. "Prepare to run, Lucius, and do not hesitate or look back. Do you understand?" she asked quietly, conscious of her surroundings and careful not to make our plans known to nearby ears which may or may not be listening. A knot grew in my stomach. Something was about to go down and evidently, there was no time to fill me. And it looked like I was about to put in some cardio with a cross-country sprint. As the knot in my stomach twisted, Mataio's voice broke through the hum of chatter amongst the travelers waiting on the side of the road with us.

"LANDSLIDE! TAKE COVER, EVERYONE! TAKE COVER!" Mataio screamed. Within seconds, he was not the only one screaming. Hundreds shrieked in terror and panic while they sprinted away from the road towards the little highway village of Kodari for cover. Maru and Terrence turned on their heels without a second of hesitation and ran past the little town, leaving me briefly in their wake. That second of hesitation left me struggling and elbowing my way through a panicking crowd, trying to head in the opposite direction of the wave of terror.

My long strides allowed me to catch up to Maru and Terrence with just a few breaths. Balancing my bag and Terrence's, one on each shoulder, made my gait off-kilter, causing stumble after stumble on the dirt road Maru led us down. The road was more of a footpath, crisscrossing between tiny homes made of rock and tin, piles of rubble, smashed cars from previous landslides, earthquakes, and other acts of mother nature's wrath dotted the way. My fear fueled me forward, faster and faster, until I passed Terrence and ran so close to Maru that I had to concentrate to avoid stepping on her heels with my proximity.

Noticing a weight suddenly lifted from my back, I silently thanked Terrence for the help. Now fifteen pounds lighter, I was less prone to trips and stumbling in the many potholes on our trail. The forest came into view as we rounded the back of this Kodari neighborhood, leaving behind all the rubble and rock and bringing into view lush forest and vast vacant land with plant life more than tall enough to camouflage our escape. Not daring to slow down even for a quick breath of much-needed oxygen, the three of us carried on through the tall weeds and plants of the vacant land with our eyes, not leaving the forest's edge for a second, our point of entry. We were just yards away from the beginning of what appeared to be a tropical rainforest when I heard it. An unknown thundering disturbance shook the ground beneath our feet and even vibrated our ears with the immense volume. Instinctively, I dove towards the ground, covering my ears and searching for Maru and Terrence to ensure their safety. Instead, I saw Terrence's hand reaching down through the tall plants to grab me.

"We have to continue, Lucius. We're nearly there. Let's go, mate." Confused by his calm demeanor, I grabbed his hand and continued. They weren't surprised or frightened by the sound at all. They seemed to know exactly what it was. Forgetting our desire for concealment, I yelled at Maru from the back of the pack, "What was that, Maru? Was that you?" Not knowing how or why, I knew Maru was behind the mysterious thunder. With nothing to acknowledge my screams but a slight glance over her shoulder, I followed them into the forest, expecting and willing to demand answers if necessary.

The heat of the rainforest struck us immediately as we all stopped for our first full breath since our mad dash began. Bent forward with our hands on our knees, we all sucked in air, but it was me who spoke first, my curiosity winning out over my need for more oxygen. "Did you create that landslide, Maru?" It surprised me just how matter-of-factly this question sounded to my ears, considering how crazy it sounded. I already knew Maru could perform incredible acts. She could manipulate the universe in ways I could scarcely understand, but I believed it to be true even if my comprehension had not quite caught up with this belief.

"Yes, Lucius… don't worry, everyone was clear. It was just a small one to facilitate our escape with more room for comfort." Even in her younger body, Maru was still working on catching her breath while I decided how to respond to this strange revelation. "It doesn't matter whether you think Maru should've created a landslide or not, Lucius," Terrence said. "It worked. We're here, and it hurt no one. Now let's look forward instead of backward, if you don't mind because I'm getting tired." He smiled.

Drawing in a long breath, Terrence stood upright again. The three of us stood out of place in the middle of this tropical environment. The sweat was already pouring out of our pores as if we were in the middle of a rainstorm.

"Alright, Lucius, lead on," Maru urged confidently as if this had always been the plan.

"Excuse me?" was all I could muster in response. I was so taken aback.

CHAPTER 9

An alien entity in this subtropical forest, I stood without flinching while my body and mind attempted to get on the same page. The weight on my chest was palpable. Although I couldn't see the elephant, I could certainly feel it. I took deep breaths and concentrated on the oxygen entering my body while I watched as the clouds from above merged with the fog hugging the ground. Experiencing the moisture on my face was refreshing, but it was another strange illusion this forest perpetrated. It wasn't raining, but the water dripping from my face suggested it was. The blend of sweat and humidity in this forest had me drenched in minutes.

As my body adapted to this strange environment, I scanned our surrounding area without addressing Maru's proclamation that I was now in charge of this expedition. Coming from the concrete jungle of New York City, I felt as though we had hopped dimensions; again. I was in awe of this natural landscape, and even with my impatient travel companions, I had to take the time to absorb this forest. Any number of different species of leafy trees encircled us and intertwined above us to envelop us within its green sphere. The sunlight poked through here and there, reminding me it was still daylight, but not for much longer. Fatigue set in as the darkness of the forest enveloped us, and the heat embraced us.

"Lucius? We don't have the luxury of standing around and sightseeing. We need to cover some ground before nightfall. The Tibetan border security will begin scanning the surrounding forests, especially after that unexpected landslide." Emphasizing *unexpected,* Maru's eyes were wide, and her eyebrows lifted in expectation as if she wished she could scream at me to get moving and quit endangering the mission. Still, she remained silent, although her facial expression continued to speak volumes.

Kneeling on the verdant forest floor, I rummaged through my carry-on bag. "What are you looking for now?" Terrence asked.

"I'm looking for my phone so I can use the compass app and see which way I should lead us," I answered in a tone that suggested it was a ridiculous question.

"Lucius, buddy… you really think we got this far by carrying personal tracking devices with us? Come on, man." Shaking his head, Terrence reached into his deep pants pockets and pulled out a real compass; old school. Spinning round and round, I tried to get my bearings in the forest. Just as I was about to go through true embarrassment on my fifth spin, the needle held its own and showed me the way.

Without a word, I started heading west for the meager reason I remembered Maru stating earlier that Ourania was to the west of Kodari. To maintain my air of confidence, I needed to portray I knew the way, so I walked deeper and deeper into the darkness of the forest, my t-shirt clinging to my body, now fully dampened by perspiration. My body temperature continued to rise while I focused on the elephant on my chest again. With each step I took, I awaited word from Terrence or Maru—confirmation that we were heading in the right direction. I got nothing but their silence.

"So… are we good to go here, guys?" My casual way of inviting their input in the direction I chose was meant to conceal the fact that I never actually used a compass before. "You're the boss," Terrence announced with amusement, making me turn to face him. Sweat was pouring down his face as well, but it was the smile that prickled my submerged anger. "What? Come on… what's so damn amusing? Am I leading us the wrong way?"

Terrence simply looked at Maru to respond. Clearly, his instructions were to remain quiet on the subject, so he simply continued to smile, gesturing for Maru to take the lead.

"Lucius, we've been over this, I believe." Wiping sweat from her forehead and out of her eyes, she continued with a deep breath, showing her exasperation. "You are leading us to Ourania. There will be signs, not traditional in their obviousness, but there will be signs. And I promise I will not allow you to get too far off track, but it is you who must read and find the signs. It is time to open your eyes, Lucius, and no one can do that for you. There is much to see here if you are looking, but it can be difficult when you are constantly distracted by passing thoughts. Silence them and pay attention." The three of us stood in the forest lit by the dying light of the day, drenched in sweat and exhaustion, but it was Terrence's smile that sparked a light at the end of the tunnel for me. It was no longer a mocking grin, but a but a 'you can do it' smile. This insignificant gesture delivered another boost of confidence my way, enough to continue forward for a bit longer.

There was no full moon on the horizon, not that we could see anyway, but there was certainly no light in the sky bright enough to penetrate this canopy of trees. Maru and Terrence lit the way from behind with their flashlights while I struggled to maintain a close watch on the compass. Hours had passed since we ran from Mataio and the main road of Kodari to the cover of this Tibetan tropical forest. No longer enthralled by the splendor of the forest, it had only taken a few hours for me to get used to our surroundings and ultimately see past its beauty with my focus on my discomforts. As this thought passed through my mind, I was stunned alert, and my eyes left the compass needle for the first time in hours.

"What is it?"

"Terrence, I forgot I was supposed to be looking for signs! Who knows what I might've missed?" I made a three-sixty turn, surveying the surrounding area. I looked at every branch, each pile of leaves, each moss deposit in case it would reveal something important. As my heartbeat amped up, I felt Maru's hand on my shoulder. "Turn around, Lucius. Look at me." Obeying without question, I hoped for some reassurance from her, even though I knew that was not what I was about to get.

"This isn't a test where you can memorize the answers and get an A. You need to feel this forest, our company, and everything around you. Sometimes, in order to see and think differently, we need to cease thinking altogether and *see* instead. Do you understand?" Maru's words soothed my heartbeat as they always did, and the look in her eyes invigorated me as if willing me to not only understand her words but put them into motion. "Alright, we're all exhausted. Let's set up a little camp over there tonight." Maru pointed towards a collection of mossy rocks piled high. "Those rocks should help keep some of the moisture off of us for the night. Lucius, have you seen any signs of animals since we've been walking?" Her casual tone temporarily distracted me from the fact she was testing me and, for the first time in perhaps all my life, I remembered back but not with my mind, my feelings, and something else I couldn't quite place. Our journey thus far through the forest flashed before me, but not on my mental movie screen, as expected; it flashed through my feelings, each footstep taken, each bush passed, and rock kicked out of the way, remembered in a new way and with details never so vibrant when played through my mind's eye.

"No, no trace of animal life so far. But there must be some in this forest?" I asked my friends, confident in my assessment of our journey so far. "Oh, of course, but I imagine much deeper into the mountains than we are now. We'll get there, though, so we all must be on our guard," Maru stated while she unrolled a small blanket from her bag, and began setting up her nest for the night. Terrence and I followed suit, making small talk about our adventure, wondering about Mataio and how his journey across the border had gone, or if the landslide had even allowed his crossing at all.

Maru and Terrence fell asleep and snored quietly while I lay awake, listening to the sounds of the forest. The light breeze rustled the leaves and vines. Nocturnal insects sang their songs happily while I thought about what I was doing in a Tibetan rainforest. My life in New York was a distant memory, a story I had read once. The more time I spent merging with this timeline, the less connected I was with my old life. It was slowly becoming someone else's story, and mine was becoming much more fantastical and dream-like.

Drip, drip, drip. Cold water beads repeatedly fell on my face, waking me from a temporary sleep I'd barely realized had happened. I wasn't sure how long I had been asleep, but my counterparts were awake and surveying the area in the fresh daylight glow. I stretched my legs and stood, evoking loud popping sounds from my back and spine as they worked to return to their natural station. Twisting left and right, I stopped only when the popping stopped, assuming I was back in place.

"Morning, Maru. Terrence," I whispered as I walked in their direction, careful not to disturb too much of the underbrush and draw ears to our location. Terrence turned and shook my hand as if we were mere acquaintances and Maru smiled pleasantly, but they both looked as though they spent the entire night worrying about a certain someone in charge of their fate and, to be honest, this was a beetle burying in my brain as well.

"We were looking for animal tracks. We have a little food in our bags, but we are going to have to hunt and stockpile. It's a long way to Ouriana," Terrence said casually.

The clouds appeared to fall out of the sky and hang around our heads instead of resting miles up where they were supposed to be. The moisture hung in the air alongside the clouds, blocking whatever sunlight the early morning sun was struggling to provide us along with the growing entities of the forest. With a few quick motions, I peeled my t-shirt off my skin to reassert a bit of space between the two. Terrence looked to be in the same boat, but Maru was completely on her own playing field as usual. She looked tired, yes, but not disheveled.

"Well, it doesn't look like we will find any game here. Likely once the rainforest ends, and the coniferous forest begins in the North, there will be more options, but there will also be more predators, so… tit for tat, I guess," Maru said as she wandered back to our "camp" in search of whatever food she had the foresight to pack.

"I hear water though… did you guys spot a stream in that direction?" Listening closely, I could pick up the subtle crashing of water on water, suggesting a small waterfall perhaps, but fresh water most definitely. "No, we didn't see it, but we can hear it, too. We may find it today, and then we can stock up on water as well. Did you find your provisions in the bag, Lucius?" Terrence asked while he was taking out his own and biting into an energy bar that would hopefully keep him going until we could find "game," as they referred to it. I copied his movements and found the interior pocket of the black carry-on contained a handful of energy bars, a ziplock bag of trail mix, and a metal water bottle full to the brim. With a grateful smile, I thanked Maru and Terrence and the three of us enjoyed breakfast together before beginning day two of our journey in the Tibetan rainforest.

Savoring my energy bar, I was reluctant to get started. I was, after all, in charge of getting us to Ouriana, and Shangri-La, if that was even possible. After all my whining about being more involved in this crazy journey, I could finally make some decisions, and didn't have a clue if I was even capable of making them or if I was putting everyone, including myself, at great risk pretending I could do this.

"Pack up, Lucius. We've already lost two hours of daylight, and it's going to take us at least another day to make it to the northern forest," Maru said as she rolled her thin fleece blanket as tightly as possible to fit back into her pack. Between the three of us, we didn't travel with much, but a blanket was a nice amenity to have when there was nothing else between your body and the forest floor and its populous. I choked down my anticipation and did as they did. Before long we all stood with bags on our shoulders, ready to begin.

Compass in hand, I found our westward heading and began with one step after another. Maru and Terrence reminisced about old times on Easter Island. They spoke fondly about something called, The Birdman Competition.

"What's that about?" I asked, not turning back to face them. Instead, I scanned the area for signs or information that apparently I would know when I saw it.

"Oh, it's part of the ancient Easter Island culture a friend of mine was determined to recreate a few years ago. Basically, the natives would choose representatives from their individual tribes to compete, and these men or women would have to swim out to the island off the coast of Easter Island. They dubbed it *bird* island because of all the seabirds. Many people died during this tournament. As you can imagine, the sea is unforgiving. But the winner—the person who came back to Easter Island with a rock from the bird island would be crowned not only Birdman but would be the leader of the entire island for the year," Maru explained with unmistakable happiness in her voice at reliving this memory. Of course, she likely was there for the original competitions, but she was also there for the twenty-first-century version and seemed to love them both equally.

"So, who won?" I asked, smiling.

"My friend Poe won. Of course, he didn't get to control the island, but he got a whole fridge full of seafood that seemed to satisfy him just as well," she said, laughing as she recounted and remembered Poe swimming to shore, surviving this ancient ritual to celebrate.

The intensity of the heat stalled the stories as the afternoon lingered, and we carried on westward in silence. My eyes frantically darted and searched the ground and the trees, probing for some indication by nature that we were heading in the right direction. *Nothing*. My legs burned to the point I wondered if my pants were about to spontaneously combust. Although only slight, I could see we were climbing an incline. After hours and hours of trekking through the rainforest, this slight ascent was enough to do all of us in for the day.

"Incline here, guys, and it burns. The air is getting thinner at this altitude. Maybe at the top there will be a place for us to sit down and take in some water while we catch our breath." I said, trying to sound like the leader Maru was sure I was meant to be. By the time we reached even ground again, we were each panting and gasping for air. The rainforest made it seem as though oxygen were plentiful, but the humidity seemed to drag it out of your lungs before you could really reap the benefits.

Pointing to the right, we all nodded in agreement and sat in a clearing surrounded by the brightest green moss I had ever seen. Careful not to sit on the spongy vegetation, we all grabbed water from our bags and chugged silently, slowly catching our breath in between gulps. Maru grabbed a tree root and ripped it in half, using one half to tie her dirty and sweaty hair up from the back of her neck with an audible sigh of relief.

"Do you guys mind if I look around for a minute? I don't know why, but I have a feeling about this place…" I started off without finishing and wandered away without their reply. After reaching this landing pad, I noticed a strange stirring in my gut. Instinct of some sort was trying to kick in and tell me something, but aside from water and oxygen, I wasn't interested in paying attention to it, dismissing it as exhaustion. But after a few minutes of persistence, I wondered if this was the sign Maru was telling me to watch for. Perhaps not only in nature but within myself as well. The thought seemed far-fetched, but of course, that was the way of my life these days, so I thought, what the hell. I blocked out their chatter behind me and circled our area over and over again. I looked up in the trees, down at the moss growing on fallen branches and discarded rocks. I looked for patterns in the fallen leaves covering the ground beneath our feet, or openings in the canopy above that would provide some insight into that stirring—twirling my energy bar round and round.

Just as embarrassment crept up on me, my peripheral vision caught something that made me stop. Glancing back over my shoulder, I saw Maru and Terrence still sitting drinking behind me. I headed straight for a pile of rocks to my left, lining the path I had outlined in my mind's eye. The stones on top were insignificant. It was the glimmer I could see beneath the rubble that made me curious. The more water I drank, the more the sweat poured and I just couldn't keep up. I tossed rock after rock out of my way until the glimmer and sparkle that caught my eye was revealed—and it was absolutely mesmerizing.

I dropped to my knees with a thud, ignoring the jolt through my bones, and wiped my hand back and forth across the top of this alluring piece of nature. Believing it at first to be granite, I had seen many shimmering granite rocks in my time, but this was something else entirely. The shimmer was nearly blinding, and the stone's color seemed to change every time I blinked. At first, I saw black, then grey, then a midnight blue, and even white at one point, but I was sure that was the reflection of the sun and not the rock changing so drastically before my very eyes. To Maru and Terrence behind me, it must've looked like I was kissing the rock. My face was so close to its surface. The stirring and clenching in my stomach intensified to where I was debating whether it was excitement or I was going to vomit. The longer I stared at the rock, the more the nausea dissipated, and the butterflies of excitement took over. There was something about this rock… I knew it.

With a glance up at the tree canopy to see where the sunlight was hitting the rock from, I was slightly stunned to see that the sun was not breaking through this part of the forest at all. The rock was essentially glowing and shimmering all of its own accord. Just as I was about to turn and invite Terrence and Maru over to check out this interesting discovery, a magnificent butterfly landed on the top of my hand. My left hand had been resting on this unique rock and now a butterfly, sparkling as bright as the stone itself, and mimicking its color changes, sat perfectly still on that hand. When I looked up to tell Maru about it, I saw that ahead there were dozens more butterflies hovering in place, forming a line in the forest. They were forming our heading.

"Maru…" I started to say, not sure how to complete the sentence, "are you seeing this?" Turning my head toward them but not willing to move enough to disturb the constantly-changing butterfly, I was ecstatic inside. I had found a sign in nature!

"Yes, I see… amazing, aren't they?" Maru commented, provoking the thought that although this was new for me, it wasn't for her.

"You've seen these before?" I asked, half-heartedly shocked, even though I shouldn't have been.

"Of course, I too had to make this journey in my early life, you know, Lucius. I wasn't born all-knowing!" she laughed, and Terrence chuckled with her.

"Amazing." was all I could say. Amazing that Maru too had taken this journey and was now my mentor in accomplishing the same task, and amazing that nature seemed to be on my side, presenting creatures I could never have imagined existed.

"Looks like we have our heading. According to the line of Alice-in-Wonderland-style butterflies, we are turning north," I said, so elated, I couldn't help but laugh out loud. Gently, I tipped the butterfly from the top of my hand to the rock's surface and silently thanked it for its help. I genuinely appreciated the butterfly, or the whole flock of butterflies was more like it, which seemed perfectly natural in this moment.

Jacked up on adrenaline and pride, I needed no more energy bars to sustain the rest of our day. Every fifty feet, a butterfly hovered in place, marking our direction, and I noted it on the compass each time so that when the butterfly flock ended, I would still know our heading.

"The sound of the water is getting louder… we must be getting close. We can stop and refill our bottles there and maybe camp for the night, depending on how much longer it takes to get there." I announce to the group as if I were a tour guide who traveled this way daily and was going through the motions for the *tourists*.

"Sounds good, dear," Maru said, her tone steady and strong even after hours of hiking through the rough terrain of decaying tree branches, vines, and creepy-crawly critters. Time continued to roll by, although none of us knew at what speed. We determined when and where to stop by the sun's light breaking through the tree canopy. Of course, the numbness in our legs certainly aided in that decision as well. The body can only go on for so long with a single energy bar fueling the way. My breathing was strenuous. I focused entirely on reaching the waterfall before nightfall. We all needed water, and I needed a goal to focus my mind.

Walking fairly straight but at a much slower pace, I held my left hand out to the side, caressing each butterfly as I passed by. Finally, we reached what appeared to be the last butterfly, and just as my mind wondered why my eyes discovered the answer. We no longer needed guidance—the way was perfectly clear. A little off-kilter from our current heading, hiding behind a cluster of vines, clouds, and trees, laid a crossing. The billowing of water was almost deafening. I wondered how I could've possibly not heard it long ago. Lurching and bending through the vines and trees, we emerged to find the edge of the forest; presumably the edge of the rainforest, and the crossing to the northern woods. Water poured from a cliff so far above us that the top wasn't even visible. The water crashed into a rapid river, and right in front of us was our only crossing point, a footbridge made of tree limbs and vines.

"Well… we found the waterfall, just like I said we would," I said meekly, not having any idea how we would reach the water and fill our bottles.

"I think I see a way down to the river. Let me take the bottles and go, and you guys rest here a bit and see what you can of that sketchy bridge we seem destined to cross," Terrence said, slapping my back as he grabbed mine and Maru's water bottled and began his steep descent to the river below. Maru sat without a word and didn't seem interested in the footbridge before us.

"I assume you have been over this bridge before? Did you build it too, Maru?" I asked, smiling, hoping she saw my humor and not just the edge of my sarcasm.

"Haha, very funny. No, I did not build this bridge, but you might be interested to know who did, funny man." Maru teased, taking a shirt out of her carry-on to wipe the sweat from her eyes and hairline.

"Who built it? It was a long time ago, I imagine," I said, staring at the bridge and noting what appeared to be weak spots where the timbre pieces looked to be softer than the energy bars we were choking down.

"Your Father built that bridge on his journey," she said with a pride that seemed to fill her completely. Her reverence for my father was something that hadn't eluded me, but I had yet to foster those feelings myself. Sparking recognition, I remembered him saying that he took this journey at some point in his life, but I didn't really believe it at the time. This thought jolted me out of my comfortable acceptance of this memory. It wasn't mine, but I'd almost forgotten that. It was so familiar and true to me, the merger of our memories nearly complete.

"Your father was one of the first dimensional beings to take this journey through Tibet; the first of the Alvanata, Leto's disciples, as some people refer to them. And before you ask, Leto is a character you need not worry yourself about right now. Let's just say that he is the overseer of the entire universe and your father has worked closely with him as one of the three Alvanata for the past three centuries," she said, relaxing into a tree trunk. So at ease, Maru seemed to literally sink into the bark and become a part of the tree. She breathed in slowly, closed her eyes, and sat so still you wondered if there were life in her body at all. The ironic thing was, she seemed to have more energy than any of us put together.

"How long did it take him?" I asked, once again curious about the man who claimed to be my father. I bounced back and forth between love and hate for him; it was a roller coaster ride I would have to exit at some point, but I wasn't ready yet.

"He was away from Atlantis for a full three years. The city was not the same without him…" She trailed off, lost in her memories of this time—a time I could scarcely believe existed at all. "He spent two years solely building this crossing. Of course, several others managed to cross the river below and continue their journey with only a few days lost, but your father wanted to help not only himself but those who would follow in his footsteps. So, he took the time to build this crossing; easing the passage for those to come," she said, smiling brightly. The love she held for my father was apparent, and I envied her in that moment. Not sure what to say, I smiled in return and allowed her words to cycle through my mind, creating a new image of the father I didn't know.

I got up and walked away to avoid further discussion about my father with Maru. I could see Terrence at the edge of the raging river below. He was close enough to the white rapids that my heartbeat escalated tenfold at the sight of his proximity. He hung firmly off a nearby tree, a thick trunk that was likely here during the time of the dinosaurs. I observed to make sure Terrence didn't lose his footing and end up in the rapids. From my vantage point, I had to appreciate my father's work to build this crossing. Saving me and likely hundreds of others the effort of struggling across a frothing river, carrying on wet if you were lucky enough to carry on at all.

"Lucius… don't… move…" Maru warned in a whisper. Her tone was steady but firm. I froze instantly, grasping a nearby tree to steady me. I watched as Terrence began his climb back to our location on the ridge. Seconds passed, and I caught myself imagining what my current surroundings looked like. *What is going on behind me?* Listening intently, Maru hadn't said another word, but I could hear her breathing, so she was still with me. As I zeroed in on her breathing, I detected a distinct pattern of breath closer to myself. Closing my eyes, I remained still, focused on what I could hear, and sensed that I had something or someone closing in on me from behind. Just as I had decided that some animal, perhaps a large jungle cat of sorts, was standing at my heels, Terrence cleared the ridge of the landing. His eyes told me I was right.

The jaguar made a guttural growl, low but intense. Just as I thought the cat would rush us both, I heard it turn away. Its wide paws padded across the forest floor, growing further and further away until I could see in Terrence's eyes it was safe to move again.

"Well, that was a close one. Wow. I never thought I would see a jaguar that close in all my life." Terrence was amazed. Maru seemed slightly interested, and I was calm—utterly calm. This lack of reaction threw my mind into high gear. I should've been terrified, or at least experiencing what Terrence felt, amazement, to see such an animal stalking back into the rainforest. The cat disappeared, and I looked at Maru to make sure she was okay.

"I'm fine Lucius." She got up from her tree trunk lounger, dusted herself off, eager and ready to cross the bridge.

"Why didn't it attack me? It was so close to me. It could've killed me if it wanted to in a second or less." I stated out loud to anyone who wanted to venture a guess.

"You weren't scared, Lucius. It sensed everything about you except the fear it was expecting. You caught it off guard, so it left. Jaguars are beautiful creatures, aren't they?" Maru added as she shouldered her bag and grabbed her now full water bottle from Terrence. "Thank you, Terrence." She patted his head affectionately.

"Alright, well, let's get going, I guess."

We headed towards the crossing my father had built centuries ago, and I scanned the branches and connections as closely as I could. It was at least three hundred feet across, the other side of the bridge too far away for me to eyeball its condition. Maru and Terrence stood behind me, ready to follow, once I gathered enough courage to begin. Feet resting on the ground inches before the first log stretched lengthways, I looked at the vine sewing the tree branches together. The fraying concerned me, but it seemed fastened securely.

"Let's go, Lucius. We either take the bridge, or we try to swim the rapids and then struggle to get warm. We are crossing into the northern forest now. The heat and humidity are going to be a fond memory once we travel to the other side," Maru assured.

"Got it. Let's go, then," I said, sounding confident and acting as though I were waiting for them to be ready. I had been prepared all along. My smile immediately disappeared when I turned back towards the bridge. There was nothing for it but to go, so my first step took me out above the raging river below. The bridge held. I clung on tightly to the swinging vine that acted as a railing, and walked slowly, each step deliberate, watching carefully where each foot landed.

"Could we pick this up a bit, Lucius? I'm not a fan of this." Terrence spoke up from behind Maru. His words allowed me to release a bit of oxygen and tension. It was encouraging to learn I wasn't the only one dreading this obstacle. My steps accelerated, but my eyes were diligent, careful not to step on a rotten branch or a vine that was ready to split.

My nerves created a blanket of sweat. I hardly noticed I was concentrating so hard, but I could feel the chill my body was experiencing because of it. I may have been sweating, bringing my body temperature up out of pure terror, but we were heading north, and the cold breeze from the river below seemed to billow out of the forest in front of us making my perspiration feel like ice water. With the occasional glance at my feet, I watched the white-capped water flow with incredible velocity away from us, and thanked God I was up on this rickety old bridge and not fighting for my life down below.

I continued to watch my every step and once my foot hit solid ground, I exhaled all the oxygen I had been holding in. Jumping off the bridge, I stood at the beginning of what Maru referred to as the northern forest, silently thanking God and my father that the bridge had held for us. Terrence was the last to cross over, practically edging Maru along so he could reach the grass-covered land quicker.

"Awe, thank God. That was the worst thing I've ever done," he said, smiling mildly but mostly looking as though he wanted to vomit. "Should've gone for a swim instead." He laughed, but not enough to convince me he wasn't kidding. Already having caught my breath, I surveyed our surroundings. The forest was much different on this side of the bridge.

"Are we sure that bridge wasn't some type of dimensional portal, Maru? It's like another world over here." I chuckled. Maru said nothing but smiled. Suspicion all over my face, I asked again, "Did we cross into a different dimension when we crossed that bridge?" The temperature was at least fifteen degrees cooler, the trees were a different species, and the terrain looked rough. We were in the mountains now.

"You seem to think we did." That was all Maru would say. "What do you think, Terrence?" she asked, while she took more clothing from her carry-on and began layering up.

"I don't know. It sure is different on this side. I doubt a different dimension, though. Wouldn't we have felt something?" He half asked, and half stated while he looked around with just as much curiosity.

"Well, the sun is going down. I guess it doesn't really matter whether we did or didn't. Our goal is to find Ouriana." I said, following Maru's lead and layering up myself. Without the cover and warmth of the canopy, the late afternoon air seemed to blow right through me, and I dreaded what nighttime would bring. Secretly, I wondered why Terrence and Maru hadn't packed warmer clothes. They knew our destination, after all. Of course, the second this thought flitted through my brain, the answer was clear. This was *my* test, not theirs.

With little chatter, we began walking. I kept a close eye on Terrence's compass, following our heading without straying, and returned to my routine of scanning the scenery around us. There was no room for mistakes here. The cold was going to be unforgiving—this I was certain of—and the quicker we could find Ouriana, the better. There seemed to be an actual path carved into the trees. We walked where it looked like hundreds of others had. The grass was worn to the point that it didn't grow at all. The trees kept their distance, and we had ample space to walk side by side instead of single file.

Even with the old dirty clothes on top of my semi-clean clothes, the cold was cutting through as the wind picked up. The trees were not much cover and the further we walked, the more exposed we became in the open terrain.

"We need to find cover for the night, guys. Can one of you break out the flashlight?" I asked Terrence and Maru. The sun was still hovering on the horizon, but it wouldn't be long until the darkness was fully upon us. I was freezing already.

Together we looked diligently for shelter, wandering off the trail and back, in case there was something of use amongst the tall, skinny trees. After what must have been an hour of searching, the sun was gone, and the moon had taken its place. Maru continued to scan the terrain with her flashlight.

"There! Do you guys see that? I think it's a small cave or opening under that rock face." I screamed loud enough for every animal in the vicinity to know our new camp location. Maru followed my gaze and shone her flashlight on the hole in the mountainous rock face. All three of us shivered uncontrollably. There was no need to speak. We headed towards the cave we hoped was empty.

Cautiously, I stuck my head into the opening while Maru held the light. It wasn't deep, maybe fifteen feet at most, but it was a shelter from the wind, and there seemed to be no inhabitant to fight with, so we jumped in without another thought.

"I'll go get some branches, and if we're lucky, we can start a fire," Terrence said.

"I can help." I wanted to show Maru that I was changing and was a fully-fledged player in this strange game we were playing.

"No need. Rest. I got this." Terrence patted my back and headed back out into the wind. Flashlight sitting on the floor in the middle of the cave, Maru and I sat in silence. I replayed the day's events in my mind, a sense of pride washing over me like an unexpected warm blanket. I got us through a lot since we left Mataio on the highway, and we had made it this far, all the way out of the rainforest and into the northern forest, right through the Himalayans. *What an adventure!*

Terrence returned with an armload of sticks and twigs to get our fire going. He piled the sticks into a tipi and I worked my magic that no longer seemed like magic. With a little concentration, I created the fire with minimal effort—just by the focus of my mind. Within seconds we were all huddled around warm flames.

"So, what's next?" I couldn't help but to ask Maru.

"You'll see," she said smiling, rubbing her hands together over the warmth of the fire.

CHAPTER 10

We survived the first night in the cold. And it would only get worse. Colder, windier, and more challenging. Energy bars running low, we each ate half of a bar and shouldered our packs, kicked over our fire, and stood at the cave entrance looking out at the wilderness. The trees had thinned significantly. We were now looking at a low grassland valley with steep ridges on both sides, covered in bright green vegetation with the first dusting of snow still visible here and there from the night before. Unlike in the rainforest, the clouds were not falling down around us; but loomed straight above, mixing in with the clear blue sky.

We headed out, and it was time to think about food. As a New Yorker, I, of course, had never hunted in my life —unless you included the desperate search for the nearest Starbucks, which I doubt Maru would consider challenging.

"Terrence, do you know how to hunt?" I asked. With Terrence on my left and Maru on my right, it was a privilege to be in the middle. They were my wind block.

"Well, I have hunted once or twice, but I'm no pro. Just keep quiet and keep your eyes peeled. If you spot pawprints or scat of any kind, we can track it and then decide how to kill it once we have a bead on it." He looked weary. I hoped we would get 'a bead' on something this afternoon because energy bars were nearly gone and the trail mix wouldn't last much longer once the bars were out of the picture.

As we moved forward, the trees completely disappeared around us. There was an occasional odd one still alive in the valley, but it was all trunk and no branches until twenty or thirty feet in the air. I did my best to scan the landscape. I saw nothing of note, nothing of interest, until we came around a slight bend in the valley, leading us northeast. A tiny, manmade hut stood on the edge of the valley. It looked as though it was teetering on the edge, made of nothing but tree limbs and some brush for the roofing. It was rustic, and I wished we had come across it last night.

"Hey, should we go check that out?" I asked, pointing at the makeshift home as if they had not seen it. It was a vacant landscape they were traveling in now. The only thing as far as the eye could see was the hut.

"No. That's a Buddhist meditation hut. We must not disturb it—regardless if someone is in there or not," Maru said and Terrence didn't comment and didn't slow down his stride either.

"Terrence, are you okay?" I asked. He hadn't been his usual self since we left the cave, and he looked as if he might fall over at any second. "Maybe we should take a little rest over there." I pointed to just below the Buddhist hut, utilizing the ridge as a natural wind blocker.

"You're the boss." Was all Terrence managed say. We left the center of the valley floor and headed for the inclining ridge. We sat in the sparse grass and sipped on our waterfall water.

The sense of pride and accomplishment I experienced last night in the cave had abandoned me and as

I looked out into the seemingly never-ending valley, I felt lost again. It was possible I had missed some sign or marker and we were heading in the wrong direction. The valley was massive. I couldn't check every inch or we would make no headway. I wanted nothing more than to curl up into a ball and cuddle with my despair. So much so that I almost missed the most obvious sign mother nature threw at me—the biggest black bear I had ever seen. My best guess was that it weighed close to a ton. The black bear stood in the center of the valley, staring up at us on the cusp of the inclining ridge. Appearing as if from nowhere, we all stared at the bear, unsure what to think, and wondering if the bear was really there at all. Starved and sleep-deprived on only day three of our expedition, this was a rare and unexpected sight.

"I think we not only found dinner, but we found some winter coats as well," Terrence said with a sly smirk. I wasn't so sure. All my focus was on the bear. There was something gathering within me, and I couldn't quite put my finger on it. This differed from the butterflies, but something was telling me this bear was not meant to be our dinner, but rather, our guide. Terrence slowly rose from his seated position and started towards the bear. Not understanding how he thought he would even begin to bring down a bear that size, I almost sat by and watched, but in the end, I didn't want something to happen to Terrence or the bear.

"Terrence stop!" I yelled. The bear didn't flinch, keeping its eyes focused on me while Terrence nearly lost his footing completely, falling back down on his backside.

"What are you doing, Lucius? We need food," he yelled at me for the first time. At this moment, I knew for certain that Terrence was losing it. He was starving, and convincing him to spare the bear would not be easy.

"Terrence, the bear is not for us to eat. I think it's here for another reason," I said, slow-playing my way to my epiphany, trying to edge Terrence into my mindset and out of his starvation-driven rage. Staring at me with anger in his eyes, the kind of anger I had only experienced from Dax and Orpheus, made me shift backward on the grass and look towards Maru for help.

"Are you kidding me, Lucius? You don't have a clue. Not a goddam clue about what is going on here, and now you want to take a stand—when we are starving and living off of mouthfuls of oats." He started off in a whisper, his voice quickly growing in volume until he was screaming and his words were echoing off the mountains circling us.

"Please, Terrence, you have to believe me. I think this bear is here to guide us." I said, standing up now. I slowly made my way toward the bear that hadn't moved a muscle since appearing, seemingly out of nowhere. "I get that it sounds crazy, so just let me test it. Please—" I begged Terrence. If I approached the bear and it attacked me then that was that, but there was a whispering in me deep down that said I had to try.

"Your nuts… you know that, right? You are going to get eaten by a bear, and Maru and I will be left here for nothing. All because of you," Terrence growled his last words, making him unrecognizable to me. He wasn't my friend, Terrence, but someone else entirely now. Maru continued to sit in utter silence, observing our back-and-forth communication with a stony face.

Laying back against the slope, Terrence waved me on as if to say, *"Go ahead, you lunatic, and get yourself killed. Prove me right."* The smugness on his face was disheartening. We needed food, and I wanted to help Terrence, but somehow, I suspected this bear would get us further than we ever could on our own. So, I took one step at a time, slowly and deliberately, just like when we crossed that ancient twig and vine bridge. I narrowed my focus on the bear and nothing else. This monstrous animal stood in place, not moving a paw or even turning its head, but keeping its focus solely on me. As I got within feet of the animal, I thought I might panic, but again felt nothing but the same composure I noticed when the jaguar was feet away from me, deciding whether to eat me. This recent development was interesting, but it wasn't the time to examine it. This was it. I had to test my theory—and if this animal was there for any other reason than to help us, it would bite my hand off and I would likely bleed to death in a valley somewhere in the vastness of the Himalayan mountainside.

With a deep breath, our eyes locked, and I stuck my hand out towards its snout as slow as possible so as not to scare it, although it seemed to recognize exactly what I was doing. Not able to stop the tremors in my hand, it vibrated in the air for a split second before I went for it and placed my hand on the top of the enormous head of a black bear. My heartbeat increased slightly until I watched the bear slowly blink, as if to communicate something to me and then sit down on its hind legs. I stood in the center of the valley with my hand on the head of the biggest black bear in the world, and it simply blinked at me.

"Well, holy shit." I heard Terrence say loudly to no one in particular. My feelings exactly. Still holding my breath, I let it all out and absently stroked the head of the bear while I soaked in what was happening. I had followed the strange buzzing in my gut, and it brought me to this bizarre situation. I was intoxicated by this moment. It made me wonder about the type of happiness that may be in my future if I were to finish these trials and join the citizens of Atlantis—now suddenly a real possibility.

Maru and Terrence slowly climbed down the hillside, not wanting to spook the bear if this was in fact some type of aberration. Then the three of us stood around the creature, not really sure what to do next. Terrence still seemed angry with me for denying him a warm meal and an even warmer coat, but even through his anger, he knew I was onto something.

Unsure of the next step, I continued petting the bear and looking into its eyes. The idea of conversing out loud with a black bear was embarrassing so I focused on the question in my mind and hoped that somehow this bear would hear me.

"Are you here to guide us the rest of the way?" I thought with as much clarity and focus as I could muster, my eyes locking on the bear. Waiting a few seconds, when nothing of note changed in its wide black gaze, and no foreign voice spoke up inside my mind, I decided that it was useless and I needed to move on. Then I heard, "*Not the rest of the way, but part of the way.*" My hand stopped stroking the furry head, and I stared at it as if trying to confirm if a black bear had spoken telepathically to me or if I had made that entire scenario up and was about to follow this creature through the forest. The bear abruptly got up and started walking up the incline our little tribe had just been sitting on. Left standing in the valley, I said, "Let's go, guys. Our guide is on the move." Unable to stop smiling, I was extremely excited about this development. After a few strides, I looked back and noticed Terrence wasn't following us.

"Terrence, come on, man," I said, waving him to fall in behind Maru.

"No," Terrence said. He stood, feet firmly planted, and his face scowled up in anger. I tapped the bear on the behind to get her to stop, not knowing why I was sure it was a *her*. She said, "*Can't stop, we have to go to the cabin before nightfall, Lucius."* Turning back around, she continued onward.

"Terrence, we have to get moving. She is leading us to a cabin for the night. There will be food there, I'm sure of it."

"Well, I hate to burst your bubble, Lucius, but you are the last person in the world I can trust with my life. I should've never come here." Spinning in circles now, looking for something, he screamed at the top of his lungs in frustration.

"Maru, do something. We can't leave him there," I whispered to her. It hurt me worse than I would've ever thought to have Terrence lash out at me like that. We barely knew each other and yet I felt so close to him, like brothers… for a little while.

"Terrence, you are hungry and tired. If we can push a few more hours, we can find food and rest for the night in comfort. Trust me if you don't want to trust Lucius. I would not guide you to your death, my dear." She spoke calmly and softly. He stopped spinning and the tension seemed to drop from his face at her words. A few moments passed, and the bear was almost at the top of the ridge, not waiting for us. We were going to have to hurry to catch up, and it was making me anxious.

"Fine, fine, Maru. I'm not doing this for you, Lucius." Those were Terrence's last words for the rest of the day. He fell in line behind Maru, and we climbed to the top of the ridge as quickly as possible, finding the bear had waited at the top for us—maybe sensing we had temporarily resolved our differences long enough to continue.

The top of the ridge was breathtaking. We were surrounded by snow-capped mountain ranges and fields of green vegetation mixed with golden yellow wildflowers. The mountains nearly blocked the entire sky, meeting the place where the clouds hovered. Towards the base of the mountains, green had found its way up, covering portions in grass and flowers, the same as where we walked, creating a beautiful contrast between the snow-white tips and the bright green bases. Dozens and dozens of delicate-looking waterfalls flowed as the snow melted at the top of the mountains and slowly wound its way to the bottom, likely feeding a natural spring that I hoped we would run into at some point. The beauty was breathtaking, and while the others followed the bear without a word, I was stationary, taking it all in.

"What should I call you?" I silently asked the black bear, moving briskly ahead of us. I couldn't help but secretly wonder if this black bear was, in fact, the great Ouriana I was meant to find.

"Zivo is what I am called, Lucius of the Alvanata." After all, I had experienced since leaving New York, you would think something like speaking telepathically to a black bear would be commonplace, but even with very few words exchanged, I felt myself glowing from the inside out.

All negativities and doubts were gone, leaving me with a blissful sensation I didn't realize existed.

"Nice to meet you, Zivo, but I'm not of the Alvanata. I think you must be thinking of my father." The clarity of my mind during our communications was refreshing, and perhaps even this event was part of my training, I wondered. Regardless, I felt wonderful. Instead of receiving a response from Zivo, I perceived a grin in the forefront of my mind. *Is this Zivo's grin?* Something told me it was, and instead of embracing my skepticism, I found myself grinning back. Looking around at my travel companions, I seemed to be the only one grinning. Maru offered her usual neutral expression, and Terrence looked as though he were debating on launching himself across the path at me and beating me senselessly. His bushy brown eyebrows creased together as he mulled over his angry thoughts, his nostrils were flaring and a permanent frown seemed to engulf his once happy-go-lucky features. Terrence quickly became my close friend, and it hurt to watch him suffering because of me. This journey would be more arduous than I first thought.

The effects of Terrence's anger were trying to hitch a ride on my own subconscious. I took a few long strides and began walking side by side with Zivo. Terrence's scoff behind me only cemented my decision was the right one. His anger had taken over and until he could rectify that situation, I had to focus on my task, which really had nothing to do with Terrence, this much I had to remind myself of. Resting my left arm on the giant back of Zivo, we walked along a very narrow worn path in the meadow, making me wonder who or what had been keeping the path worn down in all this lush greenery.

"There are many who call these mountains home, Lucius." Zivo responded to my silent musing. "Animals such as myself but many Buddhists and spiritual men as well. They are in search of the very place you are heading, Lucius." I watched her closely while her words scrolled across the forefront of my mind. I was enchanted and wondered if Maru was catching any of this telepathic conversation with her own dimensional skills.

"Aren't you afraid they will follow us, Zivo?" I asked, looking around and seeing no one, but that didn't mean someone wasn't seeing us. A strange sight to see two men, a woman and a black bear trekking through the northern forests of the Himalayas.

"The spiritual men head down the mountain at this time of day, not up. They have not altered their routine in decades, which is exactly why they learn nothing new and understand nothing of the wonders hiding within the beauty of this secret world." Zivo stopped to look me in the eye, as if gauging whether I deserved to learn her secret. I gently patted her head and hoped she could not only see within my mind, but my heart as well. Maybe she would find in me something worthy of her guidance. When she turned her attention back to the worn-out path in the grass and wild flowers, I assumed I had satisfied her requirements and continued alongside her.

The sky darkened, and more clouds billowed in. The sun's disappearance seemed to stress my sore feet, icy hands, and numbed face, as well, my my growling stomach. "How long have we been walking, Zivo? Are we getting close to the cabin? Please tell me there will be food there." I needed to help Maru and Terrence. We were all suffering, but Terrence was taking it the hardest.

"I do not understand what you are asking, Lucius of the Alvanata. I believe you speak of time, and we of the animal kingdom do not subscribe to those beliefs."

I repeated her words over and over to myself, never having stopped to think about time and what is really means in the world. Of course, animals know nothing of time. They aren't constantly staring at their wristwatch or flicking on their smartphones to check the time, even though they just did minutes before. As if right on cue, Zivo added, *"We live by mother nature, and the universe, and these forces tell us about the weather, about the environment. We need nothing else. We are about five hundred more steps to the cabin, and yes, I have prepared provisions for you and your friends."* Without thinking, I stopped and threw my arms around Zivo's neck. The thought of shelter and food left me ecstatic. I squeezed her tight, silently thanking her. While behind me, Terrence and Maru watched me maul a humongous black bear in the middle of nowhere.

"Thank you so much, Zivo. I don't know what would happen to us if you hadn't come to us." Pausing for only a second, I had to add, "Who sent you anyway?" A question that of course should have come before agreeing to follow her into the woods, but better late than never was my way of thinking.

"*You have this information already, Lucius of the Alvanata.*" Not bothering to correct Zivo, I remained silent, marveling at how the bear had plucked Ouriana's name from somewhere in my mind, bringing it front and center so I knew it to be true. Slowly we began walking again, and as our trail curved towards the right, down the bottom of the mountainside, we spotted a small object in the far distance.

"There it is, Terrence. Lucius was right to trust his instincts," Maru pointed out quietly, yet with a confidence she wanted to convey to Terrence in her own silent manner. The four of us stood on the pathway staring off into the distance at the cabin we would find reprieve in.

"Yes! There it is!" I yelled excitedly. Any trepidation that was left inside me vanished. I trusted myself, and it paid off. I was becoming someone new and loving every second of this newfound inner-self. Maru smiled and patted my back in a silent 'you did it' acknowledgment. Not wanting to look Terrence in the eye, I returned to my position next to Zivo, and we carried on leading toward the cabin. It got easier and easier to see with each passing step, just as the clouds were beginning their descent for the night.

Thinking more in terms of steps than in time, Zivo seemed to be bang-on with her estimate of five hundred steps. By my count, we would be standing on the front porch of the wood-planked cabin in four hundred and eight-seven steps. *Amazing*. A combination of wood planks and cemented river rock made up the walls of the cabin, and nice green tin formed a perfect peak for the roof. It was much more solid than the Buddhist hut we saw earlier. So much had changed since then. As Zivo swaggered her way through the front door, a firm hand settled on my left shoulder, stopping me, and holding me back.

"I'm sorry, Lucius. This is the first time in my life that I have acted this way. I guess I'm not very good in survival mode." Turning to face Terrence, he paused to stare at his feet to avoid my gaze, embarrassed and exhausted. "Can you forgive me, brother?" Terrence asked in a meek, hesitant voice that didn't suit him anymore than his furious voice from earlier in the afternoon. Choosing to say nothing, I simply threw my arms around him as I had with Zivo and unleashed every bit of happiness and love I had inside. What a relief to once again have Terrence on my side.

"Let's go eat, brother," I said, finally withdrawing from the poor, exhausted man. We were brothers, and I didn't need to hear Terrence say it to be sure of its truth, but it was nice. Together we walked into the cabin. I wasn't sure what to expect and silently prayed to the universe that Zivo, our new guide, had found us food—any food.

Inside the cabin, a fire glowed inside a wood stove. In front of the fireplace sat an ancient-looking couch, a couple of wood-spindle chairs, and a coffee table. But it was the kitchen I was searching for, led there by my screaming stomach. We walked towards the front of the cabin, turning away from the warmth of the fire to find a dining room table covered in the most delicious food I had ever seen. There were colorful and juicy-looking fruits and vegetables, pitchers of water, and what appeared to be juice, but my sense of smell lured me to a platter piled high with steaming hot meat. Terrence and I dove across the kitchen and grabbed slabs of meat, eating them as we would popsicles without hesitating a second; manners out the window.

While I swallowed as much meat as my esophagus would allow in a single gulp, I watched Maru seated at the head of the table with a plate full of food, eating as though this were nothing more than five o'clock supper at home. She smiled and shook her head at Terrence and me, carefully forking food into her mouth, savoring the flavors. At the same time, Terence and I continued to shovel in food, caring very little for flavor and going more for quantity to quiet that raging hunger we had been traveling with for days.

After we polished off the meat platter, stopping to allow Maru her chance to grab some protein, we dove into the fruits and vegetables. At this altitude the only thing growing we had come across were the wild flowers, so we had no clue where this food came from. This was a conversation to have with Zivo when I couldn't possibly put another bite of food in my mouth— but it could wait.

"Oh my God, do I feel like a million bucks," Terrence stated as he wiped his mouth on the hem of his t-shirt and took a seat in front of the fire; surely to doze off now that he was filled to the brim with food.

"I think Zivo is waiting for you outside, Lucius. I'm going to pack up some of this food to take with us. We must leave tomorrow… you know that, right dear?" Nodding, knowing it to be true, I swung open the porch door, listening to the ancient springs scream. Zivo sat on the threshold of the stairs, watching the distant mountains and grasslands surrounding us.

"How do I thank you, Zivo? You saved our lives." Smiling broadly and unconsciously rubbing my full belly, I plopped down loudly next to the bear and looked at the landscape around us just as she did.

"You saved your traveling band of friends, Lucius. You recognized why I was there and trusted your instincts, just like Ouriana hoped you would. This is your reward. Warmth and food for the night before you carry on in the morning."

"You won't be here in the morning, will you?" I asked Zivo, my instincts telling me she was preparing to say goodbye.

"My part in your story is over for now. But I will show you the way. Can you spot that ledge on the

mountainside with the three threadlike waterfalls trickling down?" she asked.

"Yes." Following her gaze up the side of the mountain. The waterfalls were at least three thousand steps away by my estimation.

"Very good, Lucius, your estimations are correct. That ledge will allow you a place to rest before moving to the top of the mountain. You are to cross it in two days and find yourself in the small village of Alexa. There you will find a second guide to aid you in your quest upon your arrival. Good luck, Lucius of the Alvanata. We shall meet again." Zivo bowed her head and plodded down the steps of the porch, continuing on the narrow path we had followed all the way here.

"Where will you go, Zivo?"

"Home," she said without turning back. As the bear disappeared in the trees, a sadness came over me.

****

The sunrise the next morning was make-you-stop-eating beautiful. With the warmth of the fire, the comfort of pillows and blankets, and piles of food, the three of us sat back enjoying the beauty of our surroundings for the first time since running from Mataio on the Arniko highway. Hot coffee steamed in our tin mugs, and we relished it. A full night's sleep in front of a raging fire invigorated us. At one point, I was so hot I was sweating, but I didn't dare move away from the warmth for even a slight reprieve.

"Well, what did Zivo tell you, Lucius? Before she left?" Terrence asked while he sipped his coffee and admired the environment we were currently lost in—lost to civilization anyway. After Zivo left, there wasn't much chatter in the cabin. All tired and full, we each took to our chosen sleep areas and were out for the night. Either Terrence or Maru had gotten up at some point to stoke the fire, but I didn't hear them; all I knew was I awoke to a fire the same size as when I fell asleep.

"She told me that Ouriana sent her. It was a test," I said with an edge of bitterness I didn't realize I was harboring over the idea of being tested by this mysterious woman I was risking my life to find in this cold wilderness. "We continue over the mountain. We have to get to a city called Alexa in two days, where another guide will be waiting to help us with the third leg of the journey. I don't know who or what to look for, but I guess we will know them when we come across them," I said, staring intently at the ridge we were meant to climb and wondering just how treacherous this leg of the journey would be.

"Is there an easy crossing over the mountain somewhere? Did she give you directions?" Terrence asked while Maru stood quietly, listening as always. She probably already had all the information about this journey, anyway. She didn't seem to need the info Terrence and I was grasping for.

"She did, but it doesn't look easy. I can tell you that." Pointing to the ridge and the threadlike waterfalls at least three thousand steps from us, it looked like a long way away.

"Well… that looks… technical," Terrence said with a great deal of hesitation as he too stared at the ridge that looked to be days away from the cabin. He was right. This seemed to require much more than your average hiking skills. We were going to need supplies like ropes and harnesses to start.

"There will be no need for ropes, Lucius. The Demeter pass is quite doable without the use of tools. We must make this journey with nothing more than what we already possess," Maru stated. Terrence and I stared at her and then back to the ridge Zivo had pointed out to me the day before. It did not seem possible, and it seemed incredibly dangerous to attempt with ropes and harnesses, let alone with nothing more than my pitiful Nikes that had seen better days.

"I wish you would stop reading my mind, and if you already know these things, just tell us, Maru," I said with a smile, although my words were serious. "You already saw how all of this is going to end, didn't you?" I asked. I set down my warm cup of coffee, balancing it on the railing. I turned away from the mountain range to face Maru. "There is a lot you don't tell us, Maru, and I get that. This is my test. You've made that clear, but just tell me… do you know how this is all going to end?"

"Of course not. I am a dimensional being, yes, but I don't get to see the future any more than you do. With each decision made, the future changes… it changes by the second. There is no way to know how anything will turn out, Lucius," she explained while she fiddled with her ponytail. "I am here to guide you, just as Zivo did yesterday. I can tell you things like we can't use tools, but I can't tell you that Zivo was there to guide us if you didn't realize it for yourself. Do you understand?" Now with both her hands on my shoulders we stood face to face, even though her face only reached my chest.

"Got it. Well, I guess we should pack our bags and say goodbye to the comforts of home." Pulling Maru close, I kissed her cheek and whispered a *thank you* in her ear. I loved Maru deeply. She had saved me repeatedly, but more than that, it was hard not to love Maru. There was something that drew me to her that was invisible, but powerful. As if an unseen rope tethered us together, and I had no desire to sever it. If I could accomplish this journey and become a dimensional being like Maru, we could spend eternity side by side, and that sounded alright to me. Interrupting this thought were sporadic memories of my father, but I brushed them aside. He wasn't here to help me, Maru was, and she was quickly taking the place of any parent figure I had ever had or dreamt of.

Inside the cabin, we all stood by the fire for a minute with our bags filled with leftover food from Zivo's prepared feast. It was time to get going. The sun had been up for at least an hour already, but it was hard to tear away from the warmth and comfort of that fire.

"Zivo said there would be a ridge at about the height of those waterfalls. Perhaps if we are watchful, we can collect some dry timber along the way and have a little bonfire before attempting to climb the mountain," I offered, thinking positively and trying to imagine a smooth and enjoyable journey, even though my instincts told me we were all about to be tested to our limits—especially Terrence.

"Good idea. I found a canvas bag around here somewhere. I'll carry it and fill it along the way. We might have a chance for a warm night, after all," Terrence said with a smile full of hope. Visually, it was already obvious that Terrence was suffering. He appeared to have lost a significant amount of weight since we left Mataio, so it was a blessing Zivo thought to provide us with so much food. We were stocked until we reached Alexa. Hopefully, I had proven myself enough to Terrence to help ease his mind continuing forward. With this thought, I witnessed a look of hesitation and doubt on Maru's face. She read my thoughts and didn't seem as confident as I was trying to be. *Now I was worried.*

We pried away from the fire, doused it in water, and closed the door behind us. Although Zivo had provided us with food and warmth for the night, she didn't provide us with any more clothing or winter gear to shelter us through the cold, so we all donned every piece of clothing we had, which didn't amount to much. The winds whipping through the valley were fierce, bringing tears to my eyes so often I could barely see where we were going most of the time. Constantly swiping at my eyes to clear them before they froze completely, my focus was split.

"I'll take the lead for a bit, Lucius. We'll take turns." Terrence set his hand on my shoulder as he stepped out from behind me and began etching a path through the wind. His tiny stature was enough of a windbreaker to stop the tears from flowing. Finally, out of the valley and making vertical progress, we walked on soft green grass, and my despair was alleviated at the sight of a small trail heading up to the ridge Zivo had shown me.

"Look at that, guys. There is a trail to the ridge. Perhaps we won't have to free climb after all," I said, exhilarated. I had imagined tumbling rocks, sharp surfaces, and plummeting to my death trying to reach this ridge, so it seemed like a win to see a semi-easy trail before us. Terrence glanced over his shoulder, offering a slight smile, and then turned back with his head down and shoulders tucked, fighting the invisible but strong force of the wind.

"I believe the mountain will shield us from the wind once we get to the ridge. Power through, Terrence!" Maru shouted over the howl of the gusts. Terrence raised his hand, giving her a thumbs-up, and carried on briskly. We would definitely need a break from the wind, and soon. My skin was burning. Oh, how I wished it were sunburn instead of a windburn. I wore my socks on my hands to protect them from the cold. I rubbed my ragged face repeatedly, creating friction with my beard stubble to induce the tiniest bit of warmth. We needed to make a kill in the wild. We needed fur to make hats and gloves if we could. Coats would be nice too, but that was likely a pipe dream. It was enough to imagine myself not only killing a wild animal, but then being able to skin it and create winter garments for myself and my friends—a very unlikely scenario.

The burning in my thigh and calf muscles monopolized my thoughts. The incline was increasing steadily, and my legs were blazing with pain and exhaustion. Working harder and harder with each step, our effort was audible as we gasped for air and groaned under the pain of our muscles straining.

"We're almost to the ridge, guys," Terrence hollered in excitement as if we had come across a Starbucks or, even better, a box of winter gear. Terrence hunched over in an agonizing effort to climb. I could see right over him and the ledge he was referring to. Only a hundred or so more steps to go, and we could rest and attempt to build a fire. As I struggled to keep my legs moving, I almost missed how the mountain was beginning to shield us from the wind, trading one struggle for another without skipping a beat.

"Maru, are you okay back there?" I asked. Maru had been pulling up the tail end of our little train since we started going vertical without a peep.

"Yes, thank you." Her voice sounded even, unbothered, making me wonder if she was suffering as much as Terrence and I were. Perhaps this was another situation where she delighted in her new, younger body. I flexed my fingers and toes to keep my extremities moving, attempting to avoid frostbite. I trudged on, knowing we would at least be able to sit, if not in front of a fire, but rest at the very least and soon. Then my focus shifted from the effort of my steps to the swaying Terrence ahead of me. At first, I was sure I was the one swaying back and forth, creating the illusion Terrence was as well. I was exhausted, and my legs were defying me to take another step. But the longer I watched, the more certain I became. Terrence was taking one step forward and then two or three steps to the left and then back again, nearly stumbling forward on his face a few times. I yelled out, "Terrence, are you okay?" Cupping my hands around my mouth to make sure he heard my words. With no response but a weak wave, I knew he was in trouble, but if he could make it just a few more steps over the ridge, we would rest and address the situation.

Inching closer to Terrence's heels, I walked as close as possible without tripping him up or stumbling myself. If he took a header, I could either catch him or at least be there for immediate help. He swayed back and forth for a few more feet, and then we finally scrambled over the small lip of the ridge onto flat land. Terrence dropped immediately, heaving dramatically for oxygen. Quickly, I took his bag off his shoulder and leaned him against the trunk of the sole pine tree in our midst. Eyes closed, he continued to breathe heavily and shiver uncontrollably. Maru climbed over the lip behind me and threw herself around Terrence to raise his body temperature.

"I'll start a fire," I said, rummaging through the canvas bag Terrence filled with dry twigs along the way. There were several large enough to make a suitable base and more than enough twigs to get the fire going. Cloning what Terrence did in the cave two nights earlier, I cleared away the pine needles and rocks to create a smooth surface to start. With intense focus, I built a small tipi of wood surrounded by twigs and all the dry pine needles and cones I could find. I concentrated to light the fire. As the fire caught instantaneously, I actually felt a deterioration in my energy levels. I had spent too much effort and not replenished any. Once Terrence was warming, we ate.

Maru and I helped carry Terrence over to where the small bonfire was now raging thanks to the twigs, pine cones, and needles. Unable, or too fatigued to move his legs properly, we were in fact dragging him to the fire, where it sapped even more of my dwindling strength to set him down gently.

"I'm fine, guys. I just need to rest for a minute," Terrence slurred and stuttered his words, too cold to talk— or perhaps a sign of something worse. Hugging Terrence close, Maru sat with him by the fire while I took it upon myself to unpack some of our food. We all needed an energy boost to go with the fire's heat.

Tossing around bags of unspecified meat, vegetables, fruit, and bread, we all ate our fill with plenty still left over. Terrence picked away at his food, not eating nearly enough. I was getting worried.

"Terrence, eat up, brother. You need to regain your strength. That's a steep climb we have ahead of us, man," I said, the cheer in my voice sounding false even to my own ears. Terrence continued to nibble on the food in front of him while he inched closer and closer to the warmth of the fire. His shivering had subsided, as had my own, allowing my energy levels to skyrocket. But something was wrong with Terrence. This wasn't just exhaustion. It was something much worse. Knowing little of survival in the wilderness, the few things I did know were ringing true the longer I watched Terrence struggle. His lack of coordination, slurred speech, and even the end of his shivering were all symptoms suggesting the onset of hypothermia. If we remained out in this wilderness much longer without proper gear, we were all going to die.

Getting up from the fire, I paced around the small circumference of our little resting area. The trickling waterfalls and the snowcapped mountain above were waiting for me to climb with nothing but my bare hands—not to mention, lack of experience. Adventure had never been my thing growing up. I was an intellectual, or so I told myself, and spent most of my time reading about other people's adventures. Now I sat in the absolute middle of nowhere on a Himalayan mountainside, preparing to climb to the top based on advice I received from a black bear named Zivo. Unconsciously rubbing my beard, I smiled. A solution was forming in my mind, but I didn't like it.

"*You know what has to be done, Lucius,*" Maru's voice echoed through the halls of my mind unexpectedly. Shocked by this sudden intrusion, I stumbled and regained my footing as we locked eyes. She was worried for Terrence, but didn't she already know this was going to happen? Wondering this made no difference and didn't help any of us, so I dismissed the thought, even though secretly I was wondering if this was another test setup at Terrence's expense. Our intense eye contact broke. I looked at Terrence, who was pale and disoriented, rocking back and forth while he tried to stay warm by the fire.

"He's gone hypothermic, hasn't he?"

"Yes, and I'm not sure how much time we have before we are in the same boat, Lucius." Maru stated matter-of-factly.

"I will go to the village of Alexa and bring back the proper gear we need to continue on together." Pausing, I stared at the looming mountain in front of us and wondered if that was even possible. "I don't know how long it will take me, but I promise I will be back, so—keep the fire burning," I said, taking my mind away from my fears of the mountain and focusing on the comfort of Maru's brown eyes. *How can I leave them behind?* Of course, logic dictated that Terrence was in no shape to climb over this mountain—albeit, the smallest peak of the mountain range

—but, still, it would be no small feat. I couldn't help but feel torn. Not only was I completely terrified to even contemplate the next leg of this journey alone, but it worried me to leave Maru and Terrence behind. How much time did Terrence have before the effects were irreversible? And was Maru at risk? Her body was human, but the spirit inside was something else entirely. What that meant for her safety, I had no idea.

"Lucius, you must go now before we are out of time. You need to be in Alexa in one day's time in order to meet your new guide. I can take care of Terrence until you come back. Go," Maru whispered, this time never taking her eyes off the fire.

After the food was distributed and my bag packed, it was time for me to face this task. I'd wasted enough time. The day was half over. "Bye, guys. I will be back with as many warm clothes and food as I can carry. Don't worry, Terrence." Those were the last words to my travel companions before I turned my back and began heading up the mountainside without another delay.

Twilight was upon me when I finally reached the peak Zivo had pointed out the day before. Before the daylight hours burned away, I filled my water bottle from a mountain waterfall and watched majestic birds I didn't recognize fly overhead with such unfathomable strength and freedom. I checked back on Maru and Terrence from this vantage point and spotted their fire blazing from a thousand feet away. The bright sun helped keep my spirits up, and my body remained semi-warm. But with each cloud covering and the lower the sun retreated, my mood and body temperature plummeted.

My feet dragged like they were enclosed in cement. The effort it took to lift them to clear a small rock or tree root seemed all-consuming. I was edging closer to the same fate as Terrence. My body was struggling and my mind was not far behind. The peak of that mountain saved me from my despair and pain. I saw a valley below through the thick fog that rolled in once the sun disappeared. According to Zivo, I had until tomorrow afternoon to make it to the village. I crossed my fingers they would allow me time to save my friends before we were to continue on to Ouriana.

I weighed my options, completely exposed to the elements straddling the mountain's peak. One foot stood on the side of the mountain where my friends awaited my help. The other was on the side where the mysterious city of Alexa awaited my arrival. There was nothing to speak of for shelter on my side of the mountain. I had no choice. If I wanted to survive the night, I needed to find even the smallest dip in the mountain to shelter myself from the cold. Even a bush would be better than nothing. So, with this fresh bout of determination, I began traversing my way down the back side of the crag, silently praying to the Universe for a bit of luck.

Fatigue was setting in with a fierceness I had yet to experience in life. Constantly glancing down at the valley, I searched for Alexa for a bit of encouragement to keep moving, but I couldn't see it. Attributing this to my current position and angle on the mountain, or to my incredible exhaustion that I was simply looking in the wrong direction, I carried on, regardless. Pebbles and rocks slid down the slope of the mountainside beneath my feet. Visibility was poor, almost nonexistent, but I heard the loose turf with practically every step I took. My steps were shaky and uneven, creating a constant disturbance in my equilibrium that caused me to nearly fall to my death on more occasions than I was likely even aware of. The cloud cover was thick. Not even the glow of the moon was out to aid me in my mission to reach the safety of flat ground below. The idea of Maru and Terrence huddled around a fire alone on the other side of the mountain that kept me going. Terrence was fighting off hypothermia, and God only knew what else, and Maru was awaiting my return. She had faith in me, which I didn't even have in myself when I left our camp, but it was growing—growing with every successful step taken. Just as my spirits were buoying back up again, I glanced down toward the valley. It was nothing but a well of shadows. It's the middle of the night. Of course, no one had their lights on. I tried to convince myself of this even though deep down inside I knew something was wrong.

Before I had any time to contemplate Alexa further, my feet flew out from under me, slipping on a pack of loose pebbles. I hit the ground hard with my arms and legs pinwheeling. Gasping for air, my lungs were empty. It took several tries to get some air back in them, and this immediately helped reduce a bit of my panic. Steadily breathing now, I was fairly confident I hadn't broken anything, but I was definitely going to be sore for days, if not weeks. I came to this conclusion fairly easily thanks to the sharp rock jutting uncomfortably between my shoulder blades. *No, no, no… I have to stay awake.* My eyes drooped as if I were half awake from a nightmare and ready to fall back into that deep sleep again. I struggled against it with all my might. *I have to get down to Alexa. Terrence needs me!* Hysteria had found me, and the last thing I remembered before losing consciousness was the aroma of smoked meat.

Pain seared through my entire body. My muscles ached, and my bones felt as brittle as twigs attempting to carry the weight of my damaged body. My head pounded. This was no ordinary headache; it was the aftermath of a concussion. It had to be because, for the life of me, I couldn't remember how I ended up under a pine tree at the base of this mountain. Squinting against the unkind ferocity of the sun, I raised my hand to shield my eyes, trying to find the path I had taken to get here, but most importantly, trying to locate the village of Alexa. Surrounded by a light dusting of early morning snow, I found no footprints. I got here before it snowed, but the top priority was locating the mountain village. *Where is Alexa?* Last night from the mountain top, I was sure I sighted the flickering of light. I was sure there was a village here. But then again, I had no idea how I even got under this tree, so perhaps it was all nothing but a hallucination. If that were the case, we were all as good as dead.

A vast countryside spread out before my eyes. It was filled with wilted yellow wildflowers struggling to survive the onset of winter, and the first dusting of snow of the season. The flowers weren't the only things wilting. I was too. I was unprepared to handle this terrain and these temperatures. Confusion had thoughts swimming laps in my brain. I had gaps in my memory. I tried to remember the events of the previous night and panicked when I couldn't recall anything other than waking up in a great deal of pain this morning. Covered in scrapes, bruises, and bumps, I obviously took a fall. The question was, did I fall all the way down the mountainside?

Again, I scanned the foothills but could find no discernible path. It was littered with loose rock as far as I could see. It didn't matter, really. What *did* matter was that I made it safely over a mountain pass in the Himalayas, and Zivo said there would be a village here with a new guide to help me. Yet, there was nothing but wildflowers and snow for miles, and a very dense forest that looked like a fortress about fifty miles in the distance.

Hastening away from my pine tree and out into the countryside, I looked around. Turning in circles, I braced my sore back with my left hand and scanned the entire area from the mountain range to the dense woodland ahead—nothing. A sharp, fiery pain shot up from my toes through my back. I collapsed into the foot-tall green grass and screamed out in agony. Breathing deeply through the pain, I was certain of one thing—however, I managed to get down that mountain—it wasn't graceful. And I was going to have this pain for a long time.

Just as my frustration was about to hit boiling point, it hit me; the scent of smoking meat. As I breathed in the familiar aroma, I looked around again, seeing no sign of smoke on the horizon. My confusion fluttered in my mind, and then I forced myself to focus on the scent. I recognized it from last night, likely before I passed out or rolled down the mountain, whichever came first. I focused all my energy on that mouthwatering aroma, and then something strange happened.

Is that smoke?

Right in front of me in the center of the vacant valley, I watched a strange tower of white smoke rising into the air, spiraling up from nothing but the green vegetation surrounding me. *Ok... I hit my head pretty hard. Maybe it's time to rest a bit.* Laying back into the green grass, stretched out and vulnerable to any predator in the vicinity, I examined what I was smelling and considered what I saw. Just as the words, *it can't be*, rose in my mind I thought of all the 'it can't be' situations I had already experienced— experiences that were real without question even though my mind would've liked to tell me otherwise. What really made me believe in the mystical was Maru. Maru saved my life. She came back in a new body. She knew my father, and Atlantis. I believed everything that came out of her mouth without question, and a great deal of it, if not all, was completely bizarre. My current situation was no different, and if Maru was by my side, she wouldn't be batting an eye at this mysterious smoke. She would patiently wait for me to make the obvious conclusions on my own. *Alexa.*

I watched the smoke billow towards the sky, not yet seeing the source, but knowing there had to be one lurking in that dense forest. Thinking of Maru cleared my mind, leaving me feeling peaceful as if she had her comforting hand on my shoulder this very minute. Before I realized what I was doing, I found myself in the same meditative posture I adopted in my family cave on Easter Island during my peculiar lessons with my father. Legs crossed and hands resting gently upturned at my knees, I breathed slowly and deliberately while I watched the white smoke. Easily ignoring my pounding head, throbbing back, and my growling stomach, I simply watched and focused. Diving deeper into my meditation, I was just about to fall asleep when a shimmer in the sun caught my eye. Right in front of me, two feet away at most, I noticed something flickering. It wasn't an object, yet it seemed to occupy a great deal of space. I jumped up from my meditative position and stood staring at the glittering substance hovering in the vacant space in front of me. It was like a curtain hanging from something unknown, far above my head, a curtain made of glitter that perfectly caught the sun's rays with no color, pattern, or point of origin. I pushed away the natural assumption that this had something to do with my head injury.

Bursting with the urge to communicate telepathically with Maru and ask her what I should do, I held back. *I can do this*. Hands trembling, not only with fear but with a strange excitement as well, I reached out in front of me, pausing when my fingertips were inches away from touching this mysterious sparkle. I grabbed the shimmering curtain dangling from nothing in front of me and pulled it aside. Blinking in shock, a smile slowly spread across my face as my mind unraveled the strange and amazing sight behind the mysterious curtain. *Alexa.*

CHAPTER 11

With a tentative step forward, I allowed the shimmering material to drop from my hands, and it did so with the weight of actual fabric. Some distant part of my mind noted the logistics, while the rest of me focused on what I saw behind the curtain. Hidden in plain sight, in the middle of a valley in the Himalayan Mountains, sat the village of Alexa. It wasn't bustling with people, but from the number of buildings, it was clear that many people lived here—all in mystical secrecy, without a single person aware of their existence.

The village comprised dozens of small but carefully crafted homes made of vibrant colored materials. One house was a deep red with a bright blue tin roof, its neighbor was its opposite, and every other color of the rainbow followed. Smoke billowed out of most of the chimneys, and the smell reminded me I hadn't eaten in well over twelve hours. Of course, I carried my own food, and that was when it hit me. *Where is my bag?* I spun around as if it would turn up at my feet, and my heart sank at the thought of losing all that food. What a waste, but it was gone, and there was no going back until I found my guide.

I continued further into the village and away from the strange curtain that shielded them from the outside world. I moved cautiously as if on eggshells instead of soft dirt. Tip-toeing through the valley and closer to the cluster of houses, I saw no signs of people. Perhaps it was still too early in the day, but I had to keep going—keep searching. Terrence and Maru were counting on me, and for once, I didn't want to disappoint. I ventured forward to the front of the first blue house, surprised to find that Alexa's homes surrounded me. The village was built in a circular pattern and I was presumably standing in the town center.

"Whoa!" I yelled in shock, and immediately wished I had been quieter. A small animal nudged me at my calf, startling me. I instinctively jumped back and away from the strange creature, inspecting it. "What the hell are you?" I whispered, as there was still not a soul in sight. The animal at my feet was about the size and height of a basset hound, but it looked more like a hamster with longer legs—a mutant hamster, perhaps. Crouching down, I took it in from all angles. The creature had no tail, basset hound legs, a rodent-type body, and a human-like face that startled me more than the rest of this hybrid's unique features.

Darting in and out of my legs, this *houndster*, as I decided to call it, was bursting with excitement. *Perhaps no one lives here anymore?* Contemplating this, I tried to ignore the crazy animal racing around my ankles and instead tried to inspect the village. There was smoke, so there must be people … somewhere. Passing house after house, I saw no one and heard nothing. Not the sound of birds overhead or the mountain breeze blowing through the trees. That shimmering curtain was doing more than shielding their presence. It was as if they were not on the mountain at all. The air was warmer, the sun crystal clear in a perfectly blue sky, and the only animal in sight was the houndster, dying for my attention.

Where is everyone? Whose magic is maintaining that sparkling curtain? All these questions cycled through my mind while I sat crossed-legged in the dirt, stroking the incredibly soft fur of the houndster. Its furry civilized nose pointed towards the sky as it arched its back, allowing me to pet it in just the right place. It seemed no one had paid attention to this creature in a long time. I grew concerned that it was the only survivor of some cataclysmic event.

"Ow!" I screamed when the houndster clamped his jaws around my wrist without warning. "What the hell, man?" I shook my hand as vigorously as possible to escape what felt more like the jaws of jaguar than the maws of a little dog. Finally, the houndster shook free and sprinted towards the last row of houses on the far side of the valley. Blood trickled down my wrist, but nothing life-threatening. With no other options or plan of action in place, I followed the houndster. Perhaps there was more to this than I realized. It was often the case.

My limp improving, I jogged in the wake of the houndster, not wanting to get too close but not letting him out of my sight, either. My wrist was just another ache in a body that had taken so much abuse, but my curiosity took precedence. The house at the very end of the circle seemed to be our destination. The entire front was made up of windows, not crystal-clear but fogged to where you had to look closely to know they used to be windows at all. It was less flamboyant than the others, offering a beige exterior and black roof. What was interesting about this particular house, besides the fact that the houndster was sitting on the front porch like he owned the place, was the shadow that loomed over the property. The sun blanketed the entire village, but for some reason, darkness shrouded this house.

The pounding in my head returned with a fierceness while I took in my current situation. Then it struck me that the pounding was not coming from inside my head. Quickly I scanned the neighborhood, taking in every house and every stray rock, but seeing nothing I could attribute the loud and consistent pounding to. "Okay, no problem… don't panic. There is an obvious solution here. Just keep your head on." I said out loud, without considering if someone was around to see me conversing with myself. I had to talk myself out of panicking and towards the inclination to solve this problem and get back to Terrence before it was too late.

The pounding intensified, forcing me to cover my ears to help drown out the sound and the reverberations. My body trembled and vibrated while the earth beneath my feet shuddered as if it were about to split open and swallow me whole, rendering my quest irrelevant. It was time to admit it; something was coming toward me and it had to be colossal. Praying Zivo didn't send me into a trap that I couldn't possibly survive, I tried to stand my ground and watch the horizon for what approached. The vibrations ran their course through my body, throwing me off kilter more than once. Whatever it was, it was nearly upon me, but all I saw was looming darkness. The houndster sat still on the front porch, licking its paws and watching me closely, as if this were a common occurrence. *It could be, couldn't it?*

It stopped. The vibrations stopped, and there was once again an eerie stillness in this deserted valley. I still saw nothing, but then, out of the corner of my eye, I thought I saw some brightness peek through the darkness looming over the beige house. Slowly and cautiously, I took several calculated steps backward as my mind registered what I saw. *Is that a giant eyeball?* Continuing to back away from the beige house, I studied the white of that huge eye, which exposed a mustard yellow pupil, like that of a cat. That same eye accompanied the most enormous head I had ever seen or imagined. Finally, the colossal body able to carry these monumental structures emerged from the forest behind the beige house, smiling widely.

"Ugh." I choked out when I finally backed up into a pothole and fell on my already bruised and battered behind. From this angle, I was looking right up at the giant's nostrils, and it appeared I could live in one of them quite comfortably, they were so large. A smile came to my lips at this thought, and before I knew it, I was laughing out loud. I mean, gut-clutching, bent over hysterical laughter. After a minute or two, I stopped to take a breath and noticed the giant wasn't too impressed with my reaction.

"Oh, no! I'm sorry. I'm not laughing at you at all. It's just a pretty funny situation, isn't it?" I asked the monstrosity of a human being that stood two hundred feet away, but seemed to loom directly over me just the same.

"Well… I suppose that is true… Lucius of the Alvanata." The deep, guttural tone of this being's voice was startling, yet soothing somehow, like the purring of a cat. Dusting myself off quickly, I gathered myself up from my pothole and stood as straight as possible, trying to double my size by simply stretching my neck—ridiculous, but instinct.

"You know me?" I asked, not including a customary sir or madame because I couldn't tell whether this being was male or female—or what the hell… maybe both.

"Of course. I've been expecting you." A simple exhale from this being nearly sent me flying back into my pothole. It was a gust of tornado-strength wind. I straightened my shirt and patted my hair back into proper order and smiled. If this was a dream, then I never wanted to leave. Forget the real world.

"Where's Maru, Lucius?" it asked, taking a few giant steps away from the forest and into the town center to join me. Bracing myself with arms out and my stance low, I held my balance while the ground beneath my feet trembled under the weight of this new arrival. "My apologies! I haven't introduced myself. I am Balthasar, keeper of Alexa. It's a pleasure to meet you," he said, bowing ever so slightly, nearly taking out a few houses in the process.

"Do you live here alone, Balthasar?" I asked, glancing around, surprised no one had emerged from their homes yet.

"No, no, there are many others who live here, but it is my job to see to visitors. It's not safe, you know if a stranger were to stumble in here by mistake, so I must verify if they belong here or not." Pride beamed through a smile that took up his entire face and, if laid flat, was actually bigger than the whole village itself. "Come now, folks. Lucius is here!" Balthasar bellowed. Not a second passed before the front doors were swinging open, and the town center bustled with enthusiastic villagers coming out to join us.

Chatter and laughter filled the tiny village and for a brief second, I forgot about my troubles and soaked in all the joy these villagers had to offer. Each shake of the hand. Each pat on the back. The crowd around me had grown to nearly a hundred people in seconds. As enthusiastic as everyone was, there were still some undertones of caution. Some people whispered that I was here to steal from them —that I wasn't the real Lucius because I looked too confused. Others mused that they sensed negativity oozing out of me from the outside world. An ingenious mix of happiness and distrust seemed to seep from the villagers regarding my arrival. Before allowing it to continue, I had to speak further with Balthasar.

"Balthasar—Maru and Terrence are in trouble. I had to leave them on the other side of the mountain. Terrence is sick, hypothermic, I think. I need to bring back warm clothes and food to them so they can join us here." My words spilled out of my mouth so fast even I had to recap what was just said to make sure the details were correct. A look of complete dismay blanketed Balthasar's wide face.

"Oh, Maru, always helping the humans… her heart is too big for her human body." Balthasar smiled and shook his head. "Okay, okay, no problem. Peter? Peter, where are you?" he bellowed over the chatter of the crowd; quieting it completely with his booming voice.

"Here, Balthasar." A rather large man, in height and width, answered while he made his way past me to the open space at Balthasar's feet.

"Great. You heard Lucius. He needs supplies, and fast. Can you gather what he needs?" Nodding, Peter turned on his heels, passing me again without even the slightest glance, and quickly gathered a few villagers to assist him along the way.

"Now, Lucius… come to me." Balthasar asked in as quiet a voice as he was likely capable, considering his vocal cords were probably the size of these houses. Gently Balthasar set himself down on his knees, now only the height of the beige house instead of the mountain range bchind us. I took a few hesitant steps away from the safety of the crowd, but it wasn't long before I found myself approaching Balthasar with confidence. Upon closer inspection, his features appeared much different than they did from a distance. Now that we were face to face, I could see the elongated features were full of cheer. His yellow cat-like eyes glowed in the forest's shadow and also flashed with happiness. The lines I saw on his face from afar were now much more defined, and amazingly, they were not simply the mark of aging as I wrongly assumed; they appeared to be the making of a map. Each line intersected with another, leading to a specific marking that had to mean a city or place. Very fascinating. His long blonde hair blew in the wind behind him, reminding me that not so long ago I noticed there was no trace of wind in this place. Very curious.

"Did the villagers make your clothing for you, Balthasar?" I asked, noting this shirt was big enough to cover the entire town. Patched together were a thousand different shirts and blankets of all shapes and sizes.

"Oh yes, they are kind to me—offering clothing that is no longer useful to them and quilting together this masterpiece." He smiled, displaying his shirt and matching trousers proudly. "That's not what we need to discuss, though," he said. "Come with me into the woods while Peter packs up your supplies. Quickly now." Balthasar headed back into the forest, crouched low so as not to disturb any of the trees. Disturbing meant ripping them from their roots at his slightest touch.

With the village out of sight and the sound of their chatter muted to the point of almost non-existent, he began speaking in a low whisper.

"Lucius… Ouriana is waiting for you. Your time is running out, my friend. You have merely two more days to make it to her, and my guide is not very patient about these things. He has never delivered a candidate to Ouriana late and will not start today; I'm sure of it," he said, looking around suspiciously. I followed suit, although not sure what or who we suspected.

"I know Balthasar, but I can't leave Maru and Terrence; they need me. I can get to them before nightfall tonight and the three of us will be here tomorrow by midday at the latest. How far is it to Ouriana?" I asked. For the first time I asked pertinent questions about this quest and considered my time table.

"It's not in time you need to measure this journey, Lucius of the Alvanata. There will be more obstacles along this last leg of your journey to test you more than mere time will allow." Pausing, Balthasar looked into my eyes, into my soul, and assessed my ability to actually make it to Ouriana; at least that's the impression I got. "Go to your friends, but remember your ultimate goal here because you may find yourself forced to make a choice. Allow me to show you to your guide so you can be on your way," he said, turning as gracefully as a giant was able to on his toes, and crouch-walking all the way back to the beige house on the outskirts of the village of Alexa.

"Wait a second… I thought you were going to be my guide?" I asked before thinking.

"Not very subtle, Lucius," he said, chuckling and shaking his head at my ignorance. "I think more than a few people would see us coming. I no longer leave Alexa, Lucius. The world isn't safe for me anymore." A bit of sadness poked through his good-natured spirit and it pierced me as surely as if it were my own. A prisoner to the village of Alexa, but no doubt, he, too, was a dimensional being. This started my mind turning, but there was no time to chat. Apparently, I was on a tighter schedule than I thought. I had to tackle that mountain another two times before heading on towards the mystical Ouriana and her secret intentions with me.

Upon our return, the village was once again deserted. Evidently, the fun was over and the villagers were no longer interested in the Great Lucius of the Alvanata. From the murmurs I heard, they had as much use for me as I had for an iPad right now. But Peter and his friends came through, leaving one large black backpack lying amongst the small rocks scattered in the town square. Bulging at the seams, it looked forbidding to lug up the side of the mountain, so I kept reminding myself of Terrence, wondering if he were still alive more than anything. The hefty weight of the backpack forced my shoulders to lean forward out of my usual straight posture, but with a little effort I adjusted myself accordingly to freight this extra weight. The pain in my back had to take a backseat. For the first time in my life, people were depending on me, and I would not let them down.

"Aren't you going to check the bag, Lucius?" Balthasar asked. In short, acknowledging that yes, that was exactly what I should've done, I dreaded taking the pack off now that my body was getting used to the weight.

"I'm sure Peter did fine. It feels like there are enough provisions in here for ten men. I trust him." I said, staring up at Balthasar, reluctant to say goodbye. Not really knowing the man, if you could call him that, but there was a connection between us and my urge to learn more about his life compelled me to stay.

"Well, here comes your guide. He will go with you back up the mountain in case you run into trouble again." Balthasar was looking at the beige house with a smile on his face, so I followed his gaze in search of my new guide. There was no one there. I scoured the home, the porch, and the surrounding area, but saw no one. With a questioning look back towards Bathlasar, he let loose a boisterous belly laugh. "You've already met Lucius, and he's been patiently waiting for you on the porch this entire time. Look closer." He mused, leaning against the top of a two-hundred-foot pine tree, seemingly enjoying my ignorance. Something many people did.

On the front porch sat what I had affectionately named the houndster. Smirking, I didn't know how I possibly missed this. After all, it was a black bear that led me to the safety of the cabin and laid out the next leg of my journey. *Why not this creature?*

"What do I call him?" I asked Balthasar. A rush of excitement flurried in my stomach, sending tingly sensations through my entire body. What an adventure!

"Hey man, I'm Fin." The houndster trotted down the creaky wooden front steps of the beige home. "I enjoyed the pets, by the way." He grinned like I didn't know an animal was able. In awe, I watched my new travel companion say his goodbyes to Balthasar. Not entirely sure how this hybrid animal was going to assist me along the way, I remained silent, having learned long ago to go with the flow. When I did, amazing things happened.

"Themenos, Lucius of the Alvanata." Balthasar bowed, pulling a nearby pine tree down with him. They both bounced back up together.

"Themenos? What does that mean?" I asked, watching the comical display of the pine tree swaying forwards and backward from the force of Balthasar's formal bow.

"It means good luck in Atlantean."

"So you are a dimension being. I knew you had to be." I was very satisfied with myself for coming to this conclusion without assistance. Of course, it wasn't every day you ran into a giant in a hidden city in the Himalayan Mountains, so that certainly tipped off my curiosity scale.

"My story is not to be told just yet. Your focus needs to be on Terrence, Maru, and Ouriana. Trust Fin to help you. Be off now." Balthasar smiled and turned back into the forest surrounding the village of Alexa.

"We'll meet again, right, Balthasar?" I yelled back as Fin began moving towards the mountain Balthasar was pounding his way away from, leaving me standing still in the middle.

"Time will tell, my very young friend," Balthasar said without turning back. It was time to get to Terrence, and the urgency within me became all-consuming since leaving them on that ridge hours ago. I dashed to catch up with Fin, and we maintained a brisk pace toward the foot of the mountain.

"Hey man, if I were you, I'd probably open that pack and put a coat on. Can't you see what's coming?" Fin spoke as casually as a California surfer. Following his line of sight, I saw the sky darkening in a way I had never seen before. *Snow?* With a quick twist of my body, I threw the pack to the ground with a thud. Scrambling to unzip the bag while I watched the ominous sky above, I rummaged around and pulled out a winter coat of arctic expedition quality. Fin paced around and around while I suited up, taking the time to see what else Peter and his friends had left for me since the bag was now open.

"Hey! Wake up, New Yorker. We don't have time to flit around. That is not just snow coming, that is a blizzard. We have to move… now!" Fin abandoned his casual tone, opting for something with more urgency. Now suited up in a coat, hat and gloves, I zipped the backpack up, hoping that whatever else was in the bag would be enough to help Maru and Terrence continue the journey by my side. *If I'm not too late already.*

Our progress was quick and made in silence. Fin bounded up the mountainside as if it were nothing more than a perfectly flat, cemented sidewalk in Central Park. I struggled in silence, tripping over everything but my own feet, fighting my burning instinct to turn and run from this blizzard instead of heading directly toward it. Halfway up the incline, I told Fin I had to stop for some water. Constantly breathing into the extended neckline of my parka made me feel like I was in the desert instead of on the cusp of a blizzard. Fin lingered impatiently for me to hydrate, and after walking with my head down, staring at my feet the entire time, I finally looked up at my surroundings and was overcome by the beauty closing in around me. The clouds were crammed together, leaving barely any room for sunlight to peek through, but there was one spot. Just over the mountain range was a hole in the clouds big enough for the entire power of the sun to squeak through with utter amazement. The light reflected off the snow-filled clouds in a way I didn't know was possible. All colors of the rainbow shone brightly and continued to reflect off the snow-capped mountains, the green vegetation, and especially the sporadic waterfalls that lined the mountains like a lifeline to the universe. The rays were too far away to reach us. We stood in the darkness of the clouds, staring in awe at the calm before the storm.

"Tick, tock, Lucius," Fin quietly said, almost under his breath, but I heard him. With effort, I pushed down my frustration with my new travel companion. He was right, so there was no point in arguing. Water bottle in hand, we continued. "Maybe two more hours until we reach the top and then we traverse down. Not news to you, though, am I right?" Fin said with a small laugh that seemed even stranger than an animal talking.

"Right, right," I replied, feeling more than a little sad that a part of me had been contemplating leaving Terrence and Maru to their deaths so I would be able to continue on to Ouriana. She had given me a strict timeline, and this journey in the wrong direction was seriously compromising my chances of making it to 'the next check point', so to speak. "Do you think they are still alive, Fin?" I asked, even though I didn't really want Fin's opinion, not feeling very friendly toward him.

"Maru… of course. She's a dimensional being. It takes a lot more than cold to kill one of us. Terrence… it's hard to say. Maru can keep a fire burning, but warmth isn't the only medicine for hypothermia or whatever else may be wreaking havoc inside his human form," Fin said with a bit of curiosity that made me furious. Terrence was not an experiment to see just how much a man could take before death finally won out. Nor was it a game to see how long Maru could keep him alive utilizing her powers of the universe. Everyone was a bit too relaxed regarding human life. This was not the type of dimensional being I intended to be.

"Relax, Lucius. Getting upset isn't going to get us there any faster. Focus on your steps because I don't want to be responsible for you falling to your death when you are so close to the end," Fin said. He actually stopped his forward momentum to look at me, and the expression on his human-like face was genuinely concerned. What made his face human-like were his eyes. They were not the cat eyes Balthasar possessed but closer to my own, and they were a clear window into Fin's emotions, negating his tough exterior.

"Lucius! Turn around and run. Run back to Alexa now!" The panicked voice of Maru flooded the valley of my mind. I came to a halt.

"Maru? Are you okay? What's happening?" I used every bit of strength and focus my body possessed to get my words to her. Maru never panicked. Something was happening, and they were in danger.

"Lucius, why are you stopping? Let's…" Fin trailed off when the echoing crack of gunshots interrupted him. No longer needing to be told, I dropped to the ground with Fin, and we lay flat and still. The shots sounded a decent distance away, definitely on the other side of the mountain, but I knew they had to be directed at Maru and Terrence. Quietly, I relayed my communication from Maru to Fin, and he seemed to understand immediately.

"Take off that backpack now!" Fin said as forcefully as possible in a whisper. Whispering was an instinct when you were in hiding, even if the people you were hiding from were on the other side of a mountain.

"What are you talking about?" Confused, I started taking the bag off without knowing why.

"Peter. Damn him. He put a tracker in your bag. I should've known." Fin belly-crawled towards me, and began sniffing all around the backpack.

"A tracker? Why would he do that?"

Now rifling through the bag, I carelessly threw hats, scarves, gloves, and food containers all down the mountainside. Before Fin answered, my hand brushed against something hard along the inside wall of the bag. Carefully grabbing hold of it, I pulled it out. Even in the shadows of the extreme cloud cover, I saw Fin was right. I didn't know exactly what I was looking at, but I knew it was not one of the supplies I had asked for.

I turned the small circular object over and over in my hand. The only feature to reveal this object was a tracker was the all-telling flashing red light. *Never good.*

"Set it down here, Lucius. We have little time," Fin whispered urgently. Several minutes had passed since the last gunshot, opening our imaginations up to a plethora of scenarios. Inside my mind, Maru remained silent.

The tracking device sat on the pebbles in between myself and Fin. "How are we going to get rid of it?" This was the first of many of my questions. Simultaneously, we both began scanning our surroundings. We had two choices from what I understood: destroy it or hide it. Clearly, Fin was thinking of hiding it, but aside from burying it, there were no hiding spots on the mountain. "Bury it or smash it?" I asked Fin after several seconds had passed.

"I think we ought to bury it. If they lose the signal completely, they will know all too soon that we found the tracker. If we bury it, maybe they'll think we're standing still—taking a break. We need to let them think they are still on our trail. This will help Terrence and Maru as well… for a little while." Fin said, his voice quivering ever so slightly and his eyes large and full of worry. "Damit, Peter! I knew it. I warned Balthasar, too. I thought something was going on with him, but he wouldn't listen, always giving everyone the benefit of the doubt. Well, look where that got us!" Fin was getting angry, and we really didn't have time to think about Peter; we had to think about our survival.

"Okay, we can deal with Peter later. We need to get rid of this and get to Maru and Terrence," I said to Fin, hoping his paws would be able to dig faster than I could with my hands.

"Lucius, you weren't listening. Maru told us to run back to Alexa, and that is what we are going to do. She can take care of herself and Terrence. We need to take care of ourselves, otherwise a lot of people have died for nothing if you end up dead. Get it?" Fin said while he began digging with his hind legs, creating a tornado of dirt, dust, and pebbles. Of course, I got it, but that didn't make it any easier to leave Maru and Terrence to fend for themselves.

"Alright, put it in the hole, and let's get the hell out of here," Fin instructed, panting slightly from his physical exertion. Quickly, I grabbed the strange tracker and placed it in the hole as Fin nudged dirt over it with his nose. I scattered rocks and pebbles over the fresh site as camouflage. I stooped to pick up some of the clothes I had yanked out.

"Leave all that stuff there. I think it will confuse them and make them wonder if you slipped and fell down the mountain. In any case, we don't need it now," Fin said, scanning the area one more time and listening closely. We had heard nothing in over fifteen minutes, so I asked the only thing that came to mind: *"Maru, are you and Terrence okay? What's happening?"* I thought as hard as I could to reach Maru, hoping my message would penetrate whatever danger she was in, but knowing communicating might not be her top priority. Still lying flat on the ground, staring up toward the peak of the mountain, my indecision had me frozen. Maru had risked her life for me countless times. They both had, and I was about to run the other way.

"Lucius, haul ass, man!" Fin yelled from twenty feet away, trotting down the mountain at a brisk pace already. Cringing at the volume of his voice, I checked the mountain peak one more time and decided to respect Maru's orders. She told me to head back to Alexa, so that's what I would do. With no bag to carry, I was on Fin's heels in no time, and we ran down that mountainside without hesitation. We sidestepped rocks and debris along the way, minds racing and feet rushing even faster. After traversing this side of the mountain twice, my confidence level was high, but so was my fear of the Kai-Tangata. Neither Fin nor Maru had said it was the Kai-Tangata, but who else could it be?

Full-out running down the side of a mountain taxed every muscle fiber, every tendon, and my focus had to be zeroed in completely on where each step would land, or I would be rolling down the mountain instead of running. After enough time had passed where my lungs were burning, my mouth was dry, and yet still able to conjure up a string of drool that dangled out the side of my mouth, I had to stop. "Fin?" I whisper-yelled to the animal a foot ahead of me. He paused and turned to face me. His tongue was hanging so low out of his mouth it was nearly dragging in the dirt, panting for breath. I wanted to rest, and I definitely did not expect an argument. "There is a giant boulder a few feet ahead, down there." I pointed. "Let's get behind it and catch our breath." Glancing over my shoulder, I hoped to find no men in our wake. We needed more time. Fin didn't respond, but ran straight for the boulder. There was no time for discussion. Instead, now was the time for action and quick thinking.

With great relief, we slid in behind a fifteen-foot-tall boulder for cover. We both gasped for air and wiped the sweat from our eyes. Unzipping my coat, I needed the cold air to lower my body temperature. I was pushing my athletic limits, and Fin looked to be on the same page. Luckily, I had kept my water bottle in my jacket pocket, and a sly smirk crossed Fin's face when he saw it.

"You're smarter than you look, Lucius of the Alvanata." He laughed.

"I wish people would stop calling me that," I said, getting annoyed by the title; it was harmless, but something about how people said it irked me. They weren't saying it out of respect or reverence of any kind. It was out of mockery and sarcasm.

"Sorry, man, but the prophecy has made a lot of people bitter—bitter about you. Can you blame them?" Fin asked before he chugged a good portion of our only remaining water.

"Prophecy? Oh ya, Maru told me. It's just a legend, it doesn't mean it's true, and besides, I have to earn my way just like anyone else." I said, displaying that chip on my shoulder brightly.

"Yes, exactly. Don't you get what Alexa is? It is a village full of people who thought they would be dimensional beings but didn't make the cut. They made their way to Ouriana, or not even that far, and failed. Now that they know what they know, it is nearly impossible to live in a normal society, so they stay here, hidden—and some of them, like Peter, are angry." His expression was a contradiction of anger and sadness at the same time. "No more time to talk. We need to get to Alexa before they come over that peak, which should be any minute." With that, we were both on our feet and running in a downward trajectory. My mind reeled with so many questions and scenarios that it distracted me from the burning in my muscles and the jostling in my joints.

Within the hour, we reached solid, flat ground, and I internally rejoiced! It was a miracle neither of us misstepped on our way down and broke our necks. The first snowflake of the blizzard landed on my nose. The entire sky immediately filled with giant flakes, so many that within seconds visibility was near zero; the blizzard had let loose. About a mile away from the shimmering curtain, which was not shimmering in this weather, we heard the sound that we both had been waiting for. They were coming.

CHAPTER 12

"You can't hide from the Kai-Tangata, Lucius!" The words of this unknown Kai-Tangata member echoed through the valley, surrounding me, and engulfing me completely in his hatred. Fin picked up his pace to what I assumed was his max speed, and I matched it, only steps away from the entrance to Alexa. The echo made it impossible to tell just how far away our pursuers were, but judging by the huff of that voice, I'd say they were struggling with the terrain, which made me smile. The snow swirled in all directions, blurring my vision and weighing down my eyelashes. Listening for Fin's steady breathing, I kept to my course, but the entrance to the secret city was impossible to find; hopefully, my new guide had better vision.

My desperation and panic increased my pace. I should be there already.

"Fin? Where are you? I can't see you," I whispered urgently, hoping I was loud enough for Fin to hear and not the men racing down the mountain in our wake. There was no response. Wiping the snow from my eyes and turning every which way, I couldn't see him. Somehow we had gotten separated; now things were serious. On my hands and knees, searching at Fin's level, I still saw nothing, and as the wind picked up, the only thing I noticed was fresh snowfall. The only positive was that the Kai-Tangata were having just as much difficulty, and I was currently invisible, thanks to Mother Nature.

"Lucius! Quit being a buffoon and get your ass in here!" This was Fin's voice, I was sure of that, but I had no idea where it came from. I squinted my eyes against the pummeling snowflakes and looked around. The voice was not that far away. But then something unbelievable happened. The besieging storm stopped. My entire radius and a clear path to the entrance of Alexa were free from the blinding blizzard, allowing me to easily see Fin sticking his head out from behind the curtain, urging me forward. Launching myself back onto my sore and now frozen body, I ran at full tilt toward Fin and dove right past him into the safety of Alexa. The curtain shut forcefully behind me, sounding as if it had the weight of an armory behind it as it slammed closed.

"How can we secure the entrance?" I asked virtually anyone standing in the vicinity while I drew in oxygen in large amounts while exhaling equal amounts of relief.

"Dimensional beings are the only ones permitted through those doors, or *curtains*, as you call them. No one from the Kai-Tangata is getting through," Fin said while he trotted towards the heart of the village. "It's time to have a little chat with our good buddy, Peter," he murmured to himself as he left me to compose myself alone at the entrance to Alexa. There was more than a slight vengeance in his voice. *Good luck, Peter.*

Soaked in sweat from once again running from the Kai-Tangata, I stripped off my winter things, piling them neatly behind one of the many giant boulders within range.

I leaned against it. Having caught my breath, I focused on Maru.

"Maru, where are you now? Are you okay?" I asked. A nice cocktail of guilt and worry began rolling around in my head and stomach, silently punishing me for leaving my friends behind. The point of view from my chosen boulder included only the backside of a few villagers' homes, and the top halves of the pine trees that filled the forest beyond, presumably where Balthasar lived. The sun had long ago disappeared and although the snow billowed around us in full force, not a single flake flew inside Alexa. It was as if I were a figurine in my very own snow globe and it created a nice aura of safety. The minutes passed, and the only thing floating around in my mind were the fears that somehow the Kai-Tangata would find their way into Alexa, and if that happened, all these people would be placed at risk because of me. Pushing my fear aside, I tried to focus all my attention and energy on Maru and where she might be out in that blizzard if she escaped their reach. Right on cue, I felt her enter my mind, even before she spoke a word.

"*I managed to escape, but not without some blood on my hands. I'm safe and heading your way.*" Her words were deliberate, 'I' instead of 'we'. My stomach dropped, and I gripped the sides of the boulder for stability. Terrence was gone. I didn't know how, and Maru was trying not to tell me, at least not until we were face to face. My head collapsed into my chest. I failed him, and the weight of this failure was suffocating. He was counting on me to come back with supplies so we could continue together, and after I left and the Kai-Tangata arrived, Maru had to make her own choice about going. Then it hit me. Fin said only dimensional beings were permitted to enter Alexa. This meant Terrence would never have been able to continue with us, regardless. Why would Maru invite him to come with us, then? It was a question I would most definitely be asking once we were together and safe in Alexa. Hopefully, that would be soon because Ouriana was waiting for me and not patiently.

"Lucius of the Alvanata." The bellow of Balthasar's voice shook the very boulder I rested against. "Back so soon, and with a great deal of trouble on your tail, I see." Balthasar smiled as he strolled out of his forest. I wondered if the secret magic of this village also contained the thunder caused by Balthasar's every move. His torso towered above the town as he made his way over to me, five steps in all to cover the length of Alexa. There was great concern in his yellow eyes as he leaned against his own boulder. I, of course, was the cause.

"Head up, Lucius. None of this is your fault. Is it your fault who your father is? Is it your fault you were born with gifts that few others can even imagine? Of course not! There are causalities in life we simply have no control over. Now pull yourself together. We have work to do, and Maru needs your help." His giant hand on my back, meant to be a sign of comfort, fell with far more weight and aggression than the sentiment implied. Collapsing forward under the weight, I couldn't help but laugh; even in our current predicament.

"Wait, how do you know about Maru, Balthasar?"

"I can see well beyond the borders of Alexa. She's been able to escape the Kai-Tangata's grasp thanks to the storm, but they are closing in on where they believe you escaped, exactly where Maru needs to be to enter," he explained as if discussing chess pieces on a game board instead of real people ready to kill if they didn't get their way.

"What about Peter? Did Fin tell you what happened?" Never one to want to start trouble or throw someone out to the wolves, but in this situation, it was the only thing I wanted to do—for Terrence.

"We will deal with him. There is no escaping Alexa. Perhaps his failures will become clear to him one day, but that day is far away, I fear." Balthasar stared over the village, seeing much more of it than myself from this position. "Peter is not our top priority. Fin was right when he said only dimensional beings may pass through the portal."

"Wait! Portal? What do you mean by that?" I interrupted, unable to stop myself when I overheard him use the mysterious word 'portal'.

"We are dimensional beings, Lucius. I understand there is much about us you haven't learned yet. This is where Ouriana comes in. But know this, our ability to tap into the Universe and utilize its energy as our own is our key to survival. We can create portals and dimensions anywhere we want in the Universe. Even in the smallest world, such as yours, in order to hide in plain sight from those with no capacity to understand—yet. Can I continue?" Balthasar asked with such formality. I had seen movies and cartoons featuring giants that had the brains of a pebble. Meeting Balthasar put an entirely new spin on my preconceptions, not to mention my belief that giants were the work of science fiction. Nodding and raising my hands to show surrender, I was ready to listen. He continued, quieter than before.

"There is one amongst them who may enter. Has this crossed your mind yet?" His whisper was an average decibel for human conversations, and as my mind connected to what he was implying, I immediately wished his volume had a lower scale.

"You mean Dax?" I asked tentatively, knowing in my heart that this was who he meant. If Dax was, in fact, my brother, then he was also a dimensional being. "I can't believe I never even considered him," I said quietly, embarrassed by my naïveté.

"Your brother has similar abilities to your own; however, I am inclined to say his are stronger right now. His anger fuels him like nothing I have ever seen in a dimensional being. The longer he remains lost to himself and his people, the stronger his anger and abilities become. You are the driving force behind his rage, Lucius. If it weren't for you, Dax would have died long ago—

completely consumed by his own anger and the negativity of the human world around him. There is no longer anywhere for the darkness within him to go. He is close to his end and therefore has nothing to lose." Balthasar shook his head sadly. It seemed every dimensional being knew the sad story of my family. "We need to fortify the portal, Lucius, and only you can do that, but first, we need to get Maru inside these walls, and Fin has a plan." Fin came out from nowhere, or I had been so engrossed in Balthasar's tale that I hadn't seen him. I imagined an invisible tail wagging as he trotted over to us. His demeanor seemed so happy compared to when he left on the hunt for Peter.

"Where is she now, Balthasar?" he asked with the seriousness of a military commander about to lay out his plan of attack to his soldiers. It was an odd contradiction to the cute dog body he possessed.

"She is hiding out on the east side of the valley floor. About fifty feet from the portal entrance, but the Kai-Tangata members are closer and more spread out," he added quickly, insinuating just how little time we had left before Dax was close enough to make his move. It stunned me to think that Dax would come personally, but if Balthasar was right, and I was the core of his anger, then nothing would stop him. "The blizzard is saving us all right now. We need to move," Balthasar said, and Fin nearly rolled his eyes. Thanks for stating the obvious.

Fin quickly laid out his plan. It was crude, but we were not only running out of time; we had none to start with, and hesitation was no longer in the cards. Fin's plan was all we had. It had to work.

"Lucius, this is not a suggestion. This has to happen. You need to create an Erebus right now. We are going to send it out for Maru, and Balthasar can create a cover for it. He can control the snow, as he did for you, and throw it towards the Kai-Tangata members, temporarily blinding them to your Erebus' presence," Fin explained quickly, allowing me no time to interrupt or question him. "She is going to die, Lucius. Dimensional beings aren't impervious to death," he added, in case I was under the impression Maru could outlast the storm and the Kai-Tangata somehow. After all, I had seen her die already, and through some power, she was back to guide me. I couldn't take the risk she had the power or energy left to make another return. I needed to save her, but I had never created an Erebus on purpose.

"Close your eyes, Lucius. I can smell your fear. Fin's request is well within your range of skills. We believe that. Now it is time you believe it as well… for Maru," Balthasar said quietly so as not to attract the villager's attention. Eyes closed, I imagined my fear running from the Kai-Tangata, running to escape their underground layer, running with several members on my heels. Not knowing what else to do, I imagined an Erebus, imagined Maru on the outside of Alexa's walls, waiting for my help, and most importantly, I concentrated on that deep-seated loss I felt for my friend Terrence.

A shiver ran through my entire body, leaving me covered in goosebumps. I trembled uncontrollably to the point where my conscious contemplated whether I was having a seizure or not. This thought managed to merge my conscious and unconscious self back together, and when I opened my eyes, I was on the ground but in front of me stood something of my own creation; an Erebus.

"Okay, no time to congratulate you. Give it it's orders!" Fin screamed, not able to maintain his composure for the sake of the villagers like Balthasar had done. Before I had a chance to ask how to give an Erebus orders, I produced a thought in my mind of Maru on the other side of our walls, awaiting guidance into Alexa. Immediately, my Erebus turned towards the curtain and disappeared on the other side without a word. I stared in awe at what had just happened. It sapped me of nearly all my energy, but I had enough left to marvel at my accomplishment and cross my fingers. The Erebus was following the thought I placed in its mind, leading it to Maru.

"Balthasar, you're up, old buddy," Fin said in a softer tone, now that the hardest part was over. He had gotten me to accomplish something of dimensional quality. Balthasar nodded, but outwardly he looked the exact same. There were no visible changes in him, so I had to assume he was manipulating the snow on the other side to further hinder our enemies. A skill I secretly hoped to possess myself.

The three of us stood at the threshold of the entrance into Alexa and waited. While Balthasar worked to manipulate the snow for as long as possible, I couldn't interrupt him to ask if he saw Maru and my Erebus advancing towards us, so we had to hope and pray in silence. Fin paced back and forth, kicking pebbles and stones out of his path and occasionally sighing deeply in his nervousness. Not knowing if it was dangerous to speak with Maru, I tried to refrain from doing so, until finally, I couldn't wait any longer. They should've made it through already. Something was keeping them.

"Maru, did my Erebus find you? You are fifty feet or less from the entrance of Alexa. He can guide you." I focused what little energy I had left. A wave of immense fear washed over me and I immediately wished I hadn't spent what little energy I had left on communicating with Maru. If the Kai-Tangata outsmarted us, I would need every ounce of energy if I were to survive.

"It's gone, Lucius. Dax spotted it immediately, and his men showed it no mercy. It did not fool Dax; he knows it wasn't you. Hang on… I'm coming."

"Lucius, are you okay? You're looking pretty pale?" Fin asked, standing still in front of me and my boulder with concern in his human eyes.

"Maru is alive, but the Kai-Tangata spotted my Erebus and killed it without hesitation. I hope Balthasar can keep the snow in his command for a while longer. She says she is coming." Wiping sweat from my brow, surprised how it got there in all this cold weather, but my body was suffering in ways it never had before; I was testing it in ways I didn't know possible.

There was little doubt that Balthasar picked up our conversation and was now working twice as hard to aid in Maru's disappearance. All Fin and I could do was wait and hope it would be enough. Fin paced back and forth again, trying to work out his anxiousness, and I bounced my feet, heel to toe, heel to toe, and incessantly tapped my fingers on my boulder, literally bursting with nerves. Maru was an extraordinary being. I had little doubt she would make it, but there was always room for error.

It happened. Balthasar thrust himself skyward as if an actual rocket were beneath him and flew his arms open with purpose, and the whirlwind of sound that accompanied this action threw me from my boulder and down onto the ground with Fin. The turf beneath me was incredibly still, but the sound hovering above me was so strong and palpable, a disturbance that was actually visible in the air above me—an earthbound frequency gone awry. The pressure bearing down on us was overpowering, and just when I felt my consciousness wavering, I glimpsed a somewhat familiar face, a face covered in blood spatter. It burst through the curtain, and thankfully the sound ceased, and the thundering of the curtain clinching shut was a welcomed relief. For the first time in minutes, Balthasar relaxed his posture and collapsed against a huge boulder, propelling it backward several feet, leaving a deep crevasse in the ground.

"Balthasar, can you hear me?" Fin rushed over to his friend and mentor. Between the three of us, we had spent a great deal of energy on rescuing Maru. We were in trouble.

"I'm fine, Fin." Panting, eyes closed, Balthasar didn't move a muscle, but Fin seemed reassured at least to hear his voice.

"Lucius?" A small, meek voice emerged from the thick silence hanging over Alexa. I shook my head to remove the stars from my eyes and the buzzing from my ears and was able to climb unsteadily to my feet. Around me, I saw an exhausted Balthasar, a worried Fin, and right in front of the curtain entrance stood a bloodied Maru.

"Maru! Oh my God!" I hollered in a voice that I didn't recognize as my own. Its pitch was so high and desperate. Racing to her side, I scooped Maru up into my arms.

"Are you hurt?" I asked while I scanned the visible parts of her, unsure if the blood on her face and hands belonged to her or someone else. Not sure which was worse, I turned her this way and that but realized these maneuvers were causing her pain.

"I'm okay, Lucius. I'm okay… set me down." Maru said, with little strength in her voice to bolster her command. Reluctantly, I set Maru down on her feet and tried to assist her, stabilizing her with my arm around her torso.

"I'm fine now, Lucius, just let me catch my breath, dear," Maru said with a bit more power. Her arms were stretched out to her side to stabilize herself. Balthasar, Fin, and I watched Maru while she dusted off her clothes, brushed the hair back from her face, and scrambled to the ground to grab her water bottle from her bag she had somehow managed to save during her escape. She gulped back enough water to drown a person. I sat back quietly, working hard to give Maru time to breathe and heal before I bombarded her with questions. No doubt she sensed my conflict.

"Lucius, Maru is going to be fine. In the meantime, you need to fortify that entryway." Balthasar nodded his head towards the curtain, gesturing for me to get to it, even though I didn't know what 'it' was.

"How?" My voice came out horse and gravelly, which I attributed to exhaustion.

"Let's all do it, Balthasar." I heard Maru say from behind, her voice sounding more and more like herself. The two of them lined up in front of the entrance to Alexa. I followed suit, not having the energy to say a word against it.

Fin stood in the background, watching three-dimensional beings attempt to seal the curtain from the powers of darkness in Dax on the other side.

"Follow our lead, Lucius. Create an image in your mind of the door sealing itself shut and focus on that with whatever energy you have left. Balthasar, do you have enough left?" she asked gently, like a concerned mother. The giant nodded, his face creased with concentration. Huddled this close to the entrance, the Kai-Tangata's sharp voices wafted through the air. They were too close for comfort and getting desperate from the sound of their strained and urgent shouts. Maru grabbed my hand and Balthasar's in her other and nodded. It was time to begin. Working hard, I cleared my mind, and formed the image Maru suggested of the door sealing itself shut—never to open again. I imagined the hinges crusting up with rust, the door knob falling off and a thick black tar dripping down the crevasses all around the door, sealing the door shut while it clumped and dripped from all angles. The image in my mind was strong. I opened my eyes and saw Maru and Balthasar reciting something quietly and in sync under their breath. Determined to do my part, I continued concentrating on the image of the tar-sealed door, but a glowing aura from the corner of my eye distracted me. I swung my head around as if on its hinges, and saw my two friends wearing haloes of the brightest white light I had ever seen. Struggling now to maintain my concentration, I forced my eyes closed to hold up my end of the bargain. We would not let the Kai-Tangata through this portal. It would not be because of my weakness… not this time.

CHAPTER 13

I awoke in the village, feeling not only dizzy but ill. Nausea stirred in my stomach, my head pounded and the stars dancing in front of my eyes had far too much energy for my liking. As my eyes slowly focused and my hearing advanced from completely plugged to merely muffled, I recognized the sound of commotion and chaos. Immediately the stirring sensation of whatever food was in my stomach increased tenfold by the mere thought that the Kai-Tangata may have defeated our attempts at security; one member in particular. With great effort, I attempted to lift the invisible elephant sitting on my chest and straighten myself upright, leaving the tiny bare cot empty save for the wrinkled imprint of my body.

"Lucius, how are you?" I heard Maru say but didn't immediately see her. At first, I wondered if she were elsewhere, and her words were merely in my mind and then her smile engulfed my entire line of sight as she closed in on me, wrapping her tiny arms around my chest, not able to make them reach all the way around but her sentiment was strong, and I melted. In the presence of Maru, I couldn't help but feel like a little boy, basking in the love of a mother and relishing in the undivided attention that was so hard to find in any other relationship in life. This regression into youthful innocence always revitalized me, and even in this state where mind and body alike were suffering together on wavelengths I never realized existed, Maru uplifted me.

"I think I'm okay. What happened? The last thing I remember was the sight of you and Balthasar glowing and the image of the door tarred shut in my mind…" I trailed off, trying to remember any other details, like if the ritual worked or how I had gotten into this small hut.

"After all the energy used to create your Erebus and to communicate with me, it's no wonder the sacred homa drained you so completely. Don't worry, it's only been a couple of hours. We are still safe, but I sense our metaphorical deadbolt on the door has only infuriated your brother further. He gains his strength from his anger, and as Balthasar told you, his wick is nearly burnt to the end; such a waste," she said, shaking her head in disappointment. We stood toe to toe, and I picked through the large basket of questions in my mind, trying to organize the most pertinent, leaving the ones that could wait until we were safe. Before I had the chance to ask Maru anything, she interrupted my thought process with a much-needed progress report.

"Balthasar and Fin are arming the villagers with what few weapons they have here. In the history of its existence on Earth, we have never allowed a breach in this village. It will be up to the three of us, Balthasar, you, and I, to take down Dax, and hopefully, the others will flee because we don't have soldiers at our backs. We have scared men and women who failed their dimensional tests and remained in Alexa for safety and security, which we have now taken from them," Maru said, void of emotion. Nothing in her expression revealed her thoughts on the outcome of the vague action plan.

"What of Peter?" I had to ask. He was certainly not a priority, but I had to know something was being done to punish him for his betrayal.

"Revenge is not a characteristic you can take with you into the realm of the universe and its myriad dimensions. This is a human reaction. You are more than human, Lucius. Peter is Balthasar's charge, not ours." Her all-consuming brown eyes penetrated my very being, digging deep enough to detect the hatred in my heart I held for this Peter—a person I'd never met but held entirely accountable for Terrence's death. Maru turned to leave, blocking the light from the sun's rays as she paused in the doorway of my temporary lodging. I could imagine how I must look to her. Dejected by her observations even though I recognized the harsh truth she conveyed.

"Lucius, there is something you need to know." She paused, taking a deep breath. Her expression revealed disappointment again, and I hated it was because of me. "Terrence passed away in front of the fire hours before the Kai-Tangata emerged in the valley below. He simply ran out of time. Peter didn't kill Terrence. You did.'"

Gone before I could burst out a scathing retort, Maru left me standing like a broken-hearted fool in the middle of a house that wasn't mine, surrounded by villagers who hated me and now a mentor who blamed me for Terrence's death. I crashed backward on my borrowed cot, and made no attempt to stop the pity party that ensued. My emotions traveled quickly down the freeway of resentment, anger, denial, and circling back to anger again.

"I can't believe Maru just blamed me for Terrence's death! Why the hell did she bring him along, anyway? He would never have been able to enter Alexa, and if she knew we were going to the Himalayas, why pack t-shirts for Christ's sake!" I was so upset I paced back and forth and screamed at the top of my lungs, but only a few syllables were audible. The rest boomed loudly inside my head. With my anger and blame finally spent, I could almost think clearly. I was the one in charge of this expedition, and I was the one in charge of getting to Alexa and back to help get Terrence the supplies he needed to recover from his severe case of hypothermia, and I had failed. Maybe I hadn't been enthusiastic about some of Maru's choices, especially the one to bring Terrence along, but I had agreed. I had agreed to take responsibility for it all, and another life was lost because of it.

Bitter, I was still able to enjoy the sun's rays disappearing for the day. It was a poignant sight in the midst of chaos. The many voices racing around outside my room and the bellow of Balthasar's orders to his villagers to prepare for Dax's break-in invaded my attempt at peace. Clinging to my anger like a crutch, I so badly needed to hate Peter. I also wanted to blame Maru for Terrence, and more than anything I wanted to kill Dax for the havoc he'd caused on my perfectly normal and mundane life.

The surge of anger rose from a small current within me to a giant tidal wave I could no longer contain. Flinging myself up from the comfort of my denial, I no longer wanted comfort. I wanted someone's head for all I had been through. I paced this tight house, seething with rage, stomping around so violently I shook the very wood panels covering the interior walls. I felt my face contorted in fury. My eyebrows furrowed together, and my nostrils flared wide, building one heck of an intimidating frown on my ordinarily placid face. So engrossed in my anger, I relished the pain and was more than happy to place blame on anyone and from any angle I could think of in order to relinquish it from myself.

In the background, hovering silently behind my heightened emotions, I heard something or sensed something; a presence. Certain that it was not Maru, I stopped. I slowed my breathing and halted my stomping for a minute, allowing me to focus on this sensation; it was familiar. It was impossible to stop my pounding heart on command, so I had to listen beyond the incessant thumping in my ears. My blood pressure was through the roof from my epic tantrum.

"Son, he's coming." My father finally broke the silence in my brain and penetrated my anger to acquire my full attention. For a second, I didn't breathe. It had been so long since I heard his voice, I was torn between wanting to use it to fuel the fire of my rage or allow it to cool the fires like an ice-cold waterfall. Frozen in thought, I stood like a statue in my room while outside my window frantic

villagers were racing back and forth, but I barely registered their movement or reasons for it.

"*Maru is right, Lucius. You are not just human. You can no longer rely on their conditioned responses to get you through life. With this mind, you will not bring Ouriana to Atlantis. Embrace the fact you can be the best of both worlds… only you can bring humanity to the dimensional worlds… you can live both lives… don't you understand?*" My father spoke encouragingly, slowly but surely, softening the sharp edge of my anger and bringing me back to myself. He said nothing more, but I repeated his words over and over on a never-ending cycle until they sank in and cleared my mind.

"Dax is going to penetrate the barrier?" I asked, trying to regain some logical train of thought.

"*Yes, in a matter of moments. The others are preparing. Are you prepared my son?*" he asked, as if I were getting ready for my first day of school instead of getting ready for some type of battle with opponents possessing fantastical gifts or powers or whatever the right terminology was for the things I had seen and would continue to see along this unbelievable journey.

"Of course, I'm not ready. I don't have a clue how to BE ready! I know virtually nothing about what is happening to me, about who or what I am or how I am supposed to utilize the 'skills' everyone expects me to possess. The memories I have of you are not even mine! They are another of Lucius' memories. I am completely unprepared, Father!" I yelled inside my head to a man in some other dimensional plane, watching all of this for his afternoon entertainment, I imagined.

"My goal was to continue with you on this journey, Lucius, but unforeseen circumstances have collided with my plans and I have had to act accordingly. Maru and Ouriana can help; they will help you. You just have to get through this last trial, and you do have the skills to survive." When he paused, I detected his helplessness. I once again experienced a pang of guilt for this incredible anger I carried around for just about anyone who contradicted my own thoughts. *"I was teaching you how to clear your mind, use it as your weapon, and most importantly, believe it's possible… because it is. You may not have been the same Lucius in the tunnels with me, but you are the right Lucius. There is nothing more I can do for you now. I am dealing with trials of my own. Maru will continue to guide you. Trust her completely."*

Left alone in my mind, I wanted to toss around my feelings of guilt and relief at hearing my father's voice, but reality interrupted me.

"What the hell, Lucius! We have a situation out here. Get your ass moving and get yourself armed… Dax is breaking through." Fin burst into my room yelling and barking when he found me standing nonchalantly, face blank and hands hanging lifelessly at my sides as if comatose. Without a word, I spotted the backpack on the floor used to alert the Kai-Tangata of my whereabouts and piled on my winter gear before following Fin into the village. Fully out of my stupor for the first time, I finally witnessed the fear on the villagers' faces while they stood together, each holding anything as a weapon. Everything from a garden ho to an automatic weapon was present amongst them, and I stood wielding nothing but my mind, hopefully as powerful as everyone expected it to be.

"Lucius, hurry… over here," Maru called me from across the crowd in the square. I zigged and zagged, trying to follow the sound of her voice. Everyone around me was preparing themselves to protect their sacred secret city from the darkness my very own brother threatened to drown them in. Not only did these people fail their trials to become fully dimensional beings, but they decided to remain in this precious city, safe from the world; they didn't deserve the violence I had brought to them. Quickly replacing my yearning for violence was a need to protect these innocent people from a man hell-bent on destroying anything in his way to me; Dax. Perhaps this was the perfect time to unleash my inner need for power.

Maru reached into a Rubbermaid garbage can and pulled out a shield closely resembling something out of the Roman era. As she handed it over to me, I immediately felt its weight and had to compensate and adjust my stance to maintain balance. When I glanced at Maru, she smiled, amused, while I wondered how on Earth she held this shield so easily. With the shield now in both hands, I turned it around to look at the front, my eye drawn to the center of the large circular weapon, where a tiny hole seemed to have once held something, a piece lost in time, no doubt. On closer inspection, I could tell this shield was not made of any earthly metal. I immediately catalogued it and determined it to be made from the orichalcum of Atlantis, a material I had seen much of during my time on Easter Island.

"This shield can withstand virtually anything thrown at it, Lucius. But I also have this to give you." Maru unfurled her hand, revealing a stone made of the same bright white light I had witnessed surrounding her and Balthasar during the ritual earlier.

"Moonstone?" I said half dazed and half to myself while I stared at the stone, not daring to touch it.

"Yes. You may not have earned your place as a dimensional being yet, but I believe if you can pass this test, and survive this battle with your brother, this stone will be yours permanently. For now, it is on lone, and I believe Ouriana will have no objections to this transaction." She outstretched her small hand to me, awaiting me to take the stone. "Keep it safe. Do not put it in the shield until absolutely necessary. The last thing we need is for Dax to steal that stone; I cannot put into words the amount of devastation he could create with it in his hands. Do you understand?" she asked, desperate to trust me, desperate to believe I could do this, but showing enough doubt on her face to create a pit in my stomach.

"Yes, I understand, Maru. I will keep it safe until I need it. I guess I will know when the time comes…" I uttered, again more to myself than to Maru. I took one last look at the purity and beauty of the stone, and slipped it deep into the tiny inner front pocket of my jeans, accessible when needed, but safe.

"Where's Balthasar?" I asked, scanning not the crowd around me but the skies for his towering torso.

"He's waiting in the forest beyond as our last defense if needed. If he sees we are holding Dax off, he will join the fight then," Maru said. I had missed so much stewing in my self-pity. A wave of guilt hit me with the force of this realization.

"Lucius, that's already done. Let's focus on the present, shall we? This is your chance to take all your experiences, everything you've learned and even the things you've yet to learn, to become Lucius of the Alvanata and destroy the darkness that threatens us all—brother or not." Smiling now, making Maru proud, was climbing to the top of my new priority list. That, as well as proving to myself I had what it took to save these people from needless pain and suffering. The Kai-Tangata had taken enough lives, and there was a growing belief somewhere deep within me that maybe I was the one meant to save them. Lucius of the Alvanata.

With defense in mind, I slipped my right hand through the loop on the back of the shield. To my surprise, I found it fit comfortably and oddly natural. My anger was lost in the wind. My mind was now clearer than I could ever recall. I was in tune with every piece of hair blown in the light breeze, hearing every inhale and exhale taken by me, but also by those surrounding me—those pacing their breath for what was to come. None of us were fighters or soldiers, but we were people who wanted to protect Alexa from Dax and maintain the city's ethereality. My hands held a shield made not of this world, and it invigorated me with an irresistible sensation I never wanted to lose; I finally believed in my potential and the potential of the universe around me.

Maru, Fin, and I made our way through the crowd of villagers to the very front. We were the first and last line of defense. The villagers stood ready to protect what was theirs, but they didn't possess the powers to hold off Dax, son of Ameretat, leader of Atlantis, and one of the three Alvanata. Never meant to travel further than this village, these men and women were ready to give their lives to defend their secret refuge from not just the Kai-Tangata, but the humans as well.

Maru stood by my side, empty-handed and wearing nothing more than the colorful native garments she wore upon our arrival in Tibet. Fin, on my other side, stood firm, holding his body so tight I wondered if he might pop under the pressure he put on himself. Wearing an oversized winter jacket, thermal gloves, and a tuque while holding a gladiator-sized shield, I felt completely ridiculous and as far from my comfort zone as humanly possible. As if on cue, Maru said, "Lucius, lose the winter gear. It's about to heat up in here significantly. Not to mention you're limiting your maneuvering abilities in those things." Never taking her eyes off the portal entrance, I kept my line of sight as well while I quickly shed my unnecessary layers and threw them off to the side. These were the last words spoken before chaos ensued and the fight for survival became real for me in a way it never had before. This battle was one-on-one; no one could help me, and no one could save me from Dax.

The entrance to Alexa was not visible to the naked eye. Nothing short of intuition and clarity would guide you to its door, and even with those gifts, your chances were slight. However, on the inside of Alexa, the portal door appeared to be no different from any other door I had seen in my life. In fact, it appeared ancient. Made of cracked and weathered dark wood with open crevices running from top to bottom, not big enough to snap the door in half but large enough to assume they had been growing over centuries or maybe longer. There were no panels or decorations to speak of. This door was one large slab of wood with a knob made of orichalcum, tarnished by the hands of time. In my mind, I had imagined a slick black tar covering and sealing the door shut. This same image appeared at the forefront of my mind, but I pictured something else, something more than this image. The tar was cracking, just like the door. Through these burgeoning tiny cracks emerged a shadow. As the cracks grew and lengthened at an alarming rate, the shadow spread, covering the entire door within seconds. I held my breath, unable to speak to relay what I was visualizing to the others. All I could do was watch as my pitiful attempt at security failed and failed quickly at my brother's hands.

The others did not know it was happening…that he was coming.

"He's coming through!" I warned. "Prepare to defend yourselves and your village. Balthasar?" Calling out Balthasar's name, I needed confirmation he was ready. If Maru and I failed, he was our last chance to stop Dax.

"Themenos Lucius, son of Ameratat," Balthasar said with a kind of reverence I never anticipated to hear associated with my name. Not sure what to say, I nodded and turned towards Maru, who bowed with her hands in prayer position at her chest as she looked up and smiled at me.

"You can stop him, Lucius, and you must." She spoke to me and me alone. Gripping my shield even tighter with my right hand, my left hand searched out the hidden moonstone in the pocket of my jeans. It comforted me. I savored its power surging through my body, electrifying my insides from my blood vessels all the way to the synapses in my brain. I was alive in a way I had never been before and the urge to put this stone in my shield was strong, but Maru had been clear; a time would present itself. Until then, I was on my own, but it was close.

Quiet and muffled shrieks and gasps drifted to my ears. When I turned to see what had drawn everyone's attention, I saw right in front of me what I had just prophesized in my mind. Dax was breaking through. With what power or magic I had no idea, but he had a strength I did not yet understand how to access or utilize, leaving me to be the proverbial underdog. Every villager took a few tentative steps backward, whether by instinct or intimidation. Their fear grew at the sight of their portal door being torn apart by a force legend and rumor had built up to be the equivalent of the devil. Maru, Fin, and I stood firm. Our show of strength was necessary to invoke the energies and support of the villagers. It would take an army to stop Dax. He was out for blood.

The tar sealing the door burst and split around the perimeter, revealing a dark shadow looming further toward Alexa. What little tar remained strained against the outside pressures until the door vibrated and convulsed as it struggled to protect Alexa and keep out those unworthy souls. Watching helplessly in horror, I observed the rusted hinges rising from their pins, the doorknob glowing red and convulsing with the wooden door. The ground beneath our feet took on the same qualities as we all faltered and swayed, and the world took on a new shape. Dax was no longer held back by the portal. The wooden slab flew high into the sky, trailing debris and smoke. The pressure from Dax was so enormous that the door might've rocketed to the moon. Smoke and snow poured in through the portal opening, leaving us all helpless and blind to the entrance of Dax—but I sensed him, nonetheless. My inner eye saw Dax even when my outer vision remained clouded by the smoke and a surge of snow. I watched him standing at the portal entrance. He took one deliberate step across the threshold into Alexa, and his presence altered me. I felt my confidence wavering. My anxieties resurfaced, but I shoved them back. This time I was in control. His darkness was spreading through the villagers and trying to penetrate my heart and mind as well, but my strength had grown since we last met.

"Lucius Xavier!" Dax screamed into the cloud of smoke and debris. We were still unable to lay eyes on each other through the melee, but the depth of rage in his voice was so palpable that no one was immune to its power. More gasps and shrieks from the villagers sounded while they no doubt contemplated running for Balthasar in the forest and abandoning this entire fight. I would not blame them one bit. The instinct to flee rose in me as the last timbres of Dax's voice reverberated through my insides.

"Don't move, Lucius. I don't think he can see us yet," Fin said quietly, his odd body still tense, his eyes glowing yellow, and his determination focused. With no intention of going anywhere, I nodded and the three of us stood right where we began, in front of the portal door, now only feet from Dax. Glancing towards Maru for a bit of encouragement, I felt a twinge of concern when I saw her standing with her hands behind her back as if she were about to take an afternoon stroll, her face expressionless. Whatever she planned to do, she did not seem worried, so I took this in stride. Sweat loosened my grip on the shield. With one quick motion, I reestablished my grip and dug my feet into the ground, reaffirming my stance as well. Whatever powers Dax may have, he clearly couldn't see me while my inner-eye observed him clear as day; this thought alone helped drive away his shadow, attempting to infect me with anxieties and fears.

The dust was settling, and without looking, I was aware the villagers of Alexa had backed away, creating an immense gap between them and us, but they were still there. One minute I felt like a great warrior holding this shield, and the next, as if I had just robbed a museum and was running amuck like a crazy teenager. But when Dax saw the shield, he recognized it. He was familiar with its powers, and the awareness in his eyes immediately made me feel threatened. He knew so much more than me about the secrets beyond our planet, and even our dimension. My ignorance weighed heavy on me.

"Where did you get that? That belongs to me!" he screamed. Stepping towards us out of the smoke and the thick curtain of snow, I saw him clearly but barely recognized him. The man standing before me was so distorted by rage that his face was no longer his own, scarcely human.

"That shield belongs to no one, Dax Xavier, and you know it," Maru said with strength and calmness. "Those who are deserving may use its powers. Those who are not will perish by the hands that wield it." Standing casually with her hands clasped loosely behind her back, she spoke to Dax while Fin and I stood in awe of her countenance.

With great effort, Dax dragged his gaze from me long enough to locate the face of the person so bold enough to contradict him, and his expression went from enraged to stunned in less than a second. Although Maru's body was different, her eyes were the same and had been since the day she was first born to this universe, and Dax recognized them without question.

"H-how?" he asked in a stutter that shocked me. He knew Maru, but he did not realize that she had been around for millennia and had the ability to return to Earth in a new body using the powers of the universe she had perfected centuries ago.

"Marseilles didn't teach you everything, young man. There is a great deal you still can learn," Maru said. It was obvious she was attempting to draw Dax in and help him see the error of his ways. A small spark of hope invaded my mind, but I knew it would not come to fruition. Anyone could see that Dax was too far gone to be convinced of anything other than his own ambitions, and perhaps Marseilles was to thank for that.

"I found Alexa!" he yelled. "I broke through the impenetrable barrier, and you are telling me I have a lot to learn? Look at this imbecile!" He pointed in my direction. "How he survived infancy is a mystery to me, and you place the survival of this ancient city in his hands? Who is it really who hasn't learned Maru? You or my father?"

Dax's voice bellowed through the village, bouncing off the mountains surrounding it and echoing into the wilderness. Maru maintained her silence, which infuriated Dax even more. He couldn't help himself. He had to continue. The rage was eating him from the inside out, and he wanted to release it before it was too late. "He's taken everything from me! Always the worthy one, always the wise and kind one, the one destined to follow in my father's footsteps! What about me?" he demanded, more composed now, but still teetering on the edge of losing what little control he had. "I AM WORTHY!" he screamed with all the power and rage his body could no longer contain. He collapsed to his knees as he used every bit of power and energy to scream the words, perhaps hoping our father would hear, wherever he was in the universe.

"Everyone is worthy, my dear," Maru said so quietly that Dax would have to calm down in order to hear her. "There is not a soul on this planet not worthy of dimensional travel and the immortality of the universe, Dax, but there is more to the story." Maru paused, watching the rise and fall of Dax's chest slow to a more normal cadence. His features were still full of anger, but his curiosity was now taking the front seat to his out-of-control rage. Maru continued, "Marseilles withheld from you the most important piece of information, the key to this dimension and many others…"

"Don't… you… dare insinuate Marseilles kept things from me! He was my mentor and my true Father,"

Dax said in a guttural voice that was closer to a creature's growl than a man's voice.

"May I finish? Or is your ego far too inflated to hear the truth of my words?" Maru boldly stated, the effect of her words sprouting goosebumps over my entire body. Dax appeared just as stunned as the rest of us and said nothing, but he was seething. There was no doubt about that. Fin and I were at the ready, shields held tightly. It was a matter of seconds before the lid completely burst off whatever monster was hiding within him.

"Does the name Tartarus mean anything to you?" she asked, still maintaining her casual and la-dee-da posture during this strange trade-off of power. I watched a spark of recognition in Fin's eyes when we looked to each other for silent answers, but what frightened me more than the blank I drew on the information was the transformation that came over my brother, Dax. For a split second, his jaw dropped completely open, and his eyes flared to a degree I had not seen a human accomplish before, and he appeared to stop breathing completely. This all took place in a second, not two, before the lid holding back the beast within flew off, leaving us to face only a shell of Dax Xavier; the rest of what we witnessed was something else entirely.

"That is nothing more than a fairy story, and you know it, Maru. We're done here…" Pulling out of his jacket a book so large I couldn't fathom how we didn't notice it earlier, I recognized it as the very same book he used to recite an ancient death spell from in front of my Erebus. That time seemed so long ago.

"Nothing more than a fairy story you claim, well… your eyes betrayed you, Dax."

"It's not real! These humans have embraced their inner darkness because it makes them strong. It makes *me* strong! Now hand over Lucius, and I will leave Alexa unharmed and will not return," Dax demanded, not just from Maru but from the entire village. His gaze missed no one, and deep inside, I feared at least Peter would want to betray me and hand me over, and frankly, I couldn't blame him or anyone for wanting to save their own skin. Not willing to turn around and gauge the reactions of the men and women of Alexa, I stood focusing my penetrating gaze on Dax, but I listened to the crowd for movement, for mumblings, and to my surprise, heard only silence. The courage these men and women were able to muster filled me with shame; they were braver than I. Many had to die in my wake for me to stand toe to toe with Dax. I had collected my courage day by day and at a high cost.

"Shields up!" Maru shouted as Dax opened his brown and battered leather book. Clasped with a large silver buckle, he made a production of loosening its grip on the pages held within, but I already knew to be afraid of its pages. The words within this book were able to bring about a death no human could battle.

"Devaraja, I beg of you, listen to my plea. Hear Me!

Alexa has hidden itself from your eyes, from your judgment.

They have lived by their own rules, forsaking the power of the darkness

The time for purification has come once again,

Let Alexa be the first on this God-forsaken planet to repent to you

Oh King of all Gods, repent and embrace your punishment for their gall

Devaraja wipe Alexa from the face of this planet, and show us the powers

Bestowed on you by not the universe but the darkness that surrounds us all!"

Dax held his arms out straight in front of his body, clutching the book in his wide hands. His eyes flew open at the sound of the book slamming shut and falling to the ground, seemingly not of his own doing. With an involuntary step back from his own mysterious book, Dax allowed a second to pass, then looked to the sky, ready to embrace whatever demon his words had released upon us. But nothing came. The slight breeze from the wide-open portal allowed snow flurries to flutter in, landing on our heads and cheeks, but the sky remained the same. From the sky to the brown book lying on the ground, Dax glanced back and forth, confusion and frustration growing with each failed glance.

"I thought you recognized this shield, Dax? You seemed devastated to see it in the hands of another, and yet you don't seem to understand its true powers…" Maru said, breaking the silence and startling not only Dax but all of us. All of us were on pins and needles, awaiting some response from this unknown demon Dax had summoned. It finally sank in that nothing was coming. This was what Maru was alluding to. I was holding the power to block Dax's incantations. I wondered what else this shield could do? With this new information in hand I grasped it tighter, accepting an instant rise in my confidence. Even though it was one hundred-to-one odds, Dax was a force to be reckoned with and my lack of knowledge and inexperience was constantly weighing me down, but this shield was about to level the playing field.

In one swift move, Dax twisted his torso to swing open his long black coat, and this time he pulled out not a book but an automatic weapon. In a hair of a second, I linked this weapon to something I had seen in a video game in a different lifetime and ducked behind my shield, holding it as high as possible to block as many people as I could behind its wide radius. Bullets rained down on us all, but only after bouncing off the mystical density of the shield. I had been trying to prepare myself for the impact, and after hearing the pop of several dozen bullets releasing from the cartridge of the weapon; I realized my arm was taking on no more force than hefting the shield. The shield itself was absorbing the force of the bullets and dropping them like dead soldiers to the ground, requiring no effort on my part.

With one hand clinging to the shield and the other patting down my front pants pocket for the moonstone, I took a large stride backward with every advance Dax made. The villagers were scrambling behind me. I couldn't protect them all behind one shield, so many ran for their homes or towards cover in the woods with Balthasar. The world of automatic weapons meant that one man with a gun could single-handedly destroy a village and all its inhabitants with minimal effort. Fin stood obediently by my side.

Although I was still unsure why or what he would do to help, it was a comfort to have him beside me. The thought of Maru barged into my mind and I realized my shield could not possibly be protecting her from the storm of bullets. I wrenched my head, hoping she was still with us and unharmed. She stood just as composed as she was before Dax arrived. The only alteration to her appearance was the bright white light encasing her. She had her own shield.

"Lucius, hold on tight," Maru yelled over the chaos surrounding us. The bullets stopped coming, at least for a second, and the air carried only the cries and screams of the innocent people caught in the crossfire. Unable to anticipate what was coming next, my shield covering me nearly completely, I held on tight as instructed. I wouldn't dare bring that shield down for even a second; that would be the very opportunity Dax was waiting for.

The force that hit me was immense. An unknown power struck me head-on, blowing me backward and off my feet. Dax's guttural cries bombarded my ears, and as I tried to get back on my feet, the same robust force struck me down again. It had blown Fin even further, and he was out of my sight, but Maru was closer to me now, still glowing but unable to hold her ground against whatever force Dax unleashed.

"What do we do, Maru? What are these powers?" I asked, still hiding behind my shield. Part of me was relieved to have its protection, and another part sick of hiding behind it and ready to finish this with Dax for good.

"Keep that shield up. He doesn't have much more energy left, but his anger is growing. That is his only ally now," Maru said, providing me with no concrete answer to my question except to keep this damn shield up. Back on our feet together, Dax let out a ferocious bellow—no words in particular, or none I could decipher. The screams of the villagers intensified as, one after another, their houses exploded with a force of similar strength to that of what bowled us over seconds earlier. The sky rained down debris, and the people around us were crushed under the weight of their own houses. Shingles, windows, front doors, wooden beams, and furniture fell from the sky in the strangest rainstorm ever experienced on Earth. A great deal of this debris was bouncing off my shield, but I felt nothing—nothing but a tinge of relief to not have to bear the weight of this attack in addition to the shield.

"Fall back, Maru, Lucius!" Fin's voice was distant and weak behind the soundtrack of chaos, but I heard it and followed his instructions. My rapid strides brought me to the village square in no time, where Fin stood on the porch of the original house where we first met.

"Fin, get out of there. Dax is going to blow it!" I screamed when I discovered him sitting on the porch, awaiting our regroup. His hybrid face, part-dog, part-human, smiled with a strangeness I didn't understand. With only two houses left to use as part of his arsenal, Dax was at a dead end, a blockade that housed a giant named Balthasar. The house on our right exploded into a million shards, lifting from the ground into a formidable cyclone. The house where Fin so confidently sat remained intact. I took the risk of peering around my shield for the first time since Dax erupted onto the scene. I witnessed his confusion when the last house wouldn't blow and wouldn't bow to his will. There were half a dozen villagers left in sight. The rest were hopefully under cover, but I had to admit to myself that many of them had been killed or maimed by Dax's violent display. Opening his arms straight out at his sides and forcefully closing them in together at his chest, he looked up at the house and repeated this pattern several times without a tremor affecting that home. Fin sat on the front porch, smiling with confidence, relishing in Dax's defeat—something I was not brave enough to do. Just as I was about to drop the shield and try to negotiate a deal with Dax, he screamed, "Devaraja!" Drawing out the name to last, he shouted, head back, eyes searching the skies. His plea was desperate, and the strength behind it created doubt within me. Maru was wrong. He was not losing power; he was gaining it.

CHAPTER 14

The Earth rumbled and quivered, but it wasn't from the arrival of some otherworldly demon summoned by Dax; it was the arrival of our own ally, Balthasar. Sensing our lack of control over the situation, he abandoned his post as our last resort and came to our aid. Dax was on his knees now, not concerned with who or what was making the ground beneath him spasm, focusing only on this Devaraja. He seemed to have tremendous confidence in this entity, in its ability to put an end to what little strength and power I possessed to continually resist Dax and the Kai-Tangata.

With Balthasar by our side now, I felt safe to lower my shield. *Lower it.* Nothing could persuade me to drop it altogether. This shield was now an extension of my hand. Until Dax was out of Alexa at least. Maru's bright white encasement vanished, returning to her ring, and the three of us stood watching Dax carefully. Dressed all in black, he collapsed on his knees with his head in his hands and mumbled to himself. His devious brown leather book was nowhere in sight, so he could recite no incantations, but that didn't mean we could trust his words. We stood firm, not advancing or retreating but simply watching this man as he broke down in the wake of his defeat.

"Devaraja!" Dax screamed one more time. This time with such force and power behind his vocal cords, I could feel his intensity right to my core. The anger he unleashed was no doubt the source of his powers. The question was, how much was left?

"Guys? Get back here to me…now!" Fin screamed from the minimal safety of his somehow indestructible front porch. Balthasar and I turned from Dax to look at Fin, but his gaze was up towards the sky, not on Dax. Balthasar followed his gaze, yet I hesitated—not wanting to see what was coming down from the sky—not wanting to acknowledge this new and likely indestructible obstacle coming straight for us.

"Lucius, something is happening…something that hasn't happened for centuries. We all need to take a few steps back and we will need that shield's protection," Maru said, never taking her eyes off Dax. Choosing the lesser of two evils I glanced towards Dax, simply to avoid seeing what was hurling down at us from the sky. I couldn't help looking, though. It was so unnatural and frightening that I wanted to avert my eyes, but somewhere in my mind existed a curiosity to know more about what I was looking at because it was no longer a man in front of me; not a complete man.

Blood dripped steadily out of the inner corners of Dax's eyes. He hadn't moved from his position on his knees, but I couldn't understand what I was witnessing. I saw a man being swallowed by the Earth beneath him. His knees were no longer visible, and the longer I watched, the more of him disappeared into the ground. Whatever demon he summoned did not appear to be his friend. Now completely immobilized by whatever was coming for us, Dax was just as vulnerable as the rest of us. The blood tears poured out of his closed eyes, and he continued to mumble words under his breath. Absorbed up to his waist, Dax had no visible reaction to this. Cupping his head in his hands and resting his elbows on the ground in front of him, he continued as if none of us were there—as if the Earth were not eating his body inch by inch. The three of us stood silent, watching this horrific display of darkness at work.

"Something is coming, but it can't possibly be Devaraja. I don't know what or who it is, but it is not likely going to be friendly. That house is the only thing that can save us now, Lucius. Get to it!" Maru said. She continued shouting commands to what villagers were left lingering in the square. Ordering them into hiding, into the forest— anywhere they could stay out of sight and perhaps out of range from the wrath of what approached.

"Who is Devaraja, Maru? What is happening to Dax?" I whispered, afraid another entity was already floating around Alexa, biding its time.

"Not now, Lucius. Dax has sealed his own fate. Now we must protect ourselves. Get to Fin and I will follow," Maru said with authority, and I obeyed without question.

"Fin, do you know what is going on?" I asked him, hoping for answers, information about what I was preparing to fight against, or if fighting was even an option.

"Look for yourself, Lucius. You have eyes don't you?" Fin said slowly as if in a trance, staring at the sky as he had been when I last saw him. Standing behind the splintered railing, covered in years of peeling paints of all colors, I took refuge with Fin and gathered my courage to look towards the sky. Out in the village square remained only half of Dax and Maru; the villagers needed no additional orders from Maru to get out of sight. They did so with great haste and efficiency. I couldn't see any of them.

Stepping out from under the slight overhang of the porch, I detected a slight tremor, a slight surge of energy coming from the house itself. *What is this house?* Tipping my head backward, I immediately fell into the same trance as Fin while I tried to absorb what I saw. The clouds displayed all variants of grey to black, swirling in unison at incredible speeds. One would expect to see the development of a cyclone thanks to the increased wind speeds and cloud rotation, but instead of a cyclone, the swirling clouds created a large hole in the sky—an entrance for something from somewhere else.

Looking towards the hole in the sky for any sign of what was to come and then back to Maru and Dax in the square, I was hardly surprised to see Maru glowing bright white again. She was either preparing to fight whatever was coming or trying to protect herself from the still ominous presence of Dax.

"Lucius, someone is coming," Fin said quietly.

"Where is Balthasar?" I asked frantically. We were going to need all the help we could get.

"I'm here Lucius of the Alvanata. I am not one to run from a fight." I heard him say from behind the house.

"You're closer to the sky than us, can't you do something?" I knew what I was asking was out of pure fear and desperation, but I had nothing to lose except looking a bit foolish, which I was accustomed to. Laughing slightly, he replied, "I don't think this thing is coming for me, and therefore I'm not sure what kind of power I will have over it, dear boy." Balthasar's words were both enlightening and frightening. He was implying I would be the only one to stop this thing coming down from the sky. Gulping down a giant lump in my throat, I silently prayed to the universe and any who might be listening that this was not true.

The rotating clouds above burned red as the shape of a human being floated out of the hole, dropping closer and closer to Alexa. The rotation in the clouds reduced and turned to soft shades of white the further this strange being floated from them. All that could be seen of this being was a floating black cloak that completely concealed its identity.

"Maru!" I screamed when the black cloak was only a few feet from landing on Earth.

"If you have any amount of dimensional power in your blood Lucius, now is the time to let it loose," Fin said, not bothering to disguise his terror at the sight of this newcomer.

"Do you know who that is?"

"It's not a who, Lucius. It's a *what*. It's a minion of Tartarus...it has to be," Fin said, not entirely confident of his conclusions but sure enough to warn me that it was here for me, and there was not much anyone else could do to help; it was of a different world.

When the strange black-cloaked newcomer finally landed, thunder boomed, not from the sky, but rather from the ground beneath our feet. His landing was so forceful the cloaked figure remained masked from our sights by a dust tornado that took several seconds to settle. Maru stood too close to this demon, or minion, or whatever the proper term was, and this set the wheels spinning in my mind. How do I get Maru away from Dax and the cloaked thing?

"Lucius, you do your job and allow me to do mine. Stay where you are."

"What exactly is my job?" I thought to Maru, feeling like I should know what to do when I didn't even know what was hidden beneath the black cloak yet.

"The shield is your job, Lucius. You will know the right moment." Staring at each other from across the square, fifty feet of empty land stood between a half-consumed man and us and our mystery guest. The situation was getting stranger and stranger.

"Here he is at last. Lucius of the Alvanata." A cruel voice spoke in my mind, breaking in with aggression and violence, creating feelings of invasion and violation throughout my entire body. Never had someone besides my father and Maru spoke to me within my own mind. In these circumstances, their entrances were soft and welcoming. This harsh and growling voice was unwanted, to say the least. I could feel the presence of this being exploring every

corner of my mind. Working desperately to shield my thoughts from the intruder, I pleaded silently and desperately for Maru to recognize the invasion I was experiencing. I needed help. This was the type of fight I was certainly not prepared for.

"*You are weak, Lucius, son of Ameretat. Vulnerable, confused, and worst of all far too human to ever be anything more than that. He left you here too long, boy, and now they have infected you too. You are no match against me, and you know it. I see the thought right here. I see the fear everywhere I look,*" he said with a smugness that invoked hate deep down in my soul. Whipping my head around desperately, hoping someone would have noticed what was going on—how, I had no idea, but I was hoping nonetheless. Fin seemed to be staring at the black figure. Balthasar had retreated into the forest, likely preparing for an attack from behind. Maru stood in the center of it all, glowing bright white and emitting a confidence that baffled me completely. We were up against something from a dark corner of the Universe, something that had yet to reveal itself, and she stood as firmly and calmly as ever—a trait I needed to learn and soon.

Plagued by an instant pounding headache the moment I felt the dark presence leave my mind, I raised my low-hanging head to see the creature in the village square. Similarly to Dax earlier, this figure flung open its black cloak by thrusting its body from right to left until the cloak lay on the ground and the creature stood wholly exposed to us. In contrast to the size of Balthasar, this creature was his polar opposite. I was stunned to see it rise not three feet from the ground. Long black and greasy hair hung limply off its strangely egg-shaped head, and its facial features were even more curious than the rest. He was a cyclops, or, at least this was what Greek mythology professors would have called him. One lidless yellow eye resided in the center of his forehead, double the size of any human eye and it scanned every detail of its surroundings, every face and every adversary in its path; always moving.

"Allow me to address you all. I have spoken with Lucius but I think even his friends here know that is a dead end," the creature said, smiling at his sarcastic wit. "Dax here, simple yet powerful in the darkness, did not know whom he was summoning. But you knew the whole time, didn't you, Maru?" Sauntering over to where Maru stood, glowing bright white, her radius seeming to expand with every passing minute. "You knew Devaraja was nothing but a human myth, and Dax was sure Tartarus was nothing but a myth—funny, am I right?" Now face to face with Maru, seemingly unable to enter her glowing radius, it remained at a safe distance. "And you, Dax, poor boy. So lost and confused. Your mentor did not guide you truthfully. If he had, you would not be half-consumed by the dirt beneath you and steadily sinking further and further to the core. It's a slow death, I admit, but Tartarus executes his punishments of choice. I've been sent to complete another task." Turning from Dax to face me once again, I instinctively put up my shield, but before my view was blocked completely by its perimeter, I saw Maru nod in agreement with my decision.

"Who are you?" I asked the creature making its way towards me, leaving Maru behind it.

"Well, I see your mentor has not served you well either, Lucius." Turning back to glance at Maru, the creature shook his head in disappointment before his single-eye swung back to me. "I am Nefario, humble servant of the great and powerful Tartarus." Bowing now, as if I were to be impressed by these strange credentials, I could do nothing but peer at the cyclops from behind my shield and anticipate what powers he may unleash. "I am here for you, Lucius. Tartarus wants you for his collection." Steadily approaching the porch of our safe house, I looked at Fin. Should we be moving? My expression hopefully relayed to him. Gently shaking his head, he remained, and so I followed. Looking to buy us some time, I could only think to banter with this creature, engage him in chatter, allowing him to educate me at the same time, I hoped.

"What do you mean his collection?" I asked, no part of me wanting to know the answer.

"Lower your shield, and I'll explain to you the inner workings of the Universe you so naively live in." The pretense in his voice was palpable but it did not persuade me to lower my shield.

"I will not be lowering this shield. Answer my question, or let's get on with why you are here." As the words tumbled out of my mouth, I came to regret nearly every one of them, but they were out, and I had to stand behind them. All of this was a game. His real purpose for traveling to Earth had yet to be revealed.

"Maru is on the move. She's coming towards the house, Lucius," Fin whispered. Not sure what this meant or what she knew was coming, but I took it to mean my words had likely angered the small otherworldly being, and the time for banter had passed. "She looks like an angel," he said with amazement seeping from every syllable. I could picture her floating towards us in her bubble of the brightest white light my eyes had ever seen, and agreed—she *was* like an angel.

Distracted from what was happening in the village square, a new and foreign feeling appeared within me. It wasn't dread, fear, anger, worry, or excitement alone. It seemed to be a strange morphing of all these emotions into one feeling. My body began to vibrate as if I chugged one too many Red Bulls and goosebumps blanketed my entire body. My heart raced, and yet I felt happier than I could fathom in such a situation. Was this the feeling Maru said I would know when it happened? Was it time to use the moonstone? Allowing these peculiar feelings to run free from my head to my toes, I thought deeply about each sensation and about what was playing out in front of my eyes as well.

Maru was five feet from the porch of the safe house now; the only thing stopping her progress was Nefario. Whatever his purpose here, it was all about to come to a head; it was time. Reaching into my front pocket, I carefully extracted the moonstone. Holding it inches from my face, gently twirling it in every direction, I nearly became lost in its galactic beauty. So many facets—so many dimensions to its splendor—I could stare at it for days and not feel a second pass. Sensing a nudge at my calf, I knew it was Fin, drawing me back. Nodding solemnly, I detached my gaze from the stone, hesitating momentarily before inserting it into the tiny carved-out hole front and center on the shield.

Beams of bright white light shot out of the shield like the rays of the sun itself—shooting in every direction and taking everyone off guard, including Nefario, for the first few seconds, but his retaliation was swift; his orders clear. Holding on for dear life, I now had the shield in a two-handed, white knuckled-grip. White light continued to surge from the moonstone, doing nothing more than providing a distraction that was quickly wearing off. Not able to resist the urge to peer out from behind my shield, I had to know what Nefario was doing. I had to know if my moonstone had affected him even in the slightest.

There he stood, unharmed, as a mocking smile spread across his face. With a quick motion, his arms rose above his head, creating a circle, and quickly rotated down to his chest. His grin never wavered. Sensing my confusion, he let loose a cackle that curdled my blood. Jumping up and down with joy, Nefario was quite pleased with himself, completely ignoring Maru's presence behind him. Just as I was about to come up with a snide comment about his strange movements and their lack of results, the results became clear to me. My breathing labored, and my body struggled for oxygen as it seemed to become thinner and thinner with each gasp. Frantically I looked all around, seeing nothing that could be creating this horrible feeling inside me. When my gaze reached the sky above, I glanced away quickly and then back again. My mind a few seconds behind what my eyes were processing. Nefario had created a dome around Alexa; nothing was getting in or out, not even oxygen. With each breath we took the oxygen in the dome was depleting, but this was not even the worst of it. Rain began to fall, fast and hard. We were going to suffocate or drown in this dome, and Nefario was relishing it.

Shield in hand, I raised it again and began walking toward Nefario. I had no plan in mind. I was just hoping beyond hope that this moonstone had more to offer than a mesmerizing light show. I could hear Fin screaming for me to come back, to stay away from the minion, but there was something in me driving me forward, and I chose to follow this instinct, even if it meant imminent death. Sweat poured off my face and down my back, creating a heat wave and simultaneous chills but as the rain pummeled Alexa, it became impossible to distinguish my own fluids from that produced by Nefario. Following the glow of Maru behind Nefario, nearly blinded by the torrential downpour quickly filling our dome, I sensed him before I saw him. Stopping abruptly, I stood still, shield in hand, glowing just as brightly as Maru; I had my own powers to utilize now, and this was my time to leave nothing on the table.

Closing my eyes to focus on Nefario, my mind immediately argued this action, but I ignored its pleas and continued down the path I somehow knew to be correct. I pictured the minion before me, the dome, and the water rising at my feet. With these images crystal clear in my mind, I began to feel more comfortable with my eyes closed than open. There was so much more to see. I imagined the moonstone glowing vibrantly, and I concentrated all its powers on Nefario; directed them at him as Zeus would use his lightning bolt. I could feel the stone's power penetrating Nefario but not quickly enough. Trying to dig further into my inner eye and deeper into the scene before me, it was Dax who cracked my concentration and allowed Nefario his opportunity to escape.

"Lucius! You aren't strong enough. Stop now and surrender for both our sakes," Dax screamed. My inner eye closed as my human eyes opened. Nearly swallowed up by the Earth, there was nothing left to see of Dax but his shoulders, neck, and head. His death was a certainty, and he meant to take me down with him.

"You can save us both now, brother. I need you… you need to surrender." He continued in a desperate plea to weaken my conscience, to play the guilt card by using the word 'brother'. Before I could reply to his final cries for salvation, Nefario morphed before my eyes, sprouting wings that rivaled any bird on Earth. These wings were strong enough to instantly raise him above us all and allow him to coast along the top of the dome, significantly diminishing my hopes of defeating him. As he flapped giant white wings, his feathers floated down along with the rain, and now we were nothing more than entertainment to him; he assumed victory.

My mind scrambled chaotically, desperately wanting to believe Dax, to believe that I had nothing inside me to battle such a creature. The tiniest sliver of hope existed in a far, nearly out-of-reach corner of my mind, and I chose to grab it before it was too late. Returning to my inner eye for clarity, I saw the situation not only before me but how it could play out as well. Standing strong and tall, I saw Maru straight ahead of me, Dax almost completely consumed by the Earth to my right, and I could feel the shadow of Balthasar from behind, even in the darkness of the rain and coverage of the dome. I was not alone.

"Dax!" I bellowed, wanting to make damn sure he could hear me over the pouring rain and the flap of Nefario's newly developed wings. "It was you who wasn't strong enough. I am strong enough. I have what it takes. You succumbed to Marseilles' darkness and allowed him to twist your mind until it was no longer your own. That is weakness Dax, not strength." Getting down on one knee, I lifted the golden shield toward the sky. I allowed it to act as a powerful umbrella against the rain while projecting its universal powers toward Nefario for one final stand. Screaming in determination, I let it all out; my fears, anxieties, doubts, and frustrations. I let it all out and funneled it through the moonstone, attacking Nefario with all I had left.

In the background of my anguished screams, I heard the final cries of Dax as the Earth finished the job and swallowed him whole. Unsure if this meant his eternal demise or if we would meet again on another dimensional plane one day, I still felt a twinge of pain in my heart at the loss of a brother I never really had. The power of the moonstone seemed to be fading, With my inner eye, I could see the burst of light shooting up from the stone and into Nefario. It was flickering, weakening. I was out of options. Now up to my waist in water, the dome was filling fast, and the powers Nefario possessed were perhaps wounded but not defeated. As the light went from a powerful stream to a flickering trickle, Nefario's flight faltered slightly. He gently floated back down to the ground where we were all struggling to maintain our footing in water levels trying to force us to swim. When he hit the surface of the water, I secretly hoped the weight of his giant wings would encumber and drown him, but instead, another metamorphosis took place. His wings were instantaneously replaced by a serpent's body. The tiny creature who arrived from the sky was now a giant, slithering snake; the water was a home advantage.

Feeling defeated and exhausted, I struggled to keep the shield above water and searched for Maru, always hoping she could bail me out. When I spotted her, the look on her face told me everything I needed to know. She was on the sidelines this time. Whatever was happening with Nefario was my test, and she was out of it. My inner eye closed shut with this realization, and I floated out of control through the dome of Alexa. The villagers were not able to maintain their cover thanks to the height of the water, and they, too, were floating around the dome, not able to control their position. Fear covered their faces, and they all looked to me—to my shield. The volume of the downpour continued to increase to the point where communication was impossible, but it wasn't necessary. Their faces told the whole story. *Why can't you save us?*

Now using the shield as a floatation device, I floundered in the water, taking in my surroundings. Wood planks, shingles, branches and people floated past me at dizzying speeds. Maru continued to glow in the village square. She didn't appear to be swimming or floating—just in flux. Fin remained on the safety of his front porch but the house was now mobile, floating off its foundations and swirling in the mass of debris encompassed by the dome of Alexa. There was more inside me I had to offer. I knew this, but I did not know how to access or free it, and my doubts quickly overtook my beliefs the higher the water levels rose. Scanning the water for Nefario, I could see the arc of his serpent body break the water every so often; he was playing with us, with me. The sensation of his reptile scales brushing my legs as I treaded water, trying desperately to conjure a plan made me feel sick to my stomach, and me think this was the end.

"No! I will not accept defeat. I am Lucius of the Alvanata, and I can do this. I can do this," I said more to myself than anyone. No one could hear me over the roar of the rain. Closing my eyes and opening the only eye that mattered, I witnessed something amazing. The indestructible house swirled past my vision. Fin was no longer alone on that front porch. Standing beside him was a beautiful woman in a flowing pink gown. She glowed even brighter than Maru. She walked off the front porch straight onto the swirling currents of the accumulating waters.

"Who are you?" I asked with my inner eye and mind. Now completely distracted by this newcomer, any fear I felt of Nefario took a backseat to my new curiosities. The power of this woman's glow seemed to leech onto my soul, enhancing my confidence and banishing my doubts. Just watching her stand on the water as if it were solid ground told me someone powerful had come to my rescue, and I had better prove worthy of her time.

"Balthasar, I need you!" I screamed, hoping my voice would find a frequency above the chaos I swam in. Not a second passed before I felt the waves around me tremble. He was coming out of hiding. Balthasar stood in the center of the swirling current, creating a cyclone as the water twisted around his enormous body. Desperately, I tried to swim against the raging stream to get to him. Seeing my struggle, he reached out and scooped me out of the water. The split-second rest in the palm of his hand was a relief. Treading water for what seemed like an eternity had sapped nearly all of my energy. Now that the water was no longer an obstacle, I focused on my inner eye. The shield pointed towards the water as I waited for Nefario to cross into my line of sight.

"Together, we can do this, Lucius. As soon as you see him, picture Alexa how it was when you first found it, and it will be so again." The new voice in my mind entered with softness and care, singing those words rather than speaking them. Her voice was so harmonious. Glancing towards the floating house, I saw this new and welcomed stranger twist the phosphorescent ring on her finger and direct its powers toward the water, as I did with my shield. Balthasar held firm. Standing in the palm of his right hand, I focused, and in my inner eye I could see my white light strike Nefario as he swam past my line of sight. In the same instant a dagger of light attacked him from the other side of the dome. My inner eye slammed shut, as if it didn't want to see the conclusion.

Oxygen filled my lungs as fully as it ever had. Every cell in my body begged for it. After a few deep breaths, I opened my eyes. Laying down in the palm of Balthasar's hand, I gazed at him to see the world's biggest smile.

"Lucius, you did it," he said with a tenderness that nearly brought me to tears. Looking down from my position in the sky, Alexa was in shambles, but the water and the dome were gone. Villagers walked around, and there were survivors. But most importantly, Nefario had vanished as well.

Balthasar gently returned me to land, where I was met not only by Fin and Maru but by the mysterious lady who seemed to instill within me powers I never believed I had. Gathering in what used to be the village square, I was met with nothing but smiles, even though I felt a deep stab of sadness when I saw the bodies of those who did not survive Dax's attack; more deaths on my conscience. I allowed the shield to drop to the ground and let loose a sigh of relief to be rid of its weight for the time being. I could hear the survivors around me whispering, whispering the name Ouriana. Stunned, I turned to look at the stranger. Her flowing pink gowns, unharmed by the debris and water, long blonde hair falling down her back like a golden waterfall, and piercing green eyes that had me mesmerized the second I connected with them.

"Hello, Lucius of the Alvanata. I am Ouriana," the beautiful woman said. Her voice was as melodious out loud as it sounded in my mind. Without rhyme or reason, I dropped to my knees and allowed my head to fall forward in an act of respect that I had never performed my entire life, and yet it felt like the right thing to do.

"Oh my dear, that is not necessary." Grasping my arms, she pulled me to my feet, and still feeling tongue-tied, I did nothing but stare into those green eyes. "I came to help you—help you all—but you did a great deal of the work before my arrival. When Maru alerted me as to who

Dax had summoned, I came as quickly as possible." Smiling at Maru, the two looked at each other as though they were sisters and not strangers.

"I called for aid as soon as I saw Dax sinking into the ground; I knew who was coming, Lucius. This was never meant to be a test for you. I need you to understand that. This was not supposed to be a part of your journey… not yet anyway," she said, coming towards me and embracing me. I sank into her arms and let out a long sigh as if I had been holding my breath since the moment Dax burst through the portal.

"Have I failed then?" I asked, glancing back and forth from Maru to Ouriana. Knowing that without her help, Nefario would have killed us all and feeling like no matter what tests I was meant to perform in order to get to Ouriana, this one fail was enough to trump them all.

"You passed with flying colors, my dear." Ouriana said with pride in her voice I was not expecting. "The tests meant for your advancement to Atlantis were all carried out with success with every action and decision you made the moment Dax burst through the portal." Gesturing for me to come and sit with her, I tentatively left Maru's side and joined Ouriana on the front porch of that indestructible house, now back where it belonged, solid on its foundation.

"In the face of great darkness and anger, you looked inwards. You utilized your inner eye and saw the scene around you in an entirely new light. Even in the wake of Dax's cruel words, you were able to find it within yourself to believe—to believe that, yes, you possess the powers to defeat the evils of the universe, and you are Lucius of the Alvanata. That was only ever what this journey was about, Lucius, but Nefario is an ancient soul. No young dimensional being could ever defeat the powers he has procured over his long lifetime. It had to take all three of us to send him back to his master." Nodding towards Maru, I didn't realize she had contributed, but of course, she had. I was so engrossed by Ouriana and my own strengths there was no room to think of Maru.

"I am your *alvis*, Lucius. Your mentor. I will always help you from now until the end of time." Smiling, she bowed towards me, and Ouriana and Balthasar joined her. Speechless, I couldn't collect the words to tell them to stop —that I didn't deserve such respect. But there was a part of me that believed maybe I could earn it. I had, in fact, just done something extraordinary, something a large part of me still couldn't believe.

CHAPTER 15

The sun graced us with its presence and warmed the chill in the air left behind by Nefario and his cold-blooded attack. I had wandered away from the others and their joyful reunion, finding myself standing on the very ground that somehow reached up and grabbed Dax by the feet, utterly consuming him. I couldn't help but wonder if he was, in fact, dead or alive to some extent, floating somewhere in the center of the Earth or somewhere else my mind was unable even to imagine. The ground beneath my feet was stable, with firmly packed dirt. Curiosity arose within me. What powers were capable of summoning the Earth to do its bidding? While these questions rolled around in my mind, I circled this particular patch of Earth for several minutes, going round and round and thinking of Dax and what he'd allowed himself to become.

"He sealed his own fate, you know, Lucius." A tender voice broke my concentration, and at first, I assumed it to be Maru, but when I glanced up from the dirt, I saw Ouriana smiling at me.

"I know that," was all I could muster. Hands clasped behind my back, I stood glancing at Ouriana and instinctively back to the ground. "Where did he go?" I finally asked. Between the Earth opening up and literally taking a human in its jaws and the unique skills of the small yet powerful dimensional being, Nefario, I felt more lost and confused than ever before. So much was changing and presenting itself to me in this world—information I never knew to be possible. My mind reeled with confusion, doubt, and skepticism, while only a small part of me continued to want to believe in all I had seen.

"I couldn't possibly say. Nefario commanded the Earth to consume Dax, and where he commanded him to be delivered, I could only guess… but he's not dead. Dax's anger and hatred have made him strong, and Nefario and Tartarus will not want to waste that when they can use him as a tool somewhere down the line," Ouriana said, trying delicately to explain only one of the many phenomena my mind was trying to convince me never happened and wasn't real.

"So much has happened since Dax and that dagger entered my life… I just can't understand it all and where I fit into the scheme of these crazy things." As was my custom when feeling frustrated, I ran my hands through my hair with fervor. My hair floundered around in an out-of-control nature, and I pulled a few twigs out of the nest while I was at it. The debris from the attack was everywhere, and my inner turmoil seemed to reflect the devastation in Alexa.

"You must understand, Lucius, that there is much more at work here than an average test for dimensional command of the Universe. You are not a normal candidate. You are the embodiment of an age-old prophecy about to come to fruition, and much is going to change, I'm afraid." Ouriana stood tall, confident, and beautiful, her smile never wavering, and the light in her eyes continued to penetrate my very skin, no doubt disappointed in what she found.

"Lucius Xavier! You just stepped out with a shield you did not understand, powered by a stone you didn't know existed to fight a dimensional being of immense strength that a few months ago you would not even have believed to be real! Can't you see how amazing that is and how far you have come towards understanding what lies behind the curtain of everyday life?" she said, raising her voice in her excitement. Smiling, I nodded, but couldn't think of anything to say. I had done all those things, and yet I still felt I needed more answers.

"Alright, let's see if I can't get you the answers you seek. Come now." She beckoned, outstretching her arm for me to join by her side. Together we walked back towards the safe house, and I silently added this to my list of questions; what was this place?

The villagers chattered together in excitement, smiling and waving at us while we passed. "I'm surprised they haven't tried to attack me. After all, who is more responsible for the near destruction of their beloved village?" I said in a low voice, seeping with shame and guilt.

"On the contrary, Lucius, they are thrilled!" Arms raised over her head, Ouriana spun in a tight circle, smiling and giggling all the while as if the most amazing thing had just taken place and I wasn't seeing it. "Their village is now safe, still hidden, and they will forever be a part of history thanks to your heroics. Many have waited lifetimes to meet you, Lucius. The prophecy is one they all grew up listening to, and now they have lived to be a part of it." Laughing in a loud unexpected burst, I tried not to think that explanation was completely ridiculous, but the feelings of the villagers weren't at the top of my priority list. So instead of fighting it, I joined in the smiling and waving and, for a few seconds, forgot about everything else, and relished the atmosphere like some strange celebrity amongst these not-quite humans, not-quite dimensional beings.

I hung back to take in my surroundings, a tactic derived from rushing into situations too quickly, only to find trouble. I strolled towards the safe house, watching Ouriana nearly bound up the stairs to hug Maru for the twentieth time since Nefario's disappearance and the reintroduction of oxygen into Alexa. There was a story between those two, and I definitely wanted to hear it after they answered a few more pertinent questions. I waved to a few lingering villagers who were reluctant to leave the safe house area, likely hoping to eavesdrop, picking up some interesting information to deliver to their fellow survivors.

"Come now, Lucius, we are on a bit of a schedule, after all," Ouriana said, motioning for me to pick up the pace with a twirl of her hand while Maru and Fin sat comfortably in some antique wicker patio furniture I hadn't noticed before. Trying to let out some of my negativities through a long exhale, I sighed deeply and stepped onto the front porch to join my unique group of travel companions —my friends. This thought produced a natural smile on my face.

"Now that we are all here, I think, for Lucius' sake, it's high time to answer some important questions before someone really gets hurt. Ignorance can be an ally for a short while, but the appearance of Nefario has ended that part of your journey." Ouriana said, looking to me. "I'm sorry things have turned out this way, Lucius. I believed we had more time. *You* had more time to discover the secrets and wonders of being a dimensional being on your own, but the other forces at work had other plans, apparently." Each sitting in our wicker porch chairs, we all seemed to have the same thought, as we stood and pulled the furniture closer to one another so that our knees were nearly touching. In this tight circle of chairs, excitement burst through every cell of my body. Questions were about to be answered, and I was on the precipice of a new life. I could feel it.

The porch fell silent, and all eyes turned to me. I tried to remind myself of all I had accomplished up to this point.

"You were meant to travel from Alexa to what the humans refer to as Shangri-La, which is really just a very isolated region far up in the mountains of Tibet. This is where I have lived for… well, since the humans began to establish themselves as a colony on this planet." Ouriana paused briefly to marvel at how long she'd been on Earth. Refocusing, she continued.

"Your journey was meant to test you not only physically, but more importantly, mentally and spiritually. But you have accomplished all these feats here in Alexa, but not how I would've hoped for you. The journey to Shangri-La, or Gaia as I like to call it, is beautiful and I would have you continue it now because you may not find yourself back on this planet or in this dimension for some time, and there is still a great deal to gain from making the trek," she said as if this were a normal conversation. The longer I thought about it, I supposed it was normal if the person you were speaking to was a dimensional being, like myself. It was a concept I hadn't yet fully accepted. "But before you go, there are a few things Maru and I need to tell you." The two smiled at each other, rousing my curiosity again as to what their history together might be.

"You're not coming with me, Maru?" I had to ask before either of them continued.

"Of course! I love visiting Gaia. Wouldn't miss it for the world, my dear Lucius," she said quickly, patting my hand for reassurance. There was no way I was leaving Maru behind. She had become a very strong and consistent figure in my life, and my attachment ran deep.

"When was the last time your father contacted you, Lucius?" Ouriana interrupted my thoughts of Maru with a question that jolted me deeply. I hadn't really thought of my father in a long time and had to consider this question. After deliberating, I replied, "He spoke to me mere minutes before Dax broke through the Alexa portal and the attack began," I said, trying to recall his exact words.

"What did he say to you?" Maru and Ouriana asked in unison, seeming equally interested in the last words my father spoke to me.

"He said he meant to take this journey with me, but unforeseen events derailed his plans, and he had to act accordingly. That you and Ouriana would help me through these trials. I haven't heard from him since," I said, experiencing a twinge of sadness, recalling his last words to me. After replaying them in my mind, it seemed he was in trouble. "Is he in trouble?" I asked the two ladies on either side of me. Their faces revealed that they knew more about his situation after my revelation.

"Your father is the strongest of us all. He can handle anything thrown his way. You two shall meet again —just not yet," Ouriana said, choosing her words carefully to avoid telling me anything in detail about what may be happening with my father. "Unfortunately, your father's situation is not our top priority… we need to get you to Atlantis. Time is running short." Watching Ouriana, I almost saw the wheels turning in her mind, trying to work out what to tell me and what to hold back, and a wave of old anger grew within me.

"How about we save some time and just be honest with each other?" My outburst couldn't be contained, and I no longer wanted to contain it. I was just as much a part of this group now as any of them, and I deserved some real answers, whether or not they believed I was ready for them.

"Tell me everything, not the version of things you choose to tell me by omission. Everything."

***

The sun set. Much time had passed since I demanded to hear everything there was to know about my current situation and the entirety of what it meant to be a dimensional being. Mentally and physically exhausted, a part of me sensed that not everything was revealed, but regardless, my brain couldn't absorb any more information. There was plenty I would have to learn as I went along, which created a rush of excitement within me I hadn't known since I was a child, with my entire life of possibilities ahead of me. As an adult, I abruptly lost this zest for life and adventure, and yet fate had brought it back to me in a way I would never have thought possible.

Expanding on what I knew about my father, Ouriana described the Alvanata in more detail. Of the guardians of the entire Universe, my father was the only male, and as it turned out, she and Maru were the two other members. Shock spread across my face at this discovery, making them both giggle with joy at my surprise. Knowing Ouriana and Maru had indeed strengthened my inner courage and confidence, and now, knowing I would work side by side with them as a member of the Alvanata when my father stepped down made the entire scenario far less unnerving. The purpose of the Alvanata seemed simple enough, to guard the Universe against the many dark forces constantly trying to penetrate it, and one of these dark forces was Tartarus and his minions.

Tartarus had been a problem for the Alvanata for Millenia. He was the source of the darkness spreading on Earth, infecting the humans, and creating wars that would eventually destroy the entire species. The story which Ouriana revealed here sounded so much like folklore or legend I almost forgot her words were true.

"The legend of Leto and Tartarus is one all dimensional beings know Lucius, but it is not legend in the sense of fiction but a legend in the sense that this story goes back to the very beginning of life in our Universe. Leto and Tartarus are twin brothers, both destined to rule within the Universe under the direction of their father, Chaos. Leto displayed empathy, compassion, and good sense when ruling and leading the races of the Universe, whereas Tartarus displayed small amounts of cruelty and anger. These traits grew steadily within him, and the more they grew, the more Chaos turned to Leto to make decisions and control the many dimensions within the Universe with a just and caring hand.

"Neglect and disappointment from his father only strengthened the darkness within Tartarus; forcing him into the shadows of the Universe where he learned to thrive. Over four billion years ago, when the planet Earth of this dimension flourished and evolved, the beauty of this planet and the simplicity of its inhabitants caught Tartarus' attention. While Chaos and Leto spent their time managing the dimensions and dispersing the negative energies that sought to embed themselves within the Universe, Tartarus sat uninterrupted, watching the unraveling of Earth at its very beginning, and he relished every second of it.

"There are many Earths in many dimensions, but this particular version of Earth caught his undivided attention. And to this day, his attention remains on this Earth. Because of this, the early humans started to change. The darkness within Tartarus seeped down through the atmosphere, infecting the humans of Earth. It filled them with feelings they had never experienced before. Anger, jealousy, bitterness, rage, and greed. These feelings, of course, led to unrest among the early settlers.

"Fortunately, humanity found a way to survive with this dark beast living within them, but annihilation is coming and always has been. The darkness in Tartarus is absolute now, and the longer he focuses his energies on this Earth, the worse the dark beast growing within each and every human will become. He relishes what he has done to this world and watches with great amusement. The reason he sent Nefario for you, Lucius, is because you were threatening the game he's been playing with your planet. You were threatening to expose qualities within the humans they no longer remember are there."

Hanging on her every word, I needed more, even when her story was complete. Amazed at what she'd revealed, I struggled to remind myself this was not just a story, not a myth or legend; it was a recount of events actually happening within the Universe while we sat in Alexa; Nefario should've been proof enough of that. I was sitting here on this strangely protected front porch in the hidden village of Alexa when it hit me—hard and fast. Who I was, who they meant me to be, had all been leading up to this moment with Maru and Ouriana; along with my other new friends. I was to be a guardian against darkness in the Universe, like my father. I had within me the ability to travel to different dimensions in space and time, visit different versions of Earth, and discover new and strange worlds as well. For the first time since hearing the prophecy from Maru, I knew it was real.

There was much I still had to learn on my own, and I finally accepted this. While, listening to someone explain dimensional travel or the power of moonstone was incredibly useful, it was nothing like learning it for myself. I could no longer seek to memorize answers as I did in my human life. I had to learn to live as a dimensional being. The only way to do that was one step at a time and one adventure at a time. I'd learned so much since stepping into this body that I didn't even realize how much I had changed until Maru suggested I step back and take a long, hard look at myself. I was no longer Lucius Xavier of New York City; I was now Lucius of the Alvanata, and I was embracing it fully for the first time.

"Lucius, before you and Maru head off in search of Gaia or Shangri-La, whichever you prefer. There is the mystery of this house to discuss, which I know you have been wondering about." Ouriana poked my shoulder jokingly. "Fin is the guardian of this house." Fin bowed his head towards Ouriana in reverence. "This house is a dimensional portal, Lucius. It can lead you anywhere in the Universe if you know how to use it. It's been Fin's charge for many years to keep the entrance of this portal free and clear. Many of the villagers here have yearned to use it, but unfortunately, it is not for them. This portal is for the Alvanata alone; therefore, no one else may pass, especially with Fin here to guard it." She quipped. "If someone were to slip through, they would meet a terrible and everlasting fate, floating through the darkness of the Universe for eternity, never finding admittance to any dimension; a terrible fate indeed." She said, shaking her head as if remembering a poor soul this had happened to. Ouriana paused and drifted away for a short time, lost in her own thoughts.

"Let me give you the crash course, Lucius, old buddy." Fin stepped in to finish the job while Ouriana sat quietly and somberly. "The back door of this house doesn't lead to the forest—it leads to wherever you want. All you have to do is think about where you want to go. A very clear and undisturbed thought is necessary; otherwise, who knows where you might end up? You want your mind crystal clear with only the one thought framed in the center; in this case, Gaia. I will warn you, your first dimensional travel will probably make you toss your breakfast once you arrive on the other side, but you get used to it," Fin said, grinning from ear to ear. Proud to reveal his purpose within the group as guardian of the Alexa Alvanata portal to the Universe. Amazing.

Without another word, Fin strutted confidently to the back of the house, expecting me to follow, no doubt. I happily got up from my uncomfortable wicker chair and followed him. The door looked like every other in the house. Old, chipped wood, warped from years and years of shifting, and yet behind it stood a gateway to anywhere in the Universe. We stared at the door together for several minutes in silence.

"So this is why Dax or Nefario couldn't destroy the house? Because of this portal… how did you do it?" I wanted desperately to understand how Fin protected this house from forces as strong as Nefario. Every bit of information I could get my hands on would help me as I moved forward in this amazing journey.

"Your father, Lucius. It was your father who instilled the powers within me to guard this portal from any force, weak or strong. I was a dimensional traveler just like anyone here in Alexa, and for some reason, he chose me." The pride in his voice was unmistakable. Once again, it reminded me how much people revered my father, and now I was a part of all that. "I didn't always look like this, though. I once looked ordinary, like you," he said, smiling. "I asked your father to change my appearance, so I was less conspicuous to those searching for something they shouldn't be searching for. They would never expect I was the guardian of the portal, and therefore I would have more of an edge; the element of surprise, I guess you might say." I wondered what on Earth made my father choose this strange combination of mammals for Fin, but for whatever reason, it worked. Not sure if a pat on the head was demeaning for Fin or not, it was a natural instinct. I wanted to show my appreciation for him in some way and regardless of how strange it seemed, this felt natural. The minor gesture brought tears to his eyes. Another friend I knew I could trust with my life, regardless of his small stature.

"Here—" Maru came up from behind me, handing me a black backpack with her right hand, holding an identical one in her left. I hesitated, grabbing the pack, recalling what had happened the last time I carried this bag, but Maru insisted it was free of tracking devices. Unfortunately, Peter hadn't survived the attack from Dax and Nefario. It was unclear how he passed on. Some speculated it was by Dax's hand because of his failure to kill me, while others believed he simply became swept up in the swirling waters like so many others.

"I believe we are ready to go, then?" Maru asked while she threw her own pack over her shoulders, preparing to travel.

"I have to say goodbye to Balthasar," I said, turning to head back out towards the front of the house.

"He's gone Lucius," Ouriana said quietly.

"What do you mean he's gone? I thought he lived here. How can a giant leave with no one noticing?" As soon as the words left my mouth, I realized the answer. He must've taken the portal, but how did he fit in the house?

"He was here in Alexa to help you, Lucius. Now that his job is done, he is heading back to his where and when," Ouriana said. This realization was harder to take than I would have thought. Not only was it amazing to meet a giant, but I really liked Balthasar, and it hurt more than expected to learn he was gone.

"Remember, Lucius, once you pass into Atlantis with the help of myself and Maru, you will be a dimensional being. When that happens, you can travel anywhere… you can see Balthasar again, my dear." Ouriana pointed out. Still not completely grasping what my new life entailed, I was glad she did. "I'll see you and Maru in Gaia." Ouriana and Fin bowed slightly to say goodbye and then turned back down the narrow hallway towards the front of the house, leaving Maru and I to head onward.

"I'm glad to be traveling with you, Lucius. We have much to talk about," Maru said, gripping the straps of her backpack as we stood in front of the nothing-special-looking door. My thoughts immediately wandered to Terrence, but now was not the time.

"Alright, Lucius, bring us to Gaia," Maru instructed. Of course, I had no idea what to picture in my mind to bring us to Gaia, but I did my best. First, I took a mental sweep at all my useless and repetitive thoughts that were just going to impede our travels. Then I placed an image in the center of my inner eye. An image of the kind of beauty people didn't believe existed here on Earth. Crystal blue waterfalls, vibrant green landscapes, and wildflowers as far as the eye can see—and, of course, the pure sensation of true tranquility; the reason many people dream of Shangri-La in the first place. Vague, perhaps, but it was the best I could do.

I grabbed Maru's hand and held it tight. I kept the image in my mind and concentrated on it with all my energy. Maru opened the door, and together, we walked through with one giant stride. The darkness on the other side startled me and with nothing to step onto, Maru and I were both swept into what felt like a raging water current. I held tightly onto my image of Gaia and Maru, and took in what was happening to us and around us. Together we rode the current in a seated position, never for a moment releasing the other's hand. Surrounded by an all-consuming, thick darkness I had never experienced before, it carried us in a fast-moving forward momentum.

Whatever held us in our seated position, whatever lay beneath the darkness, created a tingly sensation throughout my entire body; not entirely unpleasant, but certainly unknown to me. Seconds passed into minutes, and although I couldn't even see Maru right next to me, I had her hand firmly in my grasp. I knew she was there, and this provided more of a comfort to me than anything else would have. The momentum slowing, I scanned our surroundings again, hoping for anything other than pure obscurity, and I found it. Far ahead of us in the dark, I spotted a strange circular glow—an aura of all colors of the rainbow. This circle appeared to be traveling right for us. While I concentrated on this one, many emerged from the darkness, and within seconds hundreds of colorful glowing balls of all sizes surrounded us, lighting our way.

Their light allowed me to really see this portal for the first time, and any fear I had harbored from our leap into the darkness was long gone, replaced by a sense of amazement I had yet to experience in life. We were traveling in a long, winding tunnel and rode on a glowing substance. Bright gold shimmering threads seemed to hold us up, keeping us from falling into the nothingness of the Universe as Ouriana had warned us about. These threads sparked and glowed, creating that tingling throughout my body, sparking bursts of energy within me with each gentle shock. Maru sat smiling beside me, enjoying the ride as well as enjoying my marvel at seeing the inside of the Universe for the very first time.

The glowing circles continued to burst into existence, then disappear and reappear at their whim. Gold, green, red, purple, pink and yellow bursts of light and color popped through the now indigo blue walls of the tunnel in which we travelled to Gaia. The tunnel walls shimmered and wavered as if not completely stable themselves. Perhaps they were traveling as well, I wondered. Just as I had become too comfortable with our journey, the light disappeared in a flash as if someone, somewhere, had flicked the light switch off and we were once again flying at top speeds through the now invisible currents beneath us towards Gaia; I hoped.

I gauged our speed by the continuous dropping of my stomach, recalling Fin's statement about first-time dimensional travels being rough on the gut, and completely agreeing. Our seemingly straight tunnel turned sharply left, and whatever threads had been carrying us before dissolved, and we were now free-falling. I screamed the second I felt the threads beneath us give way. Maru and I were dropping completely vertically into a dark abyss. Falling so fast, I couldn't see anything, should there be anything to see. I desperately held onto that image of Gaia and begged the Universe to get us there safely. During the fall, I inadvertently let go of Maru's hand, but I knew she was close. Now spinning and tumbling forward and backward, I struggled to get my body back to vertical but felt more like a marionette controlled by a drunken sailor. Then it all came to a halt. Someone pulled on my strings, holding me still, allowing me to catch my breath. Suspended over nothing, surrounded by the same impenetrable darkness we entered from the house in Alexa, we hung in midair in the kind of silence that felt more like a presence than nothing at all.

"Maru?" I called out, begging for more information. Had something gone wrong?

"Take a deep breath, Lucius. We're almost there," Maru said directly beside me. Her voice was crystal clear, free from the vibrations mine had taken from the fear I was trying to keep at bay. Grasping in the dark for her hand, it was a relief to find her doing the same. Held together again, I took a deep breath and tried to focus on Gaia and how utterly amazing this all was; if not a little unnerving. With a whoosh of air, whatever had been holding us up let go without warning, and our speed of descent was so fast I could hardly breathe. Silently, I thanked Maru for her advice. The skin on my face rippled at the hands of the force of our falling speed. Unable to force my eyelids open, I clenched them shut instead, waiting for our next abrupt stop.

"Open your eyes, Lucius," Maru spoke in my mind. There was no way I heard her over the air rushing past us so swiftly. Not sure I would even be able to, I kept the picture of Gaia safe in my mind, while focusing on forcing my eyelids open. Shocked by how little effort I needed to accomplish that, I suddenly realized we were no longer falling in darkness but rising in a strange atmosphere, blue and bright all around us. Questions sat on the end of my tongue, but the more I looked, the more I understood. I assumed we would enter Gaia from the sky or through a strange door in another old, beaten-down house, but we seemed to rise up from the bottom of a lake in a large bubble, floating to the surface in the clearest water I had ever seen. Full of absolute amazement, I spun around in our bubble and found I could see for miles in all directions. This body of water housed an abundance of strange aquatic

creatures and plants, and the coral reefs were bursts of color and life—so much color and life in contrast to where we had just been. On the outskirts of the Universe, it was hard not to savor the opposites.

As we breached the surface, our bubble popped, leaving Maru and I to swim to the sandy shoreline. When I finally got my bearings and really saw my surroundings for the first time, I knew we'd made it.

CHAPTER 16

The scenery above the lake was just as beautiful as below. I got us to Gaia. Astonished by the journey and the beauty surrounding us, I couldn't speak. Maru and I sat, dripping wet from our swim to shore, and while she adjusted her pack and fussed with her clothing, I couldn't absorb enough details, my eyes darting back and forth, trying not to miss a single thing.

Just as Ouriana had told us, settled in amongst a great mountain range was Gaia, high in the Himalayan Mountains. Our altitude must've been high because the serene lake we emerged in emptied into several large, stunning waterfalls that appeared to cascade for miles below us. The crystal clear aqua lake sat in the center of Gaia, but what surrounded it was just as breathtaking. On the far side of the lake sat several small buildings that looked as though Ouriana had built them herself at the beginning of time. I was drawn to the unique architecture because of its remarkable ancient history. The first building was nothing more than a hut, with one prominent peak in the center of its roof and a chimney billowing white smoke. Its roof seemed to be constructed of coral and oceanic fossils, and a boundless vine consumed the walls. It may have been literally holding the building together. If there were stones underneath forming the walls of this hut, they weren't visible. The more I looked, the more I believed my eyes as the other buildings surrounding the lake seemed to be made from similarly peculiar materials— resources that couldn't possibly have found their way up the snowy mountains of the Himalayas.

The beauty of the man-made structures was undeniable and curious, but the natural environment here seemed to defy everything I knew or thought I knew about the Himalayas. The only snow I could find was high on the tops of the mountains; these were the few peaks that weren't shrouded by the thick white clouds that hovered above Gaia. A perfect ring of golden sand ran around the radius of the lake, and from there, a lush, lime-green grass covered the ground like nothing I had ever seen. The grass appeared to be thick like a shag carpet, and reaching out to touch it for myself, it felt just as soft. Sporadically large groups of wild purple flowers bloomed, sprouting up out of the carpet of green grass, creating incredible color bursts throughout the mountain valley.

Above flew an array of bird life, species I couldn't identify from this angle but was certain the rest of the world had never seen before. Their bright colors caught my attention first and their amazing song kept my attention until Maru spoke, reminding me I wasn't alone on this crazy adventure.

"Spectacular, isn't it, Lucius?" Maru said quietly, not wanting to pollute this beautiful environment with even the slightest foreign sound. Nodding in agreement, I continued to survey the landscape. The closer I looked, the more things I observed that my mind couldn't identify or put into a category. Tiny pink insects crawled through the lush carpeted ground, large multi-colored birds soared in the sky above us, and who knew what other amazing creatures were lurking the shadows, assessing us as I waited eagerly to assess them.

"Let's walk. There is more to explore than just the beach," Maru said, standing above me with her hand outstretched for mine.

"Let's head to that monastery there." She pointed across the lake. "We can change and prepare." So engrossed in our surroundings, I didn't even question what we were preparing for; truth be told, I could've cared less. I was flying high on my own accomplishments and on the many wonders that continued to present themselves in Gaia, and we had only just broken the surface.

We walked around the circumference of the lake. I couldn't stop myself from taking off my shoes and curling my toes in the amazing softness of this strange grass. The sound of the waterfalls seemed to complete the ambiance of Gaia. The constant splashing and roaring of the immense waters pouring down the side of the mountain had the power to calm even the darkest of souls, I was certain. It was then that I realized it wasn't just the aesthetics of Gaia that birthed the incredible wonder within me. There was something else as well. Everything about Gaia seemed to be the very definition of tranquility, peacefulness, and calm, from the grass to the trees and the inhabitants of the skies.

"I remember the first time I visited Gaia; I felt the way you do now, utter amazement. I couldn't believe a place like this could exist on Earth. I have seen many planets and dimensions during my travels, Lucius, but this particular Gaia has always been at the top of my list of favorites. Ouriana has really outdone herself here. It's no wonder she never wants to leave." Maru spoke casually while we walked, and I remembered just how little I really knew about her life and all she'd witnessed along the way.

"How long ago was it when you first came here?" I asked.

"Oh, many, many years; several centuries ago at least, but not much has changed," she said, looking around her old home. Maru remembered one of a thousand unique journeys to what I used to think were make-believe places.

"I still can't believe I actually got us here. I'd never even been here and didn't know what to imagine, but it obviously worked."

"It's not about knowing exactly where you are going. It's about knowing where you want to go even if you have no idea what it looks like or what to expect when you get there." Maru's brown hair glistened in the brighter-than-bright sun, and before I realized it, we were standing in front of the monastery I spotted from the other side of the lake. Surprisingly, my observations were correct. They made this monastery from remnants of the ocean.

"Where did Ouriana find coral and seashells in the mountains?" I asked Maru, circling the building while we talked.

"You were in that lake with me, weren't you? There is much down there that one wouldn't expect to find high in the Northern Mountains." With a shake of her head, I could tell she was a bit exasperated with me. Apparently, there were really no limits to what you could create as a dimensional being, and I had to remember that. When I touched the vines that snaked this way and that way up the sides of the monastery, their sturdiness stunned me. So many tentacles emerging from one plant, strong enough to form actual walls.

"Shall we?" Motioning for me to go first up the narrow, fossil-covered front steps. Inspecting each stair as I climbed, I saw amazing shapes embedded in the strange material that made up the stairs, creatures I could never have imagined in my wildest dreams. Someone preserved their likeness in this mystical place for only a few to glimpse. The door to the monastery was looming, made of a substance I recognized; wood. With no handle to speak of, I pushed the door open. It required a good amount of strength to do so. Cringing as the door hinges creaked from lack of use, I looked inside and found that the plainness was underwhelming compared to what we had seen so far. A small twin bed sat in the center of the room with a nightstand, a meager lamp with no shade, and a dead lightbulb blackened on top. The only other feature this hut offered was a floor-to-ceiling bookshelf containing at least a hundred books of all different languages, from what I could tell from their weathered and worn spines.

"Go ahead and change. I'll wait out here," Maru said while she dragged the large wooden door shut behind her. Left alone in the monastery, I dug around in my damp backpack, relieved to find my spare clothing still dry. I quickly changed, not wanting to waste any of my time here in Gaia on appearances. I ran a brush through my hair and exited the monastery, ready to discover more of Gaia's secret wonders. I was now an adventurer and fully embracing it.

Outside, I found Maru cleaned up and ready to go. Apparently not apprehensive about changing outdoors.

"Well?" Maru said with an accusatory tone.

"Well, what?" I asked, looking around, wondering what I had missed this time.

"Go back in, please, and don't come out until you've found it," she said, plopping down on the mattress of green grass, prepared to rest until my mystery task was complete.

"Okay..." I said hesitantly, walking back up the stairs and through the sizeable door of the monastery. I scanned the building again after setting my backpack down. The same twin bed and pitiful nightstand sat in the middle of the room. What was I missing? I took another walk along the walls of the building, looking from ceiling to floor, and with every step I took, I waited to stumble upon whatever Maru wanted me to find. A tiny square of a building. There really wasn't that much area to cover, and then something caught my attention out of the corner of my eye. Backtracking a few steps, I stood in front of what appeared to be a hidden compartment within the back wall of the monastery. Just the faintest definition of a box emerged on the surface of the wall, collecting dust on its minuscule ledge. I kneeled in front of the curious find and examined it closer. It appeared to be a simple spring-loaded door; a single burst of pressure should be enough to pop it open.

Dust and cobwebs floated lazily out of the compartment, infused with new oxygen after likely decades or longer of neglect. Wishing for a light, specifically the handy light from my long-gone iPhone, I peered into the narrow but deep compartment. I needed something that could hold a flame. So I searched around the room for anything that could be of use, but found nothing. Distracted from my search by a strange heat growing in the palm of my hand, I turned my attention to my hand. This can't be happening? Glowing in the palm of my very own hand was a flame created from nothing but my immediate need for it. Amazing. Tearing myself from yet another astonishing accomplishment—one I didn't fully understand but was surely taking credit for—I held my left hand over the compartment, illuminating it completely.

Down at the very bottom of the open compartment was a small leather album or journal and a fresh, blossoming flower. My shoulder hit the top of the compartment as I reached down, needing all my arm's length to reach these strange treasures. Carefully, I grabbed the flower, sure it would whither at my touch, but when it didn't, I had to wonder who put it here and when? The small leather rectangle was, in fact, some type of album I confirmed as I carefully drew it up from the depths. Tied shut with a small, frayed piece of string, my touch was all it took for the string to crumble, loosening its grip entirely on the book. As the cover fell open, the images took me aback. This book had been preserved all this time; for me.

"To my dear and precious son, Lucius,

I know you will find this one day and learn that once we were a happy family. For us, I kept these memories for you. I hope you are beginning to understand who you are and uncovering some of the great secrets of the Universe. There is much in store for you."

The inscription brought tears to my eyes, but what took my breath away completely was a family portrait on the first page of the album—the Xaviers—my mother and father standing and smiling behind Dax and myself, both of us surely under the age of six years old. We did indeed appear to be a normal, happy family. Turning from page to page through the album, I discovered smiling faces, brothers who appeared to be best friends and parents whose children were clearly the light of their life. My lack of memory made these images seem fabricated, even though I knew they had to be real.

"I can't look at these anymore..." I murmured to myself. The past was gone. And for me, it never existed in the way these photos depicted. Gently placing the album in my backpack, I glanced back toward the strange flower. Bright purple hues practically glowed through the rose-like petals. It was real, but why was it hidden away for me to find?

Slowly I opened the door to the monastery, flower in hand, to find Maru sprawled out in the grass, soaking in the afternoon sun.

"What's this about?" I asked, holding up the purple flower for Maru to inspect while I walked down the stairs.

"Interesting..." Maru said, sitting up now with curiosity. "May I?" she asked, outstretching her hand to grab the flower. A little more than unnerved by the strange flower, I was more than happy to relinquish it to her for observation. It surprised and worried me that she seemed unaware of this flower.

"This isn't what you wanted me to find?" I asked.

"No, no...I wanted you to find your family photo album. Which I assume you did?" She asked, never taking her eyes off the strange flower. I nodded, but of course, she wasn't looking at me. This peculiar flower had her completely in its trance, and the longer she stared at it, the more nervous I became.

"Do you know who left it?" I asked, now sitting cross-legged beside her, staring just as intently at the flower. It was a message of some kind; that much was clear.

"Oh yes, I most certainly do, but why it had to be left is what I'm worried about." She twisted and turned the flower, as if expecting to find a secret note or code somewhere on the stem or petals.

"Okay... so who left it?" I asked, trying to drag the information out of her.

"Ouriana. This flower is a distress signal, Lucius. We developed this way of warning each other when we were both new citizens of Atlantis. We would leave a single pluto rose for the other when we were in trouble or something went wrong with our plans. She left this for us as a warning but of what I'm not sure yet..." Drifting off, the look on Maru's face was of pure concern, translating into a developing fear within myself. If Maru was worried, there was a big problem. "We need to find Tess," Maru announced with urgency. She leaped up off the grass and stood, holding the magnificent rose towards the sky. She pursed her lips together, blowing on the vibrant warning flower. Right before our eyes, the purple rose-like blossom disintegrated into the light mountain breeze.

"Who's Tess?" I asked, distractedly, as I watched what was left of the rose float up towards the snow-capped mountains. Already on the move, I jumped up, grabbing my backpack with one hand and jogging to catch up with Maru. We headed back towards the Eastern Forest. Maru walked briskly and in silence. Perhaps she didn't hear me, I wondered, so I asked again who Tess was and how she could help in this situation. I did not yet understand.

"Tess was one of the original Alvanata, along with Ouriana and myself. Long before your father. She lives here in Gaia with Ouriana. Perhaps she has some insight as to what is going on," Maru said, increasing her stride and speed with each word spoken. Her worry was visible all over her face in newly visible lines surrounding her usually sparkling eyes, and in replace of her radiant smile was a grim straight line.

"Something is really wrong, isn't it?" I asked, working to maintain her pace. "What can I do?"

"We need to find Tess, and then we can assess what information we have. Right now, control your imagination and thoughts as I am trying to control mine. With little information, it will want to run out of control to scare you. Harness the reins and do not allow that." She said firmly.

We rounded the lake in silence, but instead of heading back to our starting point, we went north toward what appeared to be nothing. The north end of Gaia seemed nothing more than the base of a large snow-capped mountain speckled with a few pine trees here and there. As we left the familiar beach behind and trekked up a slight slope leading us toward the snow-capped mountain Maru seemed to target, it amazed me when the landscape went from bright green to sparkling purple from east to west. Together, Maru and I stood at the top of the slope, marveling at the expanse of color stretching from one mountain base to another. As the sun slowly lowered its position, its vibrant rays highlighted the rose field to perfection, taking the beauty of nature one step further. Watching in amazement, I quickly noticed Maru was not enjoying the scenery as much as analyzing it, scouting for something or someone.

"Are we waiting for something to happen here?" I asked, lowering my voice for no reason in particular, except

I sensed Maru was concentrating hard on something and, as usual, I didn't know what to expect. Maru continued to scan the horizon in front of us, remaining non-responsive while I glanced back and forth from her to the purple field of pluto roses that threatened to hypnotize me if I stared too long.

"Maru, for Christ's sake, what are we waiting for?" My sudden burst of frustration echoed through the valley of Gaia. If there was, in fact, anyone else here, they now knew we were there as well.

"Wait, Lucius, exercise your patience... please." Her exasperation clear, I remained silent once again and at least tried to aid her in scanning the landscape for activity or movement until she permitted me to know what was happening. Once my mind quieted, a spark illuminated within it. We were waiting for Tess.

The sun nearly completely set, shone its last remaining rays through the mountain peaks, creating an unearthly shimmer across the field of pluto roses and uncovering something from the shadow of the mountain as well. Initially, from a distance, the glimmer of the purple flowers appeared to crawl slightly up the side of the mountain base. Still, when the last of the day's sunlight hit that spot directly, it became clear these flowers were covering a door, an entrance into the mountain.

"You see it, Lucius?" Maru asked, smiling for the first time since I discovered Ouriana's distress signal.

"There is an entrance into the mountain?"

"That is where we will find Tess. We must hurry now." Maru broke into a run and headed towards the flower-covered door on the western side of the Mountain base, hurrying before the sun's rays were gone for the day and the descending darkness caused us to miss the entrance completely. Together we sprinted across the field of roses, the flowers adding a spring to our step, bouncing beneath our feet, never flattening underfoot. Over my shoulder, I saw no trail left through the flower field, not a flower bent by our intrusion. On the heels of Maru, we reached the mountain's base in no time, both a little winded by our effort to reach it in time. Maru tore at the flowers covering the door until revealing it completely. Nearly rotten over time, I suspected, the wood was the home to many species of mold, moss, and fungus, but the door handle was something of interest—a near twin to the ancient dagger that initiated this strange turn in my life. This door handle exhibited the same shape, gems, everything; I ran my fingers over it gently to confirm.

"Give it a pull," Maru spoke up from behind me, breaking my temporary trance. "Yes, there's a story to the door knob, but not now. We need to find Tess." She continued, growing in agitation.

The small mountainside door creaked open under my immense pressure; the hinges reacting as if they hadn't been forced to do anything in centuries. Continuing to push with my left shoulder, I edged the door further and further open until the inside of the mountain was in view, nothing but utter darkness. Maru sidestepped me, entering the mountain first. A flick of her wrist and a mumble resulted in a large ball of light hovering high in the center of the inner-mountain chamber, like a strange, ethereal chandelier. A fleeting explosion of excitement filled me and just as quickly abandoned me when Maru's ball of light revealed there was nothing in this mysterious mountain. The hollowed-out mountain appeared not much different on the inside than the outside, missing only the snow. The depth of the cavern seemed to go on for miles, and all we could see were boulders, rock debris, and the odd pine tree, just as on the outside.

"Tess? It's Maru. Where are you, dear?" Maru allowed her voice to echo through the chasm, reaching depths of it we could not yet see.

"I don't think anyone is here, Maru. Nobody could live in here," I said, while we walked deeper and deeper into the depths of the mountain.

"Oh, Lucius," Maru muttered. Still waiting to hear from Tess, she said no more. As the cavern turned right, the atmosphere grew brighter with each step forward. Looking over my shoulder, I saw Maru's makeshift chandelier still suspended but nearly a mile behind us; certainly not the cause of this new light ahead.

"Reveal yourselves!" A powerful female voice boomed from somewhere in the depths. I fell to my knees in sync with Maru, ready to follow her lead. This was her friend, after all. Head bowed, eyes closed, and knees folded underneath her, Maru spoke just as loudly.

"I am Maru of the Alvanata, and I am here, fearful for my friend Ouriana." Maru nodded to me. My turn to speak had come. Without direction or questions, I spoke the truth, as Maru had done, hoping this was what I was meant to do in order to prove myself to Tess.

"I am Lucius Xavier, son of Ameratat of the Alvanata, and I am on my journey to Atlantis with my mentor, Maru. We are looking for our friend, Ouriana. We believe she may be in trouble." I listened intently for what was to come with my head down and eyes closed. "You may both pass the barrier." The strange voice replied to our confessions of truth.

"What barrier?" I asked, looking around, still seeing nothing but rock and rubble all around us.

"There is an invisible barrier only a few feet from us, Lucius. To prevent the unworthy from gaining access to Tess or from trying to harm her. She's our oracle, and she only responds to the truth." We gathered ourselves from the dirt and cautiously continued to walk forward until the vivid light we had seen grew so bright my eyes squinted shut, trying to adjust to the immense golden glow.

The chamber she permitted us to enter appeared nothing less than magical. A giant ball of golden light hovered in the center of the room, and this light cast a shimmer on everything around it, adding another layer of mystery to this new discovery. Lush green trees, bushes, and vines nearly filled the space. The same colourful birds I witnessed by the lake cooed and cawed from their high perches in this strange indoor forest. Pluto roses were everywhere and shrouded in a golden glow. They took on an even more illustrious air.

"I've missed you, Tess." I heard Maru say, but to who? I hadn't spotted Tess amongst the incredible nature this chamber seemed to produce so successfully without the power of the sun.

"Oh, you are not alone, dear boy." I heard that same strange voice reply to my inner thoughts as if I had said the words aloud. Instinctively, I turned towards the golden glow in the center of the chamber; in my mind, the only potential source of the woman's voice. Maru extended her hand to steer me back from the ball of light. Together we stood amongst the trees and vines, watching from a distance as a distinct transformation began to take place before our very eyes. The darkness of the cavern was almost nonexistent now. It was driven away by the light of Tess, so bright in contrast, the beauty of Gaia seemed dim and out of focus. The pluto roses rushed up from the ground and began swirling through the air, twisting around the golden light until a figure materialized.

The shape of a petite woman emerged from the swarm of purple flowers. The outline of hair, glasses, and clothing could be distinguished, but pure golden light alone created this figure—translucent yet materialized enough to walk towards us on two feet. Or perhaps she's floating? Her long hair shimmered out behind her as if a strong wind were blowing it that way, when the stillness of the interior mountain room was thick, nearly suffocating.

Face to face now with Maru, the two women linked opposite arms and bowed towards each other in greeting; smiling all the while as if they had been waiting generations for this day.

"The greeting of Alvanata members, Lucius," Maru said, answering the question I hadn't thought to ask yet. Turning back towards Tess, she thanked her for admitting us, especially since I was not a full citizen of Atlantis yet. Maru explained Ouriana's warning and asked Tess what she knew.

"You are on your way to Atlantis now, yes? To confirm the boy's future, I suspect?" Tess asked Maru, even though it seemed clear she knew the answer already. Maru had said Tess was an oracle. In my mind, this meant she already knew everything, so perhaps these questions were more about manners than actually needing information. Regardless, Maru and I nodded together. Tess observed me carefully before continuing. Her gaze burned my flesh, tingled my bones, and stole my breath from my lungs.

"Do you believe him ready?" she asked Maru, making me immediately think she believed otherwise. Again, Maru merely nodded, awaiting more from Tess. She seemed to lose interest in my abilities to gain citizenship within the realm of Atlantis and moved on to Ouriana and her situation.

"Ouriana is with Leto and Ameratat. Tartarus' games with this planet must be stopped before it is too late. Leto has requested her presence, and the three of them intend to distract Tatartus so you can transport Lucius into Atlantis without detection. Her warning to you, Maru, is that Tartarus is aware the prophecy is in progress, and he will not relinquish his hold on this planet without a fight." Tess spoke in an oddly upbeat voice, considering the subject.

"What can you show us?" Maru asked. The shimmering golden figure before us warped from that of a woman into a large sphere, similar to what Maru had created upon our entrance to the cavern. The golden sphere floated toward us and its surface displayed colour and images—images of Gaia and Ouriana before our arrival.

Ouriana sat beautifully perched by the edge of the stunning lake, likely awaiting our arrival. The approach of a large variegated green bird with long flowing yellow tail feathers made Ouriana jump to her feet. Her expression quickly morphed from serene to uneasy, worried even by the sight of this stunning bird. Hesitantly, she outstretched her right arm, allowing the bird a landing place, which it found with ease. Ouriana and the beautiful bird stared at each other for several seconds before the image of her became distorted and wavy. She twisted and writhed in every direction before losing her body completely. What we saw before our eyes was a beautiful variegated green bird joined by a golden bird of equal size with the odd purple feather here and there to match its long purple tail feathers;

Ouriana. The two birds flew off, up into the clouds, and the images disappeared completely from the floating golden globe in front of us that was once Tess.

Tess floated back toward the middle of the room, allowing Maru time to process while she shape-shifted back to the figure of a woman.

"What did we just see, Maru?"

"We just saw your Father come and collect Ouriana, just as Tess described," Maru said, leaning her entire body weight against a tree as tall as the mountain itself.

"We didn't see her leave the rose, though?" I said.

"Unnecessary. We're running out of time. I don't need to see it to know she was the one who left it. We saw what was most important to see." Still, the concern hadn't left her face.

"Lucius, come here before you leave. There is something I would teach you," Tess said, pronouncing each word carefully, as if speaking a foreign language and wanting to get it right. I glanced towards Maru for assurance, but she displayed no expression at all, remaining lost in her own thoughts and plans. Tess waited patiently on a stone bench under a large vine-covered tree on the other side of the chamber. Not quite sitting on the bench, but hovering a few inches above it, glowing all the while. There was no reason to feel apprehensive. I snuffed out those feelings as best I could and started towards this strange glowing entity called Tess.

Taking the seat next to her on the stone bench, I waited while she appeared to be studying again.

"Do you know why I don't possess a body the same as you?" she asked. Startled by this question, I hadn't had time to wonder about this yet. Frantically, I tried to imagine how she could live without a body, but I needed mine to exist. Tess continued. "You are wrong to think you need your body to exist. It assists you, that is certain, especially in this realm so identified with the flesh, but it is far from necessary in most other areas of the Universe. Don't you see? I am the Universe, same as you." She stopped, watching me carefully while I tried to comprehend exactly what she was trying to tell me. Since stumbling into this world of Universal powers, portals, and dimensions—I had been told about the Universe within me, and all its potential. Is this glowing golden embodiment what it looks like inside me?

"Yes! Exactly, Lucius. I am simply without my shell. The body you carry is just that, a shell. We are all luminous beings, Lucius. When our shells are stripped away this is what you see. The golden light before you is the light of the Universe that energizes my very being, as well as yours and every being within the Universe. We all have the power within us, but so very few learn how to harness it." Tess' statement left me stunned and excited to think this golden, glowing power was what my lanky and awkward Lucius shell contained.

"Thank you for your help, Tess, but I believe Lucius and I are under tighter time restraints than initially thought. I fear it won't be long before the darkness of Tartarus spreads through the Universe, touching even Atlantis as it passes," Maru said, standing in front of Tess and me, still resting on the stone bench.

"You're right, Maru. Time is not on your side. Allow me to aid in your travels to Atlantis, if I may?" she asked meekly.

"Of course. You would allow us?" Maru and Tess spoke cryptically back and forth until I finally asked what they were talking about.

"Tess has her own collection of portals here, Lucius, so she can oversee virtually all that goes on throughout the Universe, alerting the Alvanata if need be, of imminent dangers. One leads directly to Atlantis, and is the most crucial phase of your journey to immortality and fulfilling your destiny." Once again, Maru held out her hand to me, waiting to continue with our journey. Without hesitation, I grasped her hand in mine, and we collected our things to leave. Maru and Tess enacted the same ritual used as a greeting to say goodbye to one another while I watched from a distance, allowing them their time for farewells.

"Goodbye to you, Lucius, and good luck on your journey. There is much before you that can derail your goals. You must be strong, but more importantly, wise,"

Tess said, the sincerity in her voice quite comforting even though her words were anything but.

"Can you tell me if I succeed or not?" I had to ask. She was an oracle, after all.

"I don't predict the future, Lucius. No one can do that. We all have free will and, decisions are ever-changing. You have everything you need to succeed. This I know for certain." As gracefully as an angel, Tess floated from Maru to me, kissing me gently on the cheek. My spirits instantly lifted as if she infused me with something mystical when really all she did was believe in me.

"You know the way, Maru." These were Tess' last words, and the golden glowing figure was gone, evaporating right before our eyes, and leaving us in the pure darkness of the cavern once again. I lit the way, my left palm radiating an orange glow as it did in the monastery, and Maru and I walked down an isolated, narrow corridor toward the Atlantis portal.

What we found was not a door but a wrought-iron gate strong enough to hold back the darkness surrounding the Universe. The other side of the gate revealed nothing. Its darkness was absolute.

"Before we enter the portal, Lucius, I need to tell you something. You are not responsible for Terrence's death. He knew his time on Earth was growing short. He wanted to come on this journey with you, to see the Kai-Tangata defeated by your side. It was his choice; unfortunately, the elements got to him before he could fulfill his journey alongside us. But know this, that is not the last you will see of Terrence. He was more dimensional being than he knew. We will see him again, I believe." Pulling me in for an embrace, she added, "I'm sorry for laying his death at your feet, Lucius. I was grieving and not in control of myself." Feeling the weight of Terrence lifted off my shoulders, I reciprocated the embrace with relief that I had not killed one of my only friends on Earth, that he had made his choice.

"I'm sorry I felt anger towards you about his death, Maru. Thank you for telling me the truth." We stood in silence, weighing the challenges to come and remembering what we had already accomplished together.

"When we step into that portal, I will guide us to Atlantis. Hold on tight. They will not admit you without me. If you let go, I will lose you in the universe's shadow for eternity. Do you understand?"

"I understand."

"The darkness is spreading, Lucius. There is much you need to learn before we can even hope to defeat Tartarus. But first, we must convince the citizens of Atlantis you are worthy."

"One step at a time."

"Exactly. One step at a time." Maru grabbed my hand. We held tight to each other, each drawing in a long breath before opening the gate and stepping into the great abyss Maru called the Universe shadow. At last, I would see

Atlantis and reconcile my human half with my Atlantis half. One step closer to Lucius of the Alvanata.

READ ON FOR AN EXCERPT
FROM THE NEXT
SHADOW STORM NOVEL,

WAR OF SHADOWS

COMING SOON!

"Oh, but you are alone, Lucius Xavier; bearer of the prophecy. You are very alone." This singular voice emerged from the chaos around me. The dozens of other voices ceased, and the darkness fell heavy on my chest. Who found me in this portal…. what do they want? Squeezing Maru's hand was the extent of my ability to communicate with her. Hoping beyond hope she was still there, and this being was not enthralling me. Attempting to hijack my travels.

Frantically, my eyes darted from one corner to the next, seeing nothing but absolute shadow. No shimmer or pop of light to illuminate the universe encircling me. Perhaps the darkness Maru spoke of had travelled further than she thought. *Is this what I am experiencing?* Darkness with a voice and a purpose here to suffocate me. My eyes burned with the strain of trying to see through the sludge-like-darkness, to no avail. Panicking, my heart raced, horrified by my lack of control over my situation. Maru was in charge of our travel to Atlantis, and our communication had been severed. What can I do? While I contemplated my options and how to regain control over our situation, two red glowing dots floated in the forefront of my vision. Spaced close enough together, they could be nothing else but a pair of eyes. This heavy darkness had eyes. My body stiffened at the sight, at the realization there was more to this darkness than what met the eye. The small hairs stood tall on the back of my neck, while the red dots burned holes straight through me. A guttural cackle interrupted my state of frozen fear. The dots remained steady, but the voice had more than a hint of humour to it when it once again boomed in my ears.

"I can sense myself in you Lucius… the Alvanata allowed you to spend too much time on Earth, boy. Now, I have a claw embedded deep within your soul. Can you feel it?" The voice took a lengthy pause to increase my dread. "Your prophecy is changing by the minute, Lucius. There will be no escape from me this time; I am no longer playing games." The darkness let out a deep sigh. The air around me swirling in response. It entwined us. I felt the weight of the shadow holding me. Traveling at speeds through the universe, I was helpless. With no idea whether Maru and I were still on track to Atlantis or if Maru was even still with me, I made a snap decision. I had to get away from the burning red dots and its guttural voice.

The memory of Maru instructing me to imagine Gaia. To picture it clearly in my mind's eye in order to engage in dimensional travel from the hidden city of Alexa crawled its way to the front of my mind. It was time to follow her advice again. I was not on the threshold of a dimensional portal and I was not a dimensional being… yet. But I had to try. Closing my eyes, I tried to imagine Tess, the mysterious oracle from Gaia. I pictured her mountain cave dwelling and all the beauty Gaia offered outside her layer. However, all I could see were those red eyes. Eyes open or closed, they were there. This unknown darkness was within, just as it was without. That this strange darkness, this obviously dark being, could be inside my mind spread a terror through my causing my blood to quiver. The strength of this fear could either throw my concentration completely or shift my focus into overdrive. I strived for the latter. Without knowing the purpose of this voice, where it would take me or what it wanted with me, I had to assume the worst and prepare to fight it.

My mind's eye opened wide, and I clearly saw the glowing golden form of Tess. I saw the beautiful lake at the base of the mountain Maru and I arrived through from Alexa. Big, beautifully colored birds soaring through a crystal blue sky, reflecting off the serene lake. The bright green grass teamed with life just as exotic on the ground. These images were fleeting. I clung to them like a man hanging from the edge of a building. Using all my mental strength to bring us back. I concentrated.

"There is nowhere in this universe left for you to hide, boy. I'm everywhere." The voice bellowed, but to my surprise, the words seemed to come from far away. Is it working? I didn't dare break my concentration by opening my eyes, but a bead of confidence was growing after hearing that voice, distant and angry. Still gripping Maru, I had a stronger sense of her now, but even she couldn't break through my focus. I was getting us out of this portal and back to Earth before the darkness' strength grew beyond my amateur abilities. Completely mentally ensconced in Gaia, it startled me when my body shuddered and my grip on Maru's hand loosened from all the jostling. Even from behind closed eyelids, I saw golden light flashing left, right and center. The force carrying our bodies through the blank spaces of the universe faltered. I briefly feared being dropped into the shadow, never to be found again. Then it all came to a standstill. No more movement, no more voices, no more darkness, and not even Maru's hand in mine. It was all golden. A brilliant ball of light encasing us.

"Lucius? Lucius, can you hear me? Something went terribly wrong… how did we end up back here?" The Maru's voice cut through my fog like a knife. I exhaled just as deeply as the darkness had, now feeling a strange connection to that wicked shadow. This quick realization jolted my eyes open. I scanned our surroundings, breathing heavy, secretly afraid some universal monster may have made the journey back with us.

"Lucius, snap out of it." Maru now had me by the shoulders, gently shaking me back to reality. "How did this happen?" She asked. Seeing confusion and concern on her face was an unfamiliar experience. One I didn't care for at all.

"You don't know?" I asked in return, baffled myself that somehow the darkness shielded Maru from its visit. Proving it was there only for me, as its threats implied. I ran through the entire experience for Maru. From my initial suspicion of the absolute darkness in the portal to the revelation it was more than just darkness—it was something in and of itself. Not knowing what else to say or which question to ask first, I slowed my breath and looked for Tess. The golden light had faded significantly since opening my eyes, but we were, in fact, inside the mountain where we had left only a short time ago.

"There is no such thing as time once you enter a portal, Lucius. On Earth, only a minute or two has gone by since we opened that wrought-iron gate." Maru said quietly, almost to herself. Obviously circulating through her own thoughts and conclusions regarding our strange and near death experience. Looking to her for the first time since telling my tale, I saw a haggard woman who looked like she'd been to hell and back. Her hair stood on end at all angles, mascara smeared under her eyes, clothes crumpled and askew. My attention now on myself, I saw virtually the same result with the addition of one frightening detail that took my breath away. My shirt was open and ripped—burnt haphazardly. As if I had narrowly escaped a fire, but it was what was on my skin that stunned me the most.

"Maru? Are you seeing this?" But she continued to pace the innards of the mountain, keeping her thoughts to herself. "Maru!" I yelled. Spinning, she looked at me. I stood with my shirt open and my chest exposed, displaying two circular burn marks right over my heart. Quickly covering the ground between us, Maru was by my side in seconds. She gently placed her hand over my heart and the burns left there by the dark entity that had leeched onto me. A slight glow omitted from under her palm and my skin heated as if her hand were a hot burner. Flinching slightly, she removed her palm, and yet another look of confusion and frustration crossed her face.

"I'm not going to lie, Maru. I don't enjoy seeing you confused. What is going on here? What are these marks and who uttered those threats to me in the portal?" Lowering the timbre of my voice, I wanted to be delicate, obviously Maru was concerned and me pointing out what seemed to be her only shortcoming would not help our situation. Searching through her own words, Maru gestured towards a small wooden table and chairs in the far right corner of the mountain cave. Together we sat, with only the golden light of Tess, to illuminate the inner sanctum of the mountain.

"Those are the marks of Tartarus, Lucius. I believe he was the darkness that surrounded you, blocking me from your consciousness. I have no memory of the events you described, but these marks verify your story without a doubt."

"Wait. Are you saying you didn't believe me until you saw these burns?" I asked, completely stunned that *my* Maru would ever doubt my word.

"It's not you or your word I doubted, Lucius. You must understand this has never happened to me in the history of my long, long life. Tartarus' strength has grown far beyond what we, of the Alvanata, previously thought. Things have become dire, Lucius." Again, her mind drifted off. Catching herself, she added, "Good for you for having the strength and the presence of mind to bring us back. Tartarus cannot exist in Gaia. He could not follow us here, even if he wanted to. At least that defence still stands." A slight but hesitant smile crossed her face. Forced for my benefit.

"What does Tartarus want with me? He threatened me, said there was nowhere in the universe for me to hide. That he was done playing games…" Trailing off, I tried to recapture his voice and words to re-examine the meaning be behind it all.

"There's no need to analyze Lucius. I assume he also mentioned the prophecy?" She asked, seemingly already knowing the answer to her own question.

"Yes, yes, he did." Pausing, I waited, expecting Maru to explain further, when the sudden appearance of Tess interrupted our deliberation. A genuine smile lightened Maru's tired features at the sight of her friend. The golden light within the mountain cave increased ten fold with her appearance. Watching her approach from the far corner of the cavern, directly from the portal Maru and I just escaped, Tess appeared to float, not walk. Traveling with a grace I had never witnessed in another human being, it occurred to me in that moment that Tess was not a human being, but something else entirely. So why shouldn't she float? Now by our side, Tess, too, appeared troubled.

"Did you see this coming, Tess?" I had to ask before she even began. She was an oracle, after all. Shouldn't she have known this was going to happen?

"Tatarus' strength is great Lucius, and he has dwelled in the shadow realm for a great many years. Harnessing its powers in a way we did not predict."

Although she spoke to me, Tess' eyes burned into Maru's while the two stared fiercely at each other. Glancing back and forth from one to the other, their alarm was making room for something frightening to bloom inside me. These two beings in front of me were supposed to be all knowing, all wise and without fear and yet here they were terrified of Tartarus. This dark monster whose only goal was to find me.

"Is there more to this story you two would like to share?" I asked after watching Tess and Maru exchange intense glances, virtually forgetting my presence. Tess assumed a seated position while still floating next to our little table. She shifted her gaze from Maru to me, and its intensity immediately jolted me. Her golden eyes sparkled, nearly hypnotizing me. Every aspect of her human image sparkled gold, but the seriousness of her expression transformed her beauty into something terrifying.

"It's time to discuss the prophecy, Lucius. Your prophecy." Tess said, her voice unfamiliar to me, no longer light and airy but deep with the weight of her worry. "There is more to your prophecy than what the Kai-Tangata believe. You are much more than a source of immortality. I expect that at the very least you have learned we all possess that power." Smiling slyly at me, Tess' comment stings a little. But in truth, I had been a slow learner. "It's not about how fast you learn, Lucius. It's about how much you retain and what you do with that information." Placing her golden hand on mine, a swell of positive energy surged through my veins. A smile bursting onto my face in response. "A shift is coming in the universe, Lucius. Tartarus has infected Earth to its breaking point and its demise is imminent. The Alvanata are moving in to protect the planet, but Tartarus' strength is far beyond what we imagined. He has been hiding in the universal shadow for millennia and not until your battle with the Kai-Tangata has he surfaced. You have forced him to show his hand, unwittingly perhaps. Nevertheless, we now have more information to help us with our mission.

'It has always been the Alvanata's mission to protect planets and dimensions that cannot protect themselves, against dangers they know nothing about. But this time is different. You make it different, Lucius." Pausing here, Tess glances towards Maru, looking for assistance. Her reluctance to continue on her own was puzzling and worrisome. Maru shifted her chair closer to mine to continue what Tess was avoiding.

"Lucius, you are the son of Ameratet. He is the greatest of us all, apart from Leto, of course. Although your Mother was not Atlantean, she was a descendant of one of the original Easter Island inhabitants. She had Atlantean blood coursing through her and didn't even know it. Tess declared your prophecy long before you were born and long before your parents found each other. The aspect you have not heard regarding this tale is the death of your father. The war between Tartarus and the Alvanata will kill him Lucius and you will take his place among the stars with Ouriana, myself and Tess to guide you. Together we will become the next Alvanata." Smiling, Maru's happiness with this information hurt me deeply. I thought she was loyal to my father. I thought she loved my father. How can she be happy to know of his death?

"Lucius, Ameretat is ready for this day. The arrival of this conflict not only means the revival of planet Earth, but it also means your ascension to your rightful place in the universe. His dream has always been for you to become a dimensional being. To be a part of the Alvanata.

'As you can see, there is a lot for you to learn and unfortunately, our time is short. If Tartarus can find you in the portal, there is nowhere for you to hide."

"Maru stop!" Tess suddenly screamed. Her voice echoing through the mountain cavern, startling us both. Before I could inquire what was happening, Maru put up her hand to silence me. Tess stared far off into the distance, clearly seeing something Maru and I could not… we waited. Not being able to stand it any longer, I got up and paced. Back and forth, I walked the length and width of Tess' home, taking in all that I missed the first time. A thick casing of vines writhed with life on the walls. The same bright green as the lush vegetation outside the mountain, speckled with yellow flowers, sharing the golden glow of Tess. The aura surrounding each bloom created a spectacular light show in the shadows of the mountain's sharp edges. Glancing back towards Tess, I could see Maru still waiting in silence while Tess glared ahead at a scene invisible to us but clearly distressing to her eyes.

Continuing my mindless pacing, I glanced from here to there but never really taking in my surroundings. My mind was so preoccupied with Tartarus, the prophecy, Tess and Atlantis; it was reeling in turmoil. The words of my prophecy cycled through my brain. Everything that used to be me disputing its authenticity and yet in my heart it all felt true; it felt right somehow.

"Lucius…" A whisper, or maybe even just a whistle of the wind, spoke to me from behind a dark corner of the mountain. The vines didn't grow around this corner, the flowers were not there to light my way. It was utter darkness; even out of reach of Tess' light. With a few tentative steps, I turned into a shadowed alcove, leaving Tess and Maru out of my sight. What I found in the shadows stunned me so entirely, I froze.